ELEANOR MAYO

I0662810

Swan's Harbor

REBEL SATORI PRESS
New Orleans • MMXVIII

Originally published by
Thomas Y. Crowell Company

ISBN: 978-1-60864-128-4

Published in the United States of America by
Rebel Satori Press

Part One

*I*T WAS SIX thirty o'clock on the seventh morning in June and Steve Swan was standing in his bedroom window looking out across the Bay and putting on his shirt. There was a lifting sensation in the pit of his stomach that told him he couldn't feel better, physically or mentally.

Yesterday had been heavy and muggy with the fog scarfing over the mountains all day long and lying in thick sodden arms along the shore. Sometime during the night he had come half-awake to hear the wind and rain pouring down through the funnel of hills to the northwest and had known what this morning would be. He had put out one hand to make sure Ann was still beside him, and after touching her satiny warm shoulder had fallen asleep.

The cold front passed just before daylight and the world he looked out upon from his window might have been a totally different one. Green was greener, blue bluer, and the saturation of everything it touched was the only thing that kept the sunlight from being blinding. The outbuildings, usually silver with age, were black and soaked with water. Drops of water glistened on every twig of the spruces in the pasture. The heavy heads of June grass were lodged with their too-great load of water.

The Bay itself was a tremendous flat mosaic of brilliance and blue green, with the far islands brushed sleek and furry by the northwest wind.

Steve buttoned all but the last two throat buttons of the white silk shirt and started downstairs, rolling the sleeves hastily as he went. Every window on the first floor was open and the wind blew through, bringing with it the scent of lilacs just coming into full bloom.

The old house on its hillside was sunk in lilacs every June. The scent of them in an enclosed room was so strong it gave him a headache; but while they were blooming every window must be open.

The stairs came down from the upstairs hall directly into the long living room overlooking the water. The eastern wall with its five floor-to-ceiling windows and the big glass front door made him feel as if there were no wall there.

He was as proud and sensitively aware of his house as a woman would have been; but it was a man's house. From the puncheon floors of age and oil-darkened oak to the low, austerely furnished bedrooms abovestairs, it was not a house a woman would have been able to live in without change.

The Swan place was one of the few original houses in the Harbor because the Swan men had always been able to change with, and adapt themselves to, the times. Envious and less successful men had called them opportunists; but they took what came and took advantage of it. They had always been property proud and the house showed it. There was no restoration here. Built along the hill above the Bay, the house gave as happily with the contour of the land as its owners had given with the times. You went up two steps from this room to the hall and kitchen, down one more to the dining room. This front room took up half of the ground floor; the rest was evenly divided between kitchen and dining room.

Steve heard sounds now from the kitchen which drew him away from his pleased contemplation of that blaze of light and perfume coming in his eastern windows.

He was a tall man and big proportionately. The silk shirt that fell limply from his broad shoulders showed off his back and chest muscles, flat as boards and as hard, and he was aware of it. His thick hair, tawny as the hay on a salt marsh in October, was clipped short. Even damp as it still was from his shower, it crinkled stiffly from his big squarish head. In the sunlight his rugged face was a mass of planes and angles, slightly darker in color than his hair, with high blazes of red over the prominent cheekbones from constant exposure to sun, wind and weather. The only lines in the firm flesh were brackets of amusement at the corners of his hard, full-lipped mouth and the rays, focusing at the outer corners of his eyes, that came from squinting for bobbing buoys on sunlit, ever-moving water. The eyes themselves were the color of that water, blue-green with dancing flecks of light. Stephen Swan felt wonderful.

Barefoot, he padded up the two steps and along the hall, arriving silent as a ghost at the kitchen door in time to hear Ann say thoughtfully:

"Lizzie, I could help you with that."

"No, thank you." Lizzie was hitting her deepest chest notes.

Steve grinned. When Lizzie used that particular voice, she could get more disapproval into one word than most women could get into a tirade.

"Well, what do you know!" he said softly. "I've got two women in my kitchen."

Ann spun to face him, startled; but Lizzie didn't move a mus-

5

cle. She was bending over the spider full of bacon on the stove and she continued to bend while managing to look unbending.

Steve looked at Ann, his wide mouth quirking, his bushy eyebrows twitching up. Even Lizzie's obvious disapproval couldn't damp his exhilaration. He went over and put his arm around her unyielding waist.

"Lizzie," he said softly.

Lizzie turned and fended him off with the fork she had been using to turn the bacon.

"Don't try to soft-soap me now, Steve. I'm busy. But the pair of you ought to have more sense than to leave that car right out in the open where anyone could see it."

"You old fraud!" Steve withdrew to a safe distance. "The only thing that's bothering you is what the neighbors'll think."

"Somebody's got to think of things like that!"

Lizabetta Edna Hawkes, at her offended best, was a woman to daunt almost any man. Drawn to her full height, she was as tall as Steve. Her long, skull-like face, powdered to a dead white under its roll of thick, lusterless, black hair was set into lines of tragedy better than she had ever managed on the stage, and she had practiced in the fine old tradition.

She had been cast up in the Harbor one summer like a seal on a rock. She was the tragedy lead of an Olive Mae Edwards Stock Company, and often hinted at Broadway triumphs in her past.

On the evening of her great weakness, there had been no part in the play for her. During intermission, after the juvenile lead, his hair marcelled and perfect, had stood in a blue spotlight on the stage of the movie theater and rendered "I Left Her by the River Sainte Marie" to his own accompaniment on the mandolin, Lizabetta Hawkes had stepped forward into the same blue spot to give a reading:

SWAN'S HARBOR

"Do they miss me at home—do they miss me?
Twould be an assurance most dear,
To know that this moment some loved one
Were saying, 'I wish she were here.' "

She gave it, in the finest tradition of show business, down to the last bitter word. Then she fainted. This added bit of business had been received with tremendous enthusiasm by the audience; but after the curtain came down, Lizabetta's fellow actors had carried her off the stage, still unconscious.

The company moved on to its next engagement, leaving its tragedy lead in the rooming house with a case of grippe and a temperature of 103. From this situation, Steve Swan's mother, who had been deeply impressed by the reading and had always dreamed of going on the stage herself, had rescued her. Lizabetta spent two weeks in the pleasant best bedroom recovering and, having discovered the almost forgotten comforts of staying in one place, made herself so indispensable that she was still here twenty-one years later, still indispensable.

"Lizabetta," Steve said placatingly, "you can't tell me you didn't have plenty of gentlemen around in your time, too. Why, a woman like you—"

"Never you mind a woman like me." Lizzie's face softened a little. Her voice did not. "I never in my life would put up with any man who wasn't willing to make an honest woman of me."

"Hmmm," Steve said thoughtfully, and fled.

No use coming up against Lizzie when she was on her high horse. He was still amused, though. When Ann came into the front room five minutes later with their breakfast on a big copper tray, he was sitting at the table waiting for her. Two places had been set, decently opposite each other; but he had moved them

7

around until they were side by side, facing the windows and the great whirl of windy weather outside.

Ann glanced at the table setting and smiled; but she wouldn't look at him. Steve watched her move around the table with pleasure. Most tall women were clumsy or gawky, but Ann had the inevitable unhurried grace of a wave breaking or a tree bowing in the wind.

He took her wrist and pulled her gently into the chair beside him. Her hazel eyes, set a little slanting under the wide low brow, met his gaze squarely, unrepentant, and for a moment he searched them intently. After five years they still had surprises for each other, and he found many of his in those eyes that looked at him serenely and still a little cloudy with memory.

Sometimes her eyes looked as old as the hills; sometimes they were like a child's, shallow and empty and thoughtless. Then they made him nervous. Now, however, he saw what he wanted to see.

"Will I make an honest woman of you?" he said abruptly.

"I believe you mean that." Her voice was thoughtfully low and clear.

"Disconcerting; but still a proposal."

Ann shook her head.

"I've wanted to hear you say that for the last four years," she said honestly. "But now you've brought yourself to it, I think you'd better wait a little."

"You think it wouldn't work?"

"I think right now the last thing in the world you want is to settle down with a wife. I wouldn't be sure of you from one day's end to the next."

"Let's consider what *you* want, for a change."

"Steve! You really have softened. Never mind. I want whatever you want."

Relieved and wondering what on earth had moved him to the

8

point of offering even a half-hearted proposal, Steve applied himself to his breakfast.

"Lord, look at the time! I won't get down to the shore now until seven thirty and poor old Art will be fit to be tied, wondering where I am."

"He'll know as soon as somebody gets around to telling him where my car was last night." Watching him, Ann saw and recognized the relief and knew that he wished all his words unsaid. It would be a help sometimes if she could be as oblivious to his feelings as he was to hers. Perhaps, eventually, she could. She looked forward to that time almost with hope, knowing from the sudden ache in her heart that it would be long in coming.

"You mind?" Mouth full, temples working, Steve stared at her thoughtfully. He swallowed and added: "I've certainly raised cain with your good name."

"You haven't really done it alone, have you?" She gave him freely the little smile that meant forgiving. "I've helped."

"You know, Ann—" Completely unaware of his unforgivable conclusion, he said thoughtfully: "If I ever loved any woman, it'd be you. Someday I'm going to propose again. Get ready."

He wondered idly what made her warm color fade; it certainly couldn't have been anything he'd said.

"I'll do that." Her voice was flat and when he looked at her again, her eyes had that old look that baffled him so.

"Bye, now," he said hastily. He got up, gave her a brief kiss, and went out, pausing at the door to add: "I'll see you soon."

She sat in silence until Lizzie came banging in to get the dishes. In Lizzie's face she found something that told her she had been partially forgiven her sins and that Lizzie was sorry for her. That was almost as hard to take as Steve's unconscious admission that she was only a pleasant convenience for him. She waited until she heard his car roar out of the yard before she went up to get herself ready to leave.

Perhaps she never should have given in to him, she thought blankly, as she came down the gracious stair case. But that was an inadmissable thought, because every time she looked at him she was quite aware that she could never have done anything but what she had.

Driving downtown, she tried hard to think about ordinary things so that she wouldn't have to think about Steve. Peter Ball never opened his real estate office before nine o'clock, claiming there were other sensible people in the world besides himself who felt that any business conducted before nine in the morning could hardly be done sanely. That gave her an hour and a half to go home and change her clothes and feed the cat before she had to go to work. It also gave her three quarters of an hour to reach the point of wishing she had never set eyes on Steve Swan and three quarters of an hour to realize she didn't really wish anything of the sort and that she couldn't be even as happy as she was without him.

Last night had not been the first night she had spent with him up there in the old house. But it happened rarely and, each time it did, Ann suffered this morning-after reaction. She tried to rationalize it by telling herself it was Lizzie's fault. Lizzie's accusing silence, Lizzie's tart hypocritical mind, Lizzie's 'what will the neighbors say?' threw a harshly unwelcome light on something that had become right and necessary to Ann.

She came out the door, set the saucer of milk on the step for the little tiger cat who coiled herself contentedly in the sun to drink, and went with her head high down the walk to the gate. As far as she was concerned the neighbors had thought and said everything they could years ago. Only Lizzie, apparently, would never accept the situation. Ann decided then and there, as she did each time the occasion arose, to see that it didn't happen again.

With the impersonal detachment of a busy man, putting behind him the thing done, looking forward to what lay ahead to do, Steve forgot her the moment he stepped out of the room. He had a living to make and daylight was for business.

He stopped in the kitchen to put on his boots, stamping into them, barefoot still, and with more noise than was necessary. He kept his eyes on that unbelievable towering pile of jet-black hair that was the back of Lizzie's head.

"Lizzie," he said tentatively, when she refused to acknowledge his presence.

"What?" Her voice was like her attitude, uncompromising.

"Don't forget, will you, Art and Minnie and their kids are coming for supper tonight."

"Much chance for me to forget it with you reminding me of it at least three times a day for the last two weeks."

"It hasn't been *that* bad."

"Well—" grudgingly, "—nearly."

"All I wanted to do was mention to you I want to give them something pretty fancy, see? Kind of like to show him, once a year, anyhow."

"If you have some idea in your head I am incapable of getting supper for five people, perhaps you'd like to hire somebody else to do it." Deeply offended, she turned to face him. "And, furthermore, Stephen Swan, I cannot understand why you go on with this silly supper. It just makes things extremely uncomfortable for everyone concerned."

Steve gave her a conquering grin.

"I enjoy it," he said. "I like to see Art's kids get at least one square meal in the course of the year."

"They don't look to me like they were anywhere near starving," she said.

"All that white fat's not good on kids. They look like little lard tubs, both of them."

"Oh, fluff! Since when have you been worried about their well-being. All that white fat, as you disgustingly call it, is something they'll outgrow. Probably you were just like that when you were their age."

He bristled, stung to the quick.

"I never in my life carried around anything like that!"

"Well," she said unkindly, searching for the thing that would sting most. "I notice you're getting quite a little—er—" Lizzie succeeded beyond her wildest desires, and her soft heart wouldn't let her finish the sentence. Steve's face told her that he knew what she had been going to say.

"Well, all right, Lizzie. I'll leave it to you," he said and went abruptly out the door.

Steve's back door, which was the one used by everybody and referred to by everybody else as 'the front door,' let him out directly from the kitchen on to the road. Thinly grassed dirt went for fifteen feet from the foundation and fell away in a steep cutbank to the macadam. Not long ago, the road had risen with the rise of the ground, making a steep, thank-you-marmy, little hill, and when a car passed, deep in the old bowels of the building ancient timbers would echo and stir to the thud of metal over the bump outside. An answering rumble would come up through wood and plaster until it was nothing but a shadow of sound in the upstairs bedrooms.

He had always hated that invasion of quiet; but a few years ago when, in the interests of safety and more comfortable driving, the town had cut the hill down, he had resented that, too.

During the cutting process the workmen had struck bed-rock and the first necessary blast that followed had smashed nearly every mirror in the house. Steve hadn't been there when it happened; but Lizzie, issuing forth like an avenging fury, had informed the roadmen volubly about what their future both on earth and in the great hereafter would amount to if they dreamed of setting off another charge of dynamite without telling her first.

After that, whenever they were about to blast, one of the men would come toiling up the hill and stand at the back door, cap in hand, his face shining with sweat and dust, to tell Lizzie. She would hail him in and together they would go from room to room, taking down every picture on the walls; putting every light piece of furniture down on its side; making fast everything that could possibly be jarred out of position by the shock. Then they would stand waiting.

The grumble, shock and jar would come upon them, working up through the house. When the dust settled, the indomitable old woman, followed by her sheepish acolyte, would go through the house once more, setting up everything that had been taken down until the next blast.

After working on that piece of road for a week, Alton Blaisdell swore he could find his way around Steve Swan's house blindfolded, and he was sure he knew where every piece of furniture went within a quarter inch either way.

Outside the door now, Steve stood looking abstractedly at his favorite lilac, an old gnarled bush that grew halfway between the house and the lip of the cut-bank. He had had a fight over that with the road crew. They had wanted to take the bank back farther, claiming if they left it too steep a heavy rain would bring it sliding down into the road. He'd fought to prevent them because it would disturb the roots of the lilac. It had been ended by his buying enough cut stone from the quarry to reinforce the bank along that particular stretch. But they'd bothered the roots at that, because the old bush was slowly dying.

He picked a spray of flowers and tucked it into his shirt pocket. It smelled like carnations, not lilacs, and the flowers were a different shape from the others that grew so lushly around the big foundation stones.

As he went striding down the hill to his car, Steve was still thinking of what Lizzie had almost said to him. Did she mean *he* was getting fat? He'd thought once or twice lately he'd noticed a slight thickening around his waist.

As he climbed into the ostentatious, black, fish-tail Cadillac, he was prodding himself anxiously, with two stiff fingers, in the area above his belt buckle. Maybe it was the power of suggestion, but it seemed to him it was slightly softer there than it had been.

"Blast it!" he said aloud and swung the car furiously out of the yard. "Women!"

In the center of town the traffic light caught him at a disadvantage. He was going too fast to stop, so he rounded the corner with a protesting squeal of rubber on macadam. In the rear view mirror he saw Jasper Brown come boiling out of the diner, official cap in one hand, coffee cup in the other, his bony red face working protestingly, his mouth open. The coffee cup smashed on the sidewalk as Jasper reached for his whistle. By the time he had the chain untangled and the pebbly blast going, Steve was out of sight, his good humor completely restored by the sight of the coffee dribbling down the leg of Jasper's hot blue serge uniform.

He ought to be out tending to business anyhow, Steve told himself virtuously, instead of in there drinking coffee and flirting with Allie. The town pays him enough. Let him do his courting on his own time.

He flourished around the last wooded curve and pulled into the white packed gravel of the parking space above the wharf. Under the unbroken glare of sunlight, the heat was already coming in shimmering distorting waves from the steel tops of the other cars parked there. The majority of the more expensive makes belonged to people from the islands, who left them here in all kinds of weather for the sake of using them once or twice a week.

Steve remembered with a tickle of amusement the summer lady, shawls floating, eyes wide, who had come rushing into the office one day to report a theft.

"Mr. Swan," she'd said breathlessly. "There's a tramp up there running off with a Packard! Call the police immediately!"

He had gone to the window in time to see Leverett Parker, as usual in a shapeless, dirty, white cap bearing the legend 'Sherwin Williams Paints Cover the Earth,' his blue, chambray shirt torn, the seat of his three sizes too large khaki pants nearly dragging on the ground, climb stolidly into his Packard. As he swung for the turn, Leverett stuck his head out the window and waved in Steve's direction.

Steve found Art's ten-year-old Ford, and pulled perversely in beside it. When the radiator caps were even, the tail of the Cadillac stuck out eight feet beyond Art's prim spare tire. The comparison wouldn't escape Art when he came to go home to dinner any more than it escaped Steve when he did it.

Nodding with satisfaction, Steve got out and walked leisurely down the wharf. It was so beautiful a morning he couldn't make himself hurry.

Alongshore there was noise and activity everywhere. The donkey engine on the marine railway over at the boat yard grumbled an undertone to all other sounds. The sardine factory, far up in the bight of the Harbor, belched oily black smoke that floated down across the water. Steve could see the *S. O. Dowdell* moored to the spidery-legged wharf with the big hoist baskets gleaming, dripping, piled with herring, coming up out of her hold. Every gull in the Harbor floated and wheeled above her.

At the coal wharf, two beam trawlers from Massachusetts were fueling.

Out on the head of his own wharf, invisible behind the neat buildings, he heard the huff-puff of the gasoline driven winch, screaming against the weight of fish. One of the draggers must have come in during the night.

The sign on the largest building said neatly: Benj. B. Swan & Sons, Lobster Dealers. Benj. B. Swan had been the old man, only he had never lived to be an old man, and Steve and Art were the Sons. They hadn't bothered to do anything about the sign. Once in business under a certain name, you lost out if you changed it. Art said so, anyhow. Steve himself didn't care, as long as the business was going right, what they called it.

He went into the noise and the coolness of the buildings. The radio-telephone was turned on full and some fellow with a gravelly accent was screaming into the deserted room that he 'hadn't seen any thus and so, pinkwhiskered, holy, old, hesitated fish in the whole indescribable, bluenippled, abortive, fatherless Gulf of Maine.'

That sounded like Joe Luccio and when he started talking like that it usually meant he had the old *Seventh Daughter*'s hold so full she could hardly waddle.

Every sliding door in the sheds was open and the wind sucked in through, concentrated by four walls into half a gale. Steve crossed to the office door, pulled it open, and looked in. Art was sitting behind the desk his head, bright as Steve's and exactly the same shape, bent over the big ledger that told him to a penny what had come in and gone out the day before. He glanced up and his face carried out the echo the shape of his head had begun. The brothers were identical in every physical feature—their only difference was in expression. Steve's face tilted up. Art's tilted down.

Neither one of them spoke and Art, after a careful examination of the white silk shirt, looked down at his ledger again, his mouth tight. Steve glanced at Jennie Chick, the bookkeeper, who sat at a smaller desk in the corner behind the door confronted by a confusion of paper of which only she could make sense. He jerked his head.

Jennie, thoroughly flustered as was normal with her, grabbed a sheet of paper and followed him out into the windy vastness of the cleaning shed. This procedure that she had gone through nearly every morning for eight solid years never failed to upset her. It just didn't seem right for two men, brothers, and looking as much like each other as the Swan twins did, not to speak to each other. She had been told they hadn't spoken before she ever came. Normally talkative herself, she simply couldn't see how they kept from it.

Jennie was forty-five and her name suited her. Her tiny body looked to be nothing but bone and tendon, like a stringy and particularly tough pullet. But she wasn't so old or so unperceptive that she didn't enjoy looking at Steve Swan. Sometimes, when she looked, she caught herself wishing that she herself looked different. Maybe— At that point she invariably stopped and thought: Heavens, what would mother say if she ever knew I had such ideas in my head!

"Well, is there a directive for me this fine morning?" Steve stood grinning down at her tiny, primly netted head. "What's the good word, Chickie?"

"Quite a long one." She held it out to him, her hand shaking with tension. "He seemed quite upset this morning."

"Damned if I know what about," Steve growled. He took the paper from her and stood frowning down at it. It was covered from top to bottom with Art's crooked, hard-to-read handwriting.

"Oh, Lord!" Steve sighed. "Do I have to read this tripe?"

"I think you'd better." She felt daring, telling this huge tawny creature what he should do. He gave her a sweet smile, anyhow, and she knew quite well she enjoyed doing it.

"Well," he grumbled; but he slouched against the wall and bent his head over the scribbled sheet. He sighed his way through half a page of figures which meant little to him; scratched his head over the conclusion, which seemed to be that they had done twice the business in the first five months of this year that they had in the first five months of last. That didn't seem to be anything that would upset a man. Then he came to it.

"*It would be appreciated if you would moor your boat to her mooring instead of alongside the lobster cars overnight. The goddamned thing is in the way there and the boys have been breaking their necks over her all morning. Unless you plan to be down here at a decent hour.*"

"Gosh, I did forget her last night," Steve said aloud. He glanced confirmingly out the window. Down at the end of the ramp was the big float and moored to it were what resembled two more floats. The only visible difference lay in the trap doors which opened into three foot deep, divided reservoirs made of boards set far enough apart to let the water run in and out freely, but too close together for the lobsters stored there to escape. At this season, when there was a big call for lobsters at the wharf, both the cars were moored at the end of the float. Later, when the traffic slacked off, one of them would be moved out into the Harbor.

Steve saw that somebody had shifted the *Eloise* around from the fairway side of the cars. They hadn't been too careful about mooring her and her stern swung out widely from the float.

"Damnation," he said, glaring, and returned to Art's note.

"The hearing on the wharf extension is going to be at three this afternoon. I remind you because I'm sure you've forgotten it."

"I had," Steve murmured, not resenting the tartness of this because he was accustomed to it and, even to him, it seemed deserved.

"It would be a good idea if you manage to be here because I've heard a couple of the fishermen are going to protest it. Besides, one of the factory fellows is coming over. There's some flummery about it interfering with their moorings.

"Also, I wish you would not hand out any more money to young Arthur. I give him everything that it is good for a thirteen year old boy to have. Any more will make him careless about it."

There it ended with a spurt of temper that had obviously resulted in a broken pencil. Steve raised his eyebrows at Jennie, nodded, crumpled the paper into a ball, and thrust it into his dungaree pocket.

"I will do my level best," he told her, his voice saccharin, "to see that no further offense is offered today. Okay, Chickie?"

"I guess so." She smiled at him doubtfully. "It would be so much easier for me if you could try to keep from making him mad."

"Does he take it out on you?" Steve's brows came together threateningly. "If he does, I'll—"

"No, no, no!" She went up in a flutter of negatives, so like a disturbed hen that he had to smile. "I just mean the *tension*, you know. It's like working with a stretched wire, or something, and you don't know when it's going to break."

She whisked away from him and disappeared into the tiny office where the stretched wire awaited her.

"Well." Art looked up at his bookkeeper with impersonal impatience. "What did he say? Was he mad? Did he say he'd be here to that blessed hearing?"

"He didn't say; but I'm sure he will." After Steve's low tenor, Art's voice, several notes higher and tight with nerves, was always a surprise to Jennie.

"Is he going out to haul with a white shirt on? Silk shirt?" Art asked accusingly.

"I guess he is," she conceded. "It makes him look handsome, though, doesn't it?"

The sound he made and the look he gave her sent Jennie scurrying to her desk where she sat holding her breath, not daring to look at him, wondering what imp had possessed her to say such a thing. She heard him get up and cross the office. A moment later the snapping blare of the radio-telephone died, leaving silence except for the roar of wind through the building.

Steve, going down the runway to the slip and the two lobster cars, also heard it go off. He knew that Art had come out and finding nobody listening, had turned it off for fear a little electricity might be wasted.

The tide was at the flood and about half full. In the cool dimness under the wharf there was a constant drip of water and slime from the fish being landed above. Presently the splash would be solider when the boys started gutting and the gulls would leave the factory and come racing across the Harbor with the sure inexplicable instinct that here they would find food more satisfying than the occasional herring they could snatch from the *Sammy O*'s well-guarded store.

Steve wrinkled his lip at the noisome flats, wishing it could be high tide all the time. Take it on a hot summer day with the tide low about noon, and it was all a man could do to keep from puking at the smell.

He started the *Eloise* and her screw, just touching the flats, sent up a cloud of gray-blue mud bursting with gas bubbles to swash in and merge with the scummed-over leaching of the tide up across the shore.

He kicked the *Eloise* into gear and jogged out past the head of the wharf slowly. Here in the saucer-shaped Harbor, the wind couldn't get much of a sweep, not enough to rough the water. He could see the change in the character of the sea off Barlow's Point. Where the bar made off from the south side of the narrow mouth there was a line of wind and tide meeting, so definite that it might have been laid down with a straight-edge.

The big dragger moored at the head of the wharf was the *Sally & Joe* and she belonged to Benj. Swan & Sons. Steve sheered well off from her, looking at her trim, shining, black sides with superstitious distaste. She was forty-five feet of beauty and she gave him cold chills. Art had bought her, out of state, without mentioning it to Steve until she had been moored at the wharf.

Fully rigged for dragging, with a one-year-old, eight-cylinder, Chrysler Crown engine, she had cost thirty-five hundred dollars and was worth six thousand.

When she had arrived Steve went aboard with enthusiasm to look her over, heard her name, and got right off fast. He had never set foot on her again and never would. She was a handsome, great Percheron of a work boat and she made his *Eloise* look like a Shetland pony; but Steve would never work her.

SWAN'S HARBOR

Out of Rhode Island originally, she had been a high-liner from the time her hull touched the water. But she was a killer, and a dirty one.

Her builder had coughed his lungs out in bed because of her. Fire had broken out around the stovepipe in her forecastle and he had gone down with the extinguisher, closing the door carefully behind him to keep down the draft. It wasn't much of a blaze and he put it out; but it took him longer than he'd counted on, and in the excitement he managed to inhale a good deal of the chemical contents of the extinguisher. It took him two years to die.

Her second owner had ended his days in the state asylum. The *Sally & Joe* pulled his right leg off at the hip in her winch.

His widow had sold the boat and Art, getting her cheap, said he wasn't superstitious three thousand dollars worth. He had hired Will Holmes to work her. Apparently the combination of discouraged man and boat with the bad name had canceled bad luck, for it seemed to be working out. The Swan brothers had owned her four years now and she was still a high-liner. Art even refused to change her register and give her another name than the one under which she had murdered.

Steve shook his head thoughtfully, looking back at her. He had to admit she was one of the best boats he had ever set eyes on. He would have liked to go in one just like her. But not the *Sally & Joe*. Superstition was a silly business; but around the water it paid to bow down to wood and stone. If you have your tongue in your cheek when you do it, don't let the wood and stone know.

He rounded the end of the bar and the *Eloise*'s sharp graceful bow came up against the chop as if she had run into a stone wall. For five minutes he was as busy as he cared to be. When he finally pulled out of the tide rip and looked back, all he could see was the low shoulder of the Point field with the mountains going up right behind it. The stubby, familiar, gleaming white tower of the lighthouse, almost more prominent in daylight than it was at night, grew smaller as he watched.

Once safely out of sight, he slowed his engine and let her idle along while he peeled off the white silk shirt. Folding it carefully, he thrust it out of the way in the cuddy and pulled out the tattered work shirt he kept there.

The first three traps he hauled yielded only a few short lobsters and some crabs. He threw them overboard in disgust, except for two crabs which escaped him and scuttled wildly up and down the cockpit until he went after them and scaled them over too. Instead of re-setting the traps, he piled them on the wide, accommodating stern.

Obviously the lobsters had moved inshore and if he stayed out in deep water, he'd settle for wind pudding and air sauce. From the next five traps, he took three legal lobsters.

They were getting ready to shed all right and they must be right in on the rocks. With twenty traps piled high on the stern, he headed in toward the bluff red headlands. He was wondering idly if they were going to act as funny this year as they had last. When they finally started moving again, right up into early winter, he'd been getting soft shells, and it was a hell of a nuisance because it meant five cents a pound less.

He put the *Eloise*'s bow in until it looked as if her nose would vanish into the boil of white water at the foot of the high ledges. As he set the first traps in the lee of the land, the drops of spray showering back from the rocks were so cold they burned against his skin.

Shifting traps was a tedious, hard job and by noon his stomach was growling with hunger. It seemed to him he could feel it rubbing against the knobs on his backbone.

He glanced into the cabin and found with disgust that he'd forgotten his lunch bucket. Then, thoughtfully patting his stomach again, he decided it was all to the good. It wouldn't do him any harm to cut down on his intake a little.

Lord amighty, he thought, I sure would hate to get fat.

Nobly, stoically, and starving, he continued to shift traps. At two, with a start, he remembered the hearing, and snatched Art's note from his pocket.

He had an hour to get in and gas up and find something to eat. Fat or no fat, it wasn't healthy for a man to let himself get this hungry. He dived into the cabin and put on the white shirt, still as clean and spotless as it had been this morning. Grinning, he tucked in the tails and went back to his wheel. That shirt would lead Art to think that his brother had been lying around somewhere in the lee all day, doing nothing.

Just then, the whiplash at the end of the note, which had gone over his oblivious head in his interest in the two more important items, stung him hornet-like.

"*Also*," he read carefully, "*I wish you would not hand out any more money to young Arthur. I give him everything that it is good for a thirteen year old boy to have. Any more will make him careless about it.*"

Now how the hell did he know I'd been handing out anything to the kid unless young Arthur told him?

Steve's opinion of his nephew was not high. The boy made him think of one of those curly white grubs you dig up sometimes, pale and fat and slimpsy. But he was only thirteen and it was too early to say he wouldn't amount to anything.

Arthur never asked him for money, he had to hand the kid that much. Especially when he knew the youngster had fifty cents a week to dissipate with. It was easy enough to tell when he was broke, though, and it usually took place the day after he

received his half dollar. Young Arthur, who was talkative enough
to drive you crazy as a rule, would appear at the wharf monosyllabic, half deaf, mouth and shoulders drooping.

Finally, Steve, when he could stand it no longer, would say:
"You broke?"

"Yeah." Arthur could hear that the first time.

"Well, then, for chrissake, take this and get that mournful
pucker out of my sight!"

Arthur would grab for the bill like a trout taking a fly and
head up the dock on the dead run, his chubby buttocks flopping
gaily in trousers that were always too tight for him.

There was an understanding between them, acknowledged by
Steve's secrecy in handing it out and Arthur's speed of departure
after receiving it, that nothing must be said to anybody about
the transaction. Steve took pains to see to it that nobody was
looking. And now that fool of a kid had gone and told his father.

He roared wide-open around the bar and into the Harbor. It
was two-thirty when he came alongside the gasoline scow,
throttling down and jamming the gear into reverse only when it
seemed impossible to avoid cutting the scow in two or smashing
the *Eloise* to flinders. Lightly as a feather coming to rest, she slid
alongside the scow and he gaffed her to a stop against the white-
painted tire casings Hank Lord used for fenders.

Hank himself, chewing something and wiping his mouth with
the back of his hand, came out of the cool interior. Steve stared
at him hungrily.

"Give me some gas and what're you eating?"

"Lobster sandwich. Want one?"

"Yes, by the lord harry, I do."

Hank reappeared with two thick slices of bread dripping juice
and handed it down, his grimy fingers clutching it firmly. Steve

settled on the gunwale with the sandwich. He took the first bite warily.

"First time I ever had a lobster flavored with gasoline," he said, his mouth full. "Adds a good deal to the taste."

"I thought it did myself." Hank's skinny, wrinkled, dead-pan face, its eyes as sad as the monkey he resembled, regarded the surrounding world thoughtfully and came back to Steve. "Quite a crowd in there." He nodded at the wharf.

Following his nod, Steve found the head of the wharf cluttered with men. He said: "Humph!"

"Yeah," Hank agreed.

"What's going on? Didn't anyone but me go out today?"

"Oh, they went." Hank drew the remains of his own sandwich wrapped in a tatter of waxed paper from his hip pocket, regarded it sadly. "Only they didn't wait till noon to start out. Want a bottle of Moxie to finish up your sandwich?"

"Lord, no!"

"Warn't that the *Sally & Joe* unloading this morning?" Hank sounded casual. He went forward and snapped on the gas tank, coming back with the nozzle. But he stood waiting, his intent look belying the casual voice.

"Yeah, she was in. Still there." Steve could see her handsome black bow moored around the wharf beside the tiny *Pillbox*.

"I should think Will Holmes would have a conniption fit every time he took her out."

"Why?" Steve scowled at him, over the shards of the sandwich, willing to think his own thoughts about the big dragger, but reluctant to have anyone else put them into words.

Hank's eyes narrowed wisely. He thrust the nozzle of the gasoline hose into the *Eloise*'s tank and began pumping.

"Everyone in the Harbor ever read the *Maine Coast Fisherman* knows that boat was a killer. A boat don't get a name like that for nothing. I notice *you* ain't going in her."

"Oh, you're all a bunch of old women," Steve said rudely. "I'm not going in her because I can't go in more than one boat at a time." He glanced down at the gas tank and let out a scream of rage. "Hank! Look what you're doing, you goddamned fool, or I won't be going in this one."

Hank, deeply interested in Steve's reaction to his comments on the *Sally & Joe*, had filled the tank to brimming and was now running it over. He jumped and let go the trigger.

"Jesus, Steve, I'm sorry!"

"Well, watch it, will you? I don't want my bilges pumped full of gas." Steve put the last of the sandwich into his mouth. "I suppose I better go in. I don't doubt they're just waiting for me."

"I don't doubt," Hank echoed solemnly.

"I'd probably be ready to kill you half the time if I could only tell when you were joking and when you weren't."

A lined suggestion of a grin passed like a shadow over the sad features drooping above him.

"That's the only thing that saves my life, then."

Steve hauled out his day's catch and Hank looked admiringly at the contents of the single tub.

"No wonder you can live off the fat of the land! You must have all of five dollars·worth there."

"The cussed things have crawled away into the rocks."

"You shift your traps?"

"Yes, I did," Steve roared. "Now be sure and tell everyone in the Harbor so they can come out and set right on top of me tomorrow. I'm going to quit and go handlining if things don't pick up."

"I don't see myself why you bother to do anything," Hank

27

said. "All you got to do is hold out your hand and that business you and Art have got will drop in it every day for you."

"Is it anything to you?" Steve's voice was icy warning that Hank had gone too far. "As long as you get paid?"

"All right," Hank said placatingly. "I like this job. I just as soon work for you as for anyone."

That was the queer thing about Steve Swan, Hank thought, watching him arc slowly in to the wharf. You could get away with murder, talking to him, just so long as you kept your tongue off that business. Once you said anything about that, he'd damn near tear your head off. Steve was a good guy to work for. Most of the time he acted as if he never thought about being the boss. Too bad Art wasn't more like him.

Hank shrugged. As Steve had pointed out, he got his pay check on the dot, winter and summer.

As Steve neared the float he perversely refused to look up at the loafers. Jacky Gott was fishing lobsters out of the far car with the long handled dip net. At the head of the runway stood the woman who was obviously waiting for them. Steve recognized her as one of the middle-aged ladies from the cabins along the Point Shore.

He climbed out of his boat and went over to put his hand on the tweed-covered shoulder of the tall man who stood staring down past Jacky into the mysterious depths of the car, watching the languid green lobsters move lazily over the slatted bottom.

"Hey, Frank," he said.

Franklin Pierce spun to face him, his pale but weathered-looking face creasing into a smile.

"Reception committee," he said. "Me. Have you any comment to make on the coming proceedings?"

"I never heard of such a fuss being made over a little extension on a wharf," Steve complained. "You representing the Associated Press, or just here on your own?"

"Don't you know any time you and Art start making changes, everyone smells money?" Frank jerked his head at the mumble of voices. "Why, any one of those boys up there would eat without salt and pepper a ten dollar bill if they thought it would pay them interest."

He waited to see if Steve would say anything to that. When he didn't, Frank grinned. "Come on, you might as well go up and face them. The town fathers are there in force."

Forgetting the subject, Steve stood staring with concern at his friend's face. Frank Pierce was a tall man and he might have been a big one if there had been any suggestion of flesh over his bones. His hands were like bundles of thin sticks; his face gained a bloodhound look from the fold of flesh at each corner of his mouth. He had a tremendous beak of nose and its high bridge ran without delineation into the ridge of bone that shadowed his eyes. They were sharp and black and aware. His hair was black, too, and he wore it quite long; usually a lock or two hung over his low forehead, pointing up the peculiar pallor of his skin.

Inexplicably the two men were friends. They had met at college. Even then, Frank's tongue, lashing and vituperative at times, had kept him from making many friends. Those he did make were achieved, and held, in spite of himself. Steve was one of them, and Steve was responsible for his presence here in the Harbor. After the war Frank had wanted to go somewhere and buy a country newspaper. Steve, knowing that Ed Ellison had been trying to sell the Harbor Chronicle for years, had told Frank.

Nowadays they didn't see each other too often; but when they did there was no necessity to go through the sparring of acquaintances who have drifted apart. The friendship existed, they both knew it, and nothing could change it.

"You feel all right, Frank?" Concerned, Steve thought there was a new paleness under the normal one. Frank had obviously shaved that morning; but the fast beginning of his heavy black beard stood out strangely against the fine-grained skin. And Frank, who seldom took a drink until evening, had been drinking heavily.

"All right? I feel fine," Frank said evasively, not bothering to ask why Steve might think he didn't. "Let's go, hunh?"

Standing aside to let him go first up the runway, Steve happened to glance back at Jacky. Jacky's freckled handsome young face was almost as red as the flaming crest of his hair. He was just standing there, the net in his hand, gazing after them, his soft, adolescent lower lip drooping. It seemed to Steve his face looked unpleasantly heavy and he couldn't think why. Jacky caught Steve's stare and turned even redder.

"Get busy there, son." Steve made his voice gentle because his impulse was to snap and he could see no reason for it. "The lady's waiting for her lobsters."

Frank's three sons, looking from above all of a size, wandered along the malodorous edge of the water down in the chasms among the wharves, in the secret dripping caves under the spider-legged spiling, from which they would climb with their ragged sneakers muddy and their clothes covered with the thin, slimy green weed that formed on every wooden surface the tide covered.

Seeing them, blond, tanned, with none of their knobbiness concealed by the fragmentary crash shorts they wore, made Steve feel ten years old. They looked so much like the summer boys who used to come to play on the float with him, the Peters, Christophers, Julians.

He could feel the ache from icy water in the marrow of his arm when he had reached over the float for the winkles that grew under water among the weeds to use for bait for their flounder lines. In his memory, those boys with their strange names, were always blond and tanned. Their rumpled linen shorts came only inches down the mosquito-bitten thighs. Their knees, bony and protuberant, would never belong to stout puffing men.

Steve had known, that long ago, that they were intended for another life than his. They would be transformed, in their late teens, by a metamorphosis that would take place invisibly and far away from this summer shore, into lithe, handsome, pipe-smoking, young men, devoted for nine months of the year to the pursuit of a great future in the fields of subsidized endeavor: estate lawyers, investment counselors, career diplomats.

For the other three months, they would sail their Class S sloops or fool with their mahogany-colored Kris-Kraft in this same Harbor where they had once stood enviously and watched him row away from them.

Frank's three boys were called Bill and Sam and Joe; but aside from that, the same difference existed between them and young Arthur as had between Peter, Christopher, Julian and young Steve Swan. As they grew older it got wider, until it became a chasm across which the young men stared with recognizing eyes; but did not speak.

Only Frank's boys, Steve knew, had no certain future awaiting them and Arthur did. That, at least, had changed.

Below the runway, the tide, once more at the halfway mark but now ebbing, revealed a surface like some horrid kind of soft gray mold.

"Look at that mess," Frank said quickly over his shoulder. "For god's sake, Steve!"

"I know it." Slowly Steve brought his bothered attention back to the moment. "I was thinking just this morning it was god-awful. And on a hot day it really stinks."

"Well, why don't you do something about it?"

"Me?" In utter amazement, Steve stared down at the porous mud beneath his feet. "You want me to get down and lick it up with my tongue?"

"I mean it," Frank told him abruptly. "I'm thinking of doing an editorial about the condition of this Harbor. Whenever I see the boys swimming off these wharves, it gives me a cold grue."

"I still don't see what you expect me to do." Steve's voice got a little shorter with his temper. Quite often, in the last few weeks, he'd seen Frank's car parked in the graveled space at the head of the slip and had wondered what he was doing. He didn't know why, but the idea of Frank sitting up there watching the boys dive off the piling into the Harbor bothered him.

"You're responsible for a lot of it," Frank said.

"It's just one of those dirty associations that go along with making money," Steve told him philosophically.

"Possibly. But if every man here in the Harbor that has anything to do with polluting the water, you and Art, the sardine factory, Knowlton and Heard, if you all got together and arranged it right, you could buy a barge between you and haul your waste outside the Harbor into the deep water and dump it on the outgoing tide."

"Ha, ha, ha."

"What's wrong with *that* idea?"

"What's wrong with it is, did you ever hear tell of the Swan brothers ever getting together with anyone else when it involved the outlay of a little more cash and nothing to come back in from it?"

"Something should be done and done fast," Frank said. "Why, when I first came here, years back, you could get a boat up into

..those gunk-holes at the head of the Harbor any time of tide. It was pleasant, too. Up in Budro's Cove, or that little bight behind Jill's Island. Now, even at this time of tide, they're both so silted in you can't get near them. Stinking mud up to your hips! You're going to lose the whole Harbor unless somebody sees far enough ahead to do something. And believe me, Stevie, it'll involve more money later."

"It won't involve mine," Steve told him firmly. "Wait long enough and the Government will dredge it out."

"Whose money will that involve, if not yours," Frank flung back at him.

Trouble with you, Steve told the tweed-covered shoulders ahead of him silently, you're a crusader who's run out of causes. Frank would probably die someday as uselessly as a man rushing back into the flaming ruin of a circus tent after his wife's forgotten hand-bag.

He was glad to come up out of the turgid atmosphere on the float into the cold heady feeling of justified tension on the wharf. He stepped past the woman waiting for her lobsters with a brief nod and a smile and she, who had grown accustomed to long, semi-flirtatious conversations with him, stared after his broad back in affronted surprise.

Art had seen him coming. As soon as he stepped over to the group waiting at the wharf-head, Art came through the long, cavernous, wind-runneled cutting shed. He walked forever peering from side to side, looking for waste effort, waste motion, anything that might be salvaged. He had done it now for so many years that even when he walked along the street uptown where the discovery of waste couldn't possibly be affected by his notice, he did the same thing. His eyes were never still on the face of anyone he spoke to; but always probing and peering, now over this shoulder, now over that, and finally concentrated on a

33

point about six inches above the head of his conversational opponent.

As he came out the sliding double door, Ansel Johnson pulled his cheap thick watch out of his pocket and glanced at it.

"Five minutes of three," he said and stopped to clear a nervous rattle of phlegm from his throat. "Near enough to make no difference. Let's get it over with."

He paused and looked about him thoughtfully, as if he fully expected somebody else to take over. Since he was the First Selectman and obviously the man to do it, nobody else said anything and he had to go on.

"Well, we've had a petition from Benjamin B. Swan & Sons for permission to extend this wharf fifty feet out from its present length. This hearing is in case anyone wants to object."

He stopped again. While he had been speaking, Steve's glance had gone the rounds of the waiting faces. He thought he had picked out those who were here out of curiosity and because they thought there might be a little excitement, and those who meant business.

Arlington Sargent was the engineer on the *Sammy O*. He leaned negligently against the sun-warmed side of the building, just there for the buggy-ride; but the two men with him were there for a purpose. One was Bill Theriault, the Harbor-Master. The other was a stranger to Steve. He wore a business suit and a fine straw hat with a flaming puggaree band, and he stood out like a sore toe among the dungarees and khaki pants and rubber boots around him.

Without lifting his eyes from the particular plank in the wharf he had been examining closely for the last five minutes, Bill said softly:

"Ansel, I've been telling you for the last three years I don't dare issue no more mooring permits in the Harbor. There just ain't room. The way they're put down now, you couldn't squeeze a pea-pod in here and expect her to ride safe. Trouble is, in the beginning everyone put down his mooring where he wanted it without considering anyone else, and I've had to issue permits for in-between, kind of. Now, when you get the wind and tide opposite, every boat in the Harbor's kissing someone else's. You take a fifty foot bite out here, it'll be hell, won't it?"

"I know you been telling me," Ansel agreed with him easily. "But I can't see much in the way of interference right here." He glanced out across the shining water.

"That's because the sardine boats ain't moored out there," Bill pointed out. "Summer-time, it's all right. You take it when those three are to their moorings, they can sweep the whole Harbor, practically."

The stranger jabbed him over the kidneys with an impatient forefinger and Bill jumped.

"Oh, yes," he said, rubbing the spot carefully. "This is Mr. Cameron."

Every man on the wharf had heard that name and knew it; but few of them had actually seen the owner of the sardine factory. As one, they turned to look their fill. Cameron took a confident step forward, bearing that concentrated gaze with the equanimity of one well accustomed to attention.

"I don't know that I needed to come to this hearing," he said easily. "But I just wanted to point out to the Selectmen that I'm not a resident of this state. And I could undoubtedly find winter mooring for my boats in almost any harbor along the coast, until April first, anyhow."

Ansel could feel himself turn pale. What Cameron said sounded like a non-sequitur, but wasn't. Ansel could visualize the page

35

in the town valuation book on which the personal property of the Peter Cameron Company was listed for purposes of taxation. The tax those boats brought, if lost, would make an awful dent in the budget. The taxation law governing boats said simply that the boats of any non-resident of the state could be taxed where found on April first.

"Well," he began carefully, trying to choose his words so nobody could get mad. "I don't think *you* have anything to worry about, Mr. Cameron. It certainly never occurred to me to make any difficulty about your moorings. They've been established a good many years. As far as I know, we're all in agreement that they can stay there."

"Thank you very much." Cameron nodded at him, coolly. "I think we understand each other perfectly. In that case, I won't take any more of your time."

He went without a backward glance. But Arley Sargent, as he gathered himself together to follow, couldn't resist giving Anse an impudent wink. Anse flushed angrily, opened his mouth, and shut it again, without speaking.

Damnation take it, he thought, this is a hell of a job!

"All right." A new voice took up the silence. "Now it's my turn."

Steve glanced over Anse's shoulder at the young man who had come up from his seat on the liars' bench along the wall to confront authority. Carl Benson might possibly have been twenty-two or three. His long narrow face had the bumpy, uncoagulated look of youth. He was still young enough to be mad before anyone had done anything to him. His fair skin under the rough blond hair was red with anger and his eyes narrowed as if he stared into the sun.

"What have you got to say, young fellow? We're here to

listen." Once more confident and assured, Anse smiled at him with the tolerance age assumes to youth and which means only that age considers youth extremely foolish, but is prepared to listen to the foolishness.

"I just like to point out if these fellers build their wharf out fifty feet, it'll bring my boat practically underneath it."

Anse and Steve turned to look at the boat in question. Art came slowly across from the door and looked with them. As far as paint and brightwork went, she was as trim as any boat in the Harbor; but she was so small she might have been a lobster boat in miniature.

"Pretty little thing, ain't she," Anse said, without thinking. "Looks kind of like a toy."

"Well, she ain't no toy," Carl said hotly.

"Now, look, son, it's this way." Anse turned to face the aggrieved owner. "A fifty foot extension on this wharf will mean a good deal to the town in taxes." Steve happened to be looking at his brother just then. Art's eyes closed slowly and an expression of deep pain flickered across his face. "You don't want to stand in the way of progress, just for the sake of a mooring, do you?"

"Yes, I do!"

"That's no way to act," Anse said soothingly.

"My mooring's been down there as long as Cameron's has or longer. My father used it. My grandfather put it there. By Judast, it's going to stay there."

"Look, bud." Steve approached him slowly, thinking the kid was almost mad enough to take a poke at him and that would be too bad because he might have to hurt him, holding him off. "You've got a steady job uptown, carpentering, haven't you?"

"So what?"

"Well, I was just getting at this, lobstering is kind of a sideline with you. You come down and haul in the morning and at night, after work."

"So what?" Carl said again, more belligerently. "I got a license. I'm not breaking any law."

"We've let you get away with it so far," Steve's voice softened threateningly. "But the fellows that make a living at it, the *fishermen*, they don't think much of the way you kids do, setting a few traps just for the fun of it. The fishermen don't like it, see?"

"Yeah, and the *fishermen*,"—Carl aped his italics insultingly— "don't think much of the dealers lobstering, neither, making five cents a pound on every one the *fishermen* bring in and ten cents a pound on their own. The *fishermen* don't like that, either."

For a startled moment Steve, looking around the circle of interested faces couldn't find an eye that would meet his. He was too surprised to say anything, and Ansel took it before he could get his mind ready to accept this news.

"All right, son," he said, still easily. "As far as I'm concerned, the permit is granted. As soon as they hear from the War Department, they can go ahead and build. You'll just have to move your boat."

"I knew damn well how it would be." Carl's voice sounded like a defective fire cracker. "All right, Theriault, blast you, you can find me another mooring."

Bill shrugged, spreading his hands, and was silent.

Steve left them there discussing it and strode up the wharf to the parking space. The idea that he himself might be resented by the aristocracy, the fishermen, had never entered his head before. Now that it had, he was having trouble with the idea.

Frank caught up with him just as he laid his hand on the Cadillac's shining door.

"Well." Frank's bloodhound face was ruefully amused. "Got a little dose of truth for your money, didn't you?"

"*Is* it truth?"

"I saw you looking them over. There wasn't one would look back, was there?"

"No-o-o." Steve's eyes, heavy with doubt, searched the familiar face. "You know, I think of almost everything; but I'll be eternally blessed if I ever thought of that. I guess I never considered myself a dealer in the first place, since Art does all that work."

"Kind of hard to take, isn't it? Finding out the fishermen don't approve of something *you're* doing. Makes it different when you're on the other side for a change."

"To hell with them," Steve said abruptly. He climbed into the car and started the great purring engine. "I've got along so far. If they don't like the way I do things, they can all go to the devil."

There was a stir of movement in the next car and Steve, leaning forward slightly, met squarely the frankly curious eyes of the girl who was, in her turn, leaning forward slightly to see him. Anger might have let him stare past her as if she had been invisible except for a teasing familiarity about her face. Her big eyes looked like a kitten's, and Steve's anger changed slowly to amusement when he thought that a kitten could never manage to look that naive.

Evidently she had heard them talking and was curious enough to want to see who they were. Steve grinned and looked at Frank, jerking his head toward the spectator.

"There's a cute little thing," he said softly.

Frank's eyes rested momentarily and without interest on the occupant of the next car. Apparently he didn't take in what Steve had said, or considered it beneath notice.

"Steve," he said, leaning in the window. "I'm on my way again."

"Oh?" Steve glanced at him thoughtfully.

"Getting a little restless," Frank said with a weak grin. "I guess it's time I took another trip."

"Well," Steve sounded agreement, not really giving it any thought. "Maybe it's a good idea."

He was used to these periodic trips that seemed to be necessary to Frank's happiness. Usually, though, Frank just lit out without telling anyone, and Steve wished he would do it that way this time.

"Maybe you'll feel better when you get back." He wasn't even hearing his own words, watching instead the unembarrassed feminine face through the window of the next car. Usually when you stared at anyone like that you could make them look away; but she seemed completely unaware of his gaze. She simply looked and kept on looking.

"Christ almighty," Frank said bitterly. "All you ever think about is women!"

Steve jumped and turned to stare at him; but Frank was gone. Hastily Steve got out of the car and yelled after him. Frank, half-way across to his own car, didn't look back.

Steve shrugged and let him go. He would cool off.

He stood hesitating, thinking of the girl in the next car, wondering what she'd do if he appeared at her window ready to talk. He glanced at the license plate, found it an in-state one, and filed the knowledge for future reference. If she were visiting somewhere in town, he'd be bound to run into her under easier circumstances.

He drove away thinking, I'm about ready for a little change myself. Maybe that's it. No harm in finding out. She had cer-

tainly seemed interested enough. He was watching the other car
in his rear view mirror, trying to see if she was still looking after
him; but he couldn't tell.

Promptly at six-thirty, Steve Swan came down from his bedroom again, using the back stairs this time. He had heard the
door-bell give its asthmatic buzz ten minutes ago; but he'd told
Minnie six-thirty and he didn't intend to show himself before
that minute.

He had also heard Lizzie go bustling to open the door, and
the ensuing hum of conversation told him that she was effectively
entertaining his annual guests. From the smells that drifted up to
him through the open register, he judged that she had also taken
steps to serve up an impressive supper.

He found that Ann had left a package of her cigarettes on the
bedside table. She smoked one of those mentholated brands and
the package was distinctively not his. He scooped it into the
table drawer out of sight and, on second thought, took it carefully back out again and put it right where he'd found it. He left
the table light on. It burned palely in the low light room; but
later on when Minnie and the kids had to make their nine o'clock
journey up to the bathroom, it would light their way past his
bedroom. He was pretty sure Minnie would notice the cigarettes.
As far as he could tell, the only reason she accepted this yearly
invitation was to see what was going on in the old house and
what changes he'd made. Might as well give her something to
think about.

They were all sitting in the big front room into which they
had come because Minnie, after having lived one year of her mar-

ried life in this house, would never make the mistake of using the back door when she came as a guest.

Steve stopped at the kitchen, glanced in, and turned to the door of the seldom used dining room. He noted that the table was carefully set with his mother's best Staffordshire that lived all year long in the corner china closet and was used perhaps twice during that time. There was no cloth to hide the deep lights in the rosewood table, only a few mats where the hot dishes would sit. That was right and the way he liked it. Lizzie must have polished the thin old silver. It did nothing so hard as glisten. Rather it had a dull sheen that was a combination of age, use, and elbow-grease.

He was nodding his head with satisfaction when he appeared in the door to look down at his company. Lizzie was standing with her back to him talking to Minnie who sat very straight in the rocker by the window. The two children, Arthur and Patty, were on their knees before the little glass cupboard that held the souvenir scrimshaw and ivory elephants, the clippers in distorting old bottles, the gew-gaws and knick-knacks from fifty voyages to odd corners of the earth.

Art himself, not listening to the clatter of the women, was staring moodily out one of the big windows across the Bay where the dying northwest wind still drew sharp lines of light and shadow across the living water.

"Well, Minnie," Steve said jovially. "How's my old girl?"

There was considerable truth in the epithet. She had been his girl fifteen years ago and still enjoyed pretending there was a special understanding between them. He went over and kissed her thin cheek firmly, not because he particularly enjoyed it but because Art would be watching this bit of by-play. She got up to meet him.

"Steve, every time I come into this house, I think what a shame there isn't a woman to enjoy it. No man deserves such a lovely place all to himself."

"You had your chance," Steve said lightly and then, lest she think he referred to their own old romance, he added, not too quickly: "You and your family could have stayed right here where you were. I was willing."

"Yes." Minnie sighed regretfully, thinking of the little six-room bungalow Art had moved her into when they left this house. It was new and close to neighbors on each side and never so long as it stood would it have the grace and light that age had given this house.

"Lizzie." Steve turned to her. "How about it? Can't we eat? I'm starving."

"Go right in and sit down," Lizzie said. "I'll have supper there as soon as you are."

He had heard her sniff when Minnie had said this house needed a woman and the sniff told him he was still unforgiven for the night before; but when Lizzie reached the sniffing stage that meant she had begun to condone and would soon forgive.

Steve stood aside and let Minnie go ahead of him. He motioned to Art who went past him with head bent and eyes going from side to side rapidly, finding enough to make him gasp at the waste of hard-earned money.

"Come on, Patty." Steve glanced at his little niece and away quickly. The little girl flipped by him; but when young Arthur would have done the same, Steve stopped him with a firm hand on his pudgy shoulder. Arthur's fat young face was startled and mournful. With surprise Steve saw that the boy was growing taller and that the face was a little less fat.

"What is it, Uncle Steve?"

"You young idiot," his uncle whispered fiercely. "How did

43

you let him find out I was giving you money? I thought you'd know better!"

"I needed some new corduroys," Arthur whispered too, casting a fearful glance after his father's back just disappearing safely into the dining room. "I—I got two pairs and a shirt with that ten you gave me and he saw them."

"Ten! I thought it was five."

Arthur's faint grin was surprisingly mischievous.

"I surmised you did; but it was ten."

"It's a mistake I won't make again. Did he lambaste you?"

Arthur looked reminiscently chastened.

"Well, yes, kind of."

"Serves you right, being so damned dumb. Look, I give it to you to teach you how to waste it. Don't spend it on anything he can see, nothing sensible. Throw it away. It's no good if you don't enjoy it."

Arthur's pale face was shocked but willing to learn. His eyes got suddenly intent and a deeper blue.

"It's kind of hard to waste all that," he said.

"You can learn if you try."

"It'd be easier if Daddy was as rich as you are, Uncle Steve."

"Get it through your thick head, will you. I haven't got anything he hasn't. I enjoy mine. All it's good for is to spend while you can enjoy it. He's saving his for a gold-lined coffin just to prove you *can* take it with you."

He saw he'd gone a little too far in too much of a hurry. Young Arthur's face took on the slightly stupid, stubborn look that Steve disliked so.

"Daddy's got a family to support," he pointed out and Steve recognized the source of this wisdom.

"Arthur." Minnie's voice called tightly from the dining room. "Are you coming?"

SWAN'S HARBOR

"Yes, mama," Arthur said and clumped hastily down the hall.
"Yes, daddy; yes, mama," Steve said softly, mimicking the obedient young voice cruelly, but unheard by anyone but himself.
Lizzie crossed the hall just ahead of him with a steaming platter and when he appeared in the door, Arthur was just settling into his chair and Lizzie was putting the platter of steak before his own place with the dignity it deserved. Opposite him, at the other end of the table, Minnie sat, very straight, and looking at her face, now harshly revealed in the light from the old overhead dome, Steve thought the last fourteen years had not been gentle with her.

When he had been nineteen and she a year younger, she had been a pretty, plump, flirtatious girl, full of life and fun to fool around with. Empty-headed as they came, though, and no one you'd want to have around the rest of your life. Now she sat there, only fifteen years older; but if looks counted, it might have been twenty-five. Her hair was still brown but no longer glossy and there was a liberal salting of gray over temples now so thin the blue veins were visible. Her entire face, once thoughtless and laughing, had fallen easily into the lines of denial and patience.

Steve glanced at his brother, wondering if Art could see what he'd done to his wife, but he found Art staring at the great bouquet of old-fashioned white narcissus Lizzie had put in the center of the table.

The two children, Patty's head barely appearing over the edge of the table, were more interested in the carving. Hastily he filled their plates, with a heavy hand.

"Don't wait," he said. "Start right in."

"Minnie," Art said. "Will you say grace, when it's time?"

"If Steve doesn't mind."

That'll show me. Steve bent his head over the steak. Perversely, when it came to Art's serving, he put half one of the tremendous

45

T-bones on the plate and handed it over. Art sat for a minute staring down at it, his eyes bulging. Look at him, Steve thought, trying to keep the corners of his mouth straight, even when he's getting it himself, he thinks it's too much.

He filled his own plate, nodded at Minnie, and bowed his head stiffly.

"Oh, Lord," Minnie said tentatively. "For that which we are about to receive, make us duly grateful. Amen."

For the next ten minutes everyone was too busy for conversation. After that, a desultory sort of talk about weather and her own physical ailments sprang up between Steve and his sister-in-law. She enjoyed talking to him because he was the only man who would listen patiently to her ills. She thought him charming, but was too much a wife actually to regret the hasty way she had rebounded from his announcement years ago that he was completely unready to marry anyone. What she felt was not as active as regret. It was only a nostalgic consideration of what might have happened.

He thought her a brainless and silly woman and let her talk simply to fill in the gulf of silence that lay between himself and his brother.

Minnie's chatter carried them through supper and back into the front room where they sat drinking coffee from the tiny, red-figured, Chinese cups that felt like a bubble in the hand.

"I don't know that we ever used these cups before, Steve." Minnie held hers up to the light. "They're lovely."

"They're valuable, too," Art told her abruptly. "Mother always kept them in the curio cabinet. She never used them."

"That's what they're for, to use," Steve said.

At nine exactly, as he had foreseen, Minnie had to take Patty upstairs. Five minutes later they came down again, Patty looking relieved and Minnie with her head high and a little unusual color across her prominent cheek-bones. A more sophisticated woman would have ignored his trap; but Minnie couldn't.

"You've changed your brand of cigarettes, Steve."

"Oh, no." Innocently he held up the familiar white and red package from which he was at the moment extracting a cigarette. "No. I stick by my favorites."

"Oh?" She persisted. "I thought you might have started smoking those mentholated ones. Easier on your throat."

"I wouldn't touch the things with a ten-foot pole," Steve assured her with exaggerated interest. "Why?"

"Nothing," Minnie said shortly. "No reason." She sat staring in silence at her bony hands. Following her glance, Steve saw that her fingers were twined so tightly together the knuckle joints showed white. Art was staring at her curiously and from her to his brother's ugly assured face.

Inordinately amused at his own childishness and the success of his silly ruse, Steve grinned secretly down at the lighted match. That was it, he thought, once you have any soft talk with a women, forever afterward she thinks she has an interest in you. He was sadly amused to find that Minnie was still jealous of him.

"Minnie." For the fourth time that evening, Art spoke, making it clear, as he had the other three, that it was his wife he addressed and nobody else. "It's nine-thirty. Time the kids were getting to bed."

"Yes, I suppose so." Reluctantly she sat for another moment looking around the room, wondering if she could ever make a room in her own home feel the way this one did and knowing she never could.

Arthur came silently and obediently to the sound of his father's voice, and Minnie, getting up, put her hand proudly on his shoulder.

"What do you think of this boy going out to earn his own living this summer, Uncle Steve?"

Steve, who disliked that particular form of address deeply, was almost too annoyed to take in what else she had said. He glanced at Arthur.

"That so? What's he going to do, caddy at the Club?"

"No, indeed." Minnie glanced with slightly tearful pride at her son whose curly head was almost level with her own. "He's nearly a grown man now." Arthur was writhing with embarrassment. "His father thinks he's old enough this summer to do his share, so he's going to let him go on the *Sally & Joe*."

Steve, completely aware of what she'd said this time, got suddenly to his feet. His motion startled them all, it was so abrupt. Minnie and the children stared at him. Art turned up the corners of his mouth in a faintly derisive grin.

"*What?*" Even to himself Steve's voice sounded queer.

"What?" Minnie echoed in amazement. "I don't— He's going on the dragger."

"I heard you." Aware that he was going to make himself look silly because he couldn't bring himself to give her the true reason for what he intended to say, Steve was defensively more vehement than he'd meant to be.

"You can't let him do it, Minnie," he said firmly, staring directly into his sister-in-law's pale surprised face. "You mustn't let that kid go on that dragger."

"I don't understand, Steve. They need a boy and there's no reason why Arthur shouldn't have the job. It's sort of silly to let a good job like that go out of the family when he's fully capable of doing it."

Arthur himself, unaccustomed to being a bone of contention, stood staring in amazed dismay, feeling that his uncle was letting him down sadly by his attitude.

"He isn't capable of it." Steve seized on the only sensible explanation for his own reaction. "The work, Minnie—it'll be too hard for him. He's a big boy; but he's only fourteen. It will be too—

"And besides," he had an altogether new thought and maybe that would soften her. "He's never been around with a couple of men like that. He's nothing but an innocent baby. You can't tell what ideas they'll put in his head."

Minnie's head lifted stiffly, warningly.

"Steve, you're too apt to judge everyone by yourself. I think I know those men and they'll have sense enough to hold their tongues a little with Arthur around."

"Oh,—" If he had said the word that hesitated on his tongue, Steve knew she'd turn her back and leave him. So he swallowed it and said instead: "Minnie, I think you are making a mistake."

"*I* don't think so." She gave a light amused laugh. "I think I can trust my own boy."

"Oh, hell!" Steve shrugged. "It's your business. If he was my kid, he wouldn't go."

"Remember there are ladies here," Minnie said, her offended gaze telling him he had gone so far now she wouldn't even hear what he said to her if he chose to say more. "Besides, he's *not* yours."

Art got to his feet as if he'd been stung.

"Come on, Min," he said. "The party's over."

He ushered his little brood out the door into the night; but he let Minnie come back to repair her forgotten manners.

"Thank you for the lovely supper, Steve. Children, you didn't remember to thank Uncle Steve for the lovely supper."

Soberly Steve accepted the prompted thanks of the two young Swans. As the family moved away down the walk and around the hill, he heard Art saying: ✦

"There is no room for superstition in business."

And Minnie, her voice high with outrage:

"But, Art, I still don't understand what it's all about."

"There's nothing to understand," Art growled. "He's got some silly idea in his head."

Their voices died and Steve, standing silently in the door, staring into the warm, lilac-scented darkness, thought perhaps he had been pretty silly. He still felt firmly that young Arthur should not be allowed to go on the dragger. Superstititon in business? Maybe not. But superstition concerning anything to do with the water was different. It wasn't business. It was simply propitiating whatever dark gods there might be. No one could be sure, himself least of all, that they didn't exist.

Will Holmes knew the *Sally & Joe* like a book. He kept his eye on the ways things were going. For four years nothing had gone wrong, chances were, nothing would. But if Steve could think of a more sensible reason why young Arthur should stay ashore, he intended to use it. A grown man stood a fair chance in an emergency; but a soft kid like Arthur would lose his head too easily.

Lizzie was putting the final touches on the kitchen when Steve went to see if the back door was locked. He glanced in at her.

"Well," she said. "Did you enjoy your evening?"

"Mmm. So-so."

"I don't see how you could, liking to talk the way you do. I don't see how you can sit there listening to that poor silly woman, with *him* like a thunder-cloud alongside you."

"It's only once a year," he protested.

Lizzie gave a last considering look around at the kitchen. Points of light shone back at her from every surface that could possibly reflect a light. Satisfied that everything was done, she permitted herself a short sigh, the closest she ever came to admitting weariness.

"I don't know," she said consideringly. "I—I realize certainly, I owe the Swan family a lot—"

"You don't owe anyone anything."

"No, let me finish. It's just—I can't understand you two boys. It doesn't seem right for two brothers not to speak to each other. If you're going to be like that, why do you have to be together all the time? If you're not going to be decent to each other, stay apart. It's so hard on everyone else."

"I speak to Art whenever I feel like it," Steve said.

"Yes; but whenever you feel like it is when you're good and mad. Oh, don't think I don't know you, Steve! I know the way you work so well I could tell two weeks ahead what you're going to do."

He glared at her, stung.

"That's silly!"

"I know," she purposely misunderstood him. "That's what I've been saying. But it's true."

"Oh, Lizzie." Steve went over and put his arm around her firmly corseted waist, smiling into her old, wise, puzzled eyes. "Would you believe it, I can't even remember now why it was he decided he wasn't going to speak to me any more. Isn't that ridiculous?"

"It most assuredly is! It's hardly even human." She let herself stay in the circle of his hard young arm just long enough to show she had forgiven him for bringing Ann into the house. Then, firmly and gently, she moved away. "I'm tired. I'm going up to bed. Why, when I first knew you two boys, you were together all the time. I remember thinking it was so nice to see two brothers liking each other the way you did. When your Ma and

Pa were living. The house was always full of happy people. It seems kind of lonely now."

"Maybe I'll bring you home somebody to keep you company one of these days," he said teasingly, more to get her mind off Art than because he meant it. He was astounded to see her eyes cloud with the sudden weak tears of age.

"It would be the making of you, to get married and settle down."

"I didn't say anything about marrying."

"Stephen Swan! I will leave this house and never set foot in it again if you ever bring a woman here to live without being married to her!"

"Give you my promise, I won't do it," he said quickly, laughing, backing away from her with his hands up protectingly and Lizzie swept past him. Halfway upstairs she apparently thought of something more to say. She turned abruptly, but then all she said was: "Good night, Stephen."

An hour later Steve turned out the last light and went to bed. In summer he slept with the three east-facing windows wide open. Tonight the wind sucked the white curtains out against the screens. He could lie in bed and look out across the moon-silvered Bay to the islands, seeing it in the incredible light as clearly as he could see in daylight. There was an entirely different spirit abroad over the Bay at night. It looked like land and water divorced from humanity, a place where men would never dare to go, knowing if they ventured out of sight of home and lights and other men, they would never come back.

He lay on his back, hands under his head, staring, not restlessly like a man who can't sleep, although it was unusual for him to lie awake.

When he had told Lizzie he couldn't remember what Art and he had quarreled about, he was telling her the truth. Thinking back, he searched the secret recesses of his mind and found only small things. Nostalgically he remembered Art as he had been and wished him back, the Art who had been ten and twelve when he was himself. But as he thought about it, he knew the suspicion, the coldness, the growing apart had been starting when they were that young.

The always-more-frequent, niggling disagreements over less than nothing had resulted in an armed truce between them by the time they were out of high school.

Art had seemed to resent everything Steve did, had behaved as if he thought Steve might be trying to take away from him something he valued. Perhaps he had, Steve thought ruefully. It had always amused him to try for the same prize Art did: the girl, the boat, the honor, whatever it might be. He'd usually managed to get it by a hair, leaving Art to brood over each successive loss. That particular young rivalry died for want of fuel when Steve went away to college and Art refused to go, claiming that a fisherman with a college education was a pretty silly sort of character.

The summer the twins were twenty, Benjamin Swan and his wife had left them in Lizzie's care and gone off on a vacation, the first one they'd ever taken without the boys.

Steve remembered as clearly as if he were living through it again, coming home at three o'clock Sunday morning from a dance at the Forks. He wasn't tight, but he was feeling high when he climbed out of his old Ford and came whistling up the path to the back door.

He'd thought at first the light in the front room had been left burning for him. But he found Art, dressed only in his pajamas, sitting in the wing chair beside the fireplace. He wasn't crying when Steve came in; but his face looked soaked, his eyes swollen. He stared sullenly and in silence at his brother's cheerful face.

Steve felt himself turn pale at first sight of Art, as though the blood had left the extremities of his body and gathered in a heavy useless pool in the bottom of his stomach.

He looked quickly from Art to Lizzie who sat opposite him, fully dressed and decent except that her hair, loose and amazingly thick, hung around her face in witch locks. Steve was astonished, never having seen her so distraught she couldn't put her hair up. Her long face, free of the coating of dead-white powder, couldn't have been whiter than it was. Her eyes looked like cigarette burns in a sheet.

"What?" Steve said blankly and, because his legs refused to hold him up, sat down on the top step.

"While you been out tom-catting around," Art said accusingly.

Lizzie stopped him with a glance. She got up like a woman in a slow-motion picture, crossed the room, and handed Steve the piece of paper she'd been twisting in her fingers.

The telegram was short because some local official had been trying to save money. It told him that Benjamin and Ellice Swan had got as far as Eastport on their way home from the Maritimes. A steep hill, a blinding rain, the early deceptive light of evening, had stopped them there. The car had turned over three times, leaving the road, and they had both been killed instantly.

The boys found, when the old man's will was read, that they had little in the way of actual cash assets; but a thriving and healthy business. After stilted discussion, they fell rather than reasoned themselves into a division of labor, governed partly by Steve's insistence on finishing his two last years at Brunswick.

Art would handle the business end of things, which he had already begun to do. Steve, when he stopped wasting time on a needless education and came home to go to work, would take care of everything else. Two years later, he came back to a smoothly

running concern where everything else seemed to be neatly
taking care of itself. That suited him. Bored by the details of
business, he would never question them as long as the income was
unflagging.

Alone, Art had far-sightedly managed to build the business into
a spider-like, minor empire that would have astounded Benjamin
Swan by its scope. From the very first he had insisted that every
penny of profit should be divided three ways: one went back
into the firm, one went to Steve, the third Art kept himself.

It seemed to Steve a grasping unpleasant process. The business
had made enemies for him he didn't even know he had. But he
could find nothing to object to in the third share that came regu-
larly to him. He enjoyed money and liked to spend it better than
most.

They still spoke to each other during the next three years
when they were getting under weigh, but Art withdrew more
and more until toward their twenty-third year, he was talking
only about things that had to do with Benjamin Swan & Sons.

The final break came the summer they were twenty-three and
at another dance at the same dance hall. Steve began to wonder
if every crisis in his life would come at the end of an evening
spent in the crepe-paper hung, shaky, old building at the Forks.

The summer before he had taken up with Minnie Palmer, liking her for the plump, jolly carelessness that had vanished so
completely. They'd had a lot of fun together, but when Minnie
started getting serious, Steve, looking about him at greener fields,
had decided that twenty-three was too young to settle down.
He simply didn't want to get married. He had an idea Minnie
still wondered what had gone wrong and why she found herself
going to dances with other young men.

He hadn't seen her for a long time, and when he spotted her
on this particular July evening, he thought as he watched her

circle the floor, he had never seen Minnie look so blooming. Her face had fined a little; but it had a new and secure happiness that went deeper than the simple jollity.

He had cut in and after one waltz they slipped out the side door together.

"Like old times, Steve." Minnie had given him a laughing glance with no trace of the coquettishness he remembered.

He had learned that night that a woman could be friendly and fun to be with and still not leave you an opening to make a pass at her. They had gone over to the Cafe in Centerville, had a sandwich and malted, and come back to the dance. That was all, and they had both enjoyed themselves.

Back at the Forks, Steve spotted a familiar figure draped over the railing outside the wide lighted door.

"Why, there's Art," he'd pointed out in surprise.

"Oh," Minnie said softly, apparently realizing something Steve didn't. She got out of the car and went over to Art with Steve trailing behind her.

"Hi, son," Steve said jovially. "I didn't know you were here. How long you been here?"

Art didn't answer him; instead he looked at Minnie and his face was dark with fury.

"Where've you been?"

"We just went over to Centerville for a sandwich."

"Yes, I'll believe that—with him!"

"Take my word for it, Art. It's the truth." Steve was too puzzled to be mad yet; but he was beginning to feel a suspicious warmth around the back of his neck. "What's it to you?"

"Plenty!" Art turned on him. "I'm damned if I want my wife running around alone with you."

The insult went right over Steve's head, completely lost in amazement.

"Wife!" He stared from one to the other.

"We were married at seven o'clock tonight," Minnie said softly. "I thought I'd get a chance to tell you; but I couldn't seem to get started."

Art's shoulders were heaving with imperfectly repressed rage.

"I would have told him in good time, believe me."

Steve felt suddenly lost and lonesome. Being away all winter, he hadn't even known that Art and Minnie were going together. And now they were married and hadn't told him!

"Art, you never even asked me to stand up with you!" Steve still couldn't believe that the rift growing between them had grown so wide that Art would do anything as important as getting married without even letting him know. He found his mistake in Art's eyes. They were icy and gray as sea water on a January day.

"I was afraid—" Art said nastily "—you might forget which one of us was the groom!"

Steve felt his right hand close into a fist; but he hesitated because it hardly seemed right to sock a man on his wedding night, and that man his own brother. By the time he'd decided he would anyhow it was too late. Art had grabbed Minnie's arm and marched her into the lighted hall, leaving Steve to glare after them in furious astonishment.

That had been the last time he'd ever heard Art's voice directed actually to him.

Lying in bed on that other night, he had heard them come up the stairs, past his door, to Art's bedroom. Their voices had gone on long into the night, Art's low, steady, unchanging; Minnie's getting higher and higher until finally he heard her crying. At that he had climbed out of bed and banged loudly on the wall.

"For pete sake, quiet down and let a guy sleep, will you?"

The voices in the other room had stopped instantly.

The four of them had lived there together in the old house for the next year, with Lizzie and Minnie to carry messages from brother to brother when it became necessary. Young Arthur had been born there.

Three months after his birth, Steve, who had been driven nearly mad by the constant squalling of his grub-like, baby nephew, was relieved to find that Art wanted to sell his share of the house. He wanted to move downtown. He made it all clear in a long note he left with Lizzie and which she handed to Steve by one corner as if it might bite her.

Steve read it under the eyes of the two women and with young Arthur's wailing in his ears.

"Do you want to move?" he asked Minnie.

"I love this house," she said evasively. "But it's *so* uncomfortable, Steve, the way you two are."

"Not *my* fault. I'll talk to him whenever he has something to say to me."

"You know he never will have."

"Humph! He says here he wants thirty-five hundred for his share of this place. I will give him twenty-five. You can tell him to have the deed drawn. I'll take it over."

That was the first of Art's notes. It had since become a bi-weekly habit. When Jennie Chick had handed him the note this morning, it was so customary that Steve no longer thought about the implications.

There had been no comment on his price-cutting; but four days later Minnie presented him with the signed deed and received his check made out to Arthur Swan for twenty-five hundred dollars.

Steve turned over, yawned deeply, and fell asleep, thinking: He ought not to let young Arthur go on that damn dragger. He would have to do something; but he didn't know what.

Part
Two

IT WAS ONLY four o'clock and short of broad daylight when Art finished dressing and came out from the little back bedroom off the kitchen he had occupied alone for the last eight years. He had told Minnie he preferred to sleep there so he wouldn't disturb her when he got up early in the morning. Actually, however, it was a queer sort of vanity that had made him move out of the double room they had used together the first few years in this house. He had never realized until he was married what people look like, just wakened and still frowzy with sleep. He didn't mind particularly the way Minnie looked; but he couldn't bear the idea that she should see him looking the same way.

Minnie had accepted the explanation calmly, as she had learned to accept his other peculiarities. Secretly she had searched her soul for the real reason, knowing well that Art expected her to be up and have his breakfast ready for him, if he had to go out at two. But after eight years, she still knew only that the reason he had given her was not the true one.

She was moving sluggishly around the kitchen now, still half-dazed with interrupted sleep. She kept telling herself that someday she would get used to this awful hour in the morning and might come to meet it with composure. But she hadn't achieved the composure yet and often felt if she had to face one more dreadful sunrise she would try to learn to walk in her sleep.

The spider was on the stove full of sputtering bacon and there were two wide-eyed eggs on a plate in the oven. Art retrieved them and went, without speaking, to the table where he sat and waited until she had put the bacon on his plate and poured his coffee. Breakfast was his best meal of the day and he enjoyed it in spite of Minnie's swollen-eyed face, her thin figure swaddled in the gray flannel bathrobe, her slippered scuffing around him.

"Where's Arthur?" he asked, after the first mouthful had received due attention.

"In bed." She stared at him, surprised into wakefulness. "Where else, at this hour in the morning?"

"Well," he said impatiently. "It's no place for him if he's going dragging, for pete's sake. The *Sally & Joe*'ll go as soon as I get down to the wharf."

"Oh, Art, you didn't mean for him to go this morning! Why, school's just out. He's only had a week or so of vacation!"

"I most assuredly *did* mean for him to go this morning."

Art's ugly face didn't change expression; but his clear, blue-green eyes bulged a little, letting her know he was as touchy on the subject as she was.

"Art." Pleadingly she said his name.

"Now, look, Minnie. If he's going dragging, he might just as well start right in. If he's not, then let's drop the whole thing."

That left the decision up to Minnie. Young Arthur had made her life miserable for the last six months with his begging her to let him go on the dragger this summer. If she spoiled his chances now, he would never forgive her, and she would have to live with his long face at her elbow all summer long.

Art, watching her fleeting changes of expression, said tightly: "Will you call him, or shall I?"

"Just a minute, Art." She sat down opposite him, in her hand the single cup of coffee that was all she could manage at four in the morning. "Before we let that *child* go on that boat, I want to know what that fuss was all about last night."

"Steve, you mean?"

"Of course I mean Steve. What other fuss was there?"

"He's a funny guy." Art sparred helplessly for time. "You know that as well as I do. He's superstitious as an old woman."

"Superstitious," she echoed blankly. "You said that last night. But I didn't see any signs of his being superstitious. All it seemed to me was he was more concerned about young Arthur's welfare. What effect it would have on him, being with those rough men, cooped up in that boat. Are those men on the *Sally & Joe* good men, Art?"

Art's eyes popped at her again and his under lip thrust out angrily.

"Dammit, Minnie, of course they're good men. I don't know what you mean anyhow. *Good!* What do you mean?"

"I mean they won't—corrupt him in any way. He's just a baby, Art."

"You're telling me! I don't know what you think goes on aboard a boat where a couple of men are working like dogs, Minnie. But I can tell you, if they wanted to corrupt him as you say, there still wouldn't be time. Whatever you mean by that!"

"Rough men," she said helplessly.

"Look, the only thing that'll happen to him is, he'll hear some strong talk. But let me tell you, Minnie, I've listened to that gang of kids that hangs out all summer down to the wharf and if you think any two men aboard one of the boats can talk any rougher than those kids do you've got another think coming."

He got up abruptly. Minnie heard him cross to the foot of the stairs leading up to the open chamber over the kitchen where Arthur slept.

"Arthur," he roared and was answered immediately by a sleep-soaked voice from above.

"Wha, Daddy?"

"Get dressed and get down here and have your breakfast, if you're going. You've got half an hour."

Young Arthur's feet hit the loose boards above her head with an alacrity he had never displayed when she called him to go to school. Art came back, gave Minnie a look of triumph, and settled into his chair.

"Steve," he said, "is superstitious as an old woman. The only thing that bothers him is the *Sally & Joe* got a bad name before we bought her. He thinks she's unlucky, that's all."

"Well," Minnie gave in reluctantly. "It certainly seems funny, a man with his education being as superstitious as that. I still feel as if he really knew something about those men."

"Education is just veneer," said Art. "You can't change a man's mind any, plastering it over with a little stucco out of books. He thinks she's unlucky and that's all there is to it. But I certainly ain't noticed any signs of it. We've had her a good four years and she paid for herself the first six months."

"Well, if it's just superstition like you say, why doesn't he worry about the men on her?"

Seeing her husband's look of bitter triumph, Minnie realized that she had left herself open exactly as he had been hoping she would.

"Perhaps he's one of those people don't worry about any but his own flesh and blood," Art said. "He's a selfish devil." He would have gone on; but young Arthur came clumping into the kitchen and, before him, Art could not say what he had been saying in one way or another to Minnie all through their married life. With Arthur's trusting eyes turned on him, he couldn't say: I don't believe this boy is my son. I think he's my brother's son. But I've acknowledged him and only you and I, Minnie, will ever know that I found you out.

And she could not deny it, as she had vehemently many times before in words and in every action of her waking hours. Since she had first realized the suspicion Art had started trying to voice to her on the night of their marriage, she had tried in every way she could think of to prove that he was wrong.

She wondered, now, if he really wanted to believe her. He had fought tooth and nail against naming the boy after himself, saying he hated hearing a kid called Junior until he was in his twenties. Once she had triumphed over the name, Art had never called his son by any diminutive. It was always Arthur, full out; and when the boy had been a baby, it had usually been preceded by 'young.'

Arthur's face, right now, was transfigured with delight and excitement. He could hardly force himself to take a mouthful of breakfast. Between infinitesmal bites, he kept looking unbelievingly at his father.

"This morning?" he kept saying. "You never told me. Really this morning, Daddy?"

Art would nod at him and grin at Minnie. Finally, unable to bear it any longer, she got up quickly.

"I'm going to get dressed," she announced. "I'm coming down with you. I want to see for myself what he's getting into."

Art opened his mouth to expostulate; but his words were drowned in Arthur's wordless wail of anguish. Minnie stared at her son, from whom she had never heard such a noise before.

"What *ails* you?"

"Mama, you can't!"

65

"I should like to know *why* I can't."

"It ain't—not like going to school the first time," Arthur pleaded. "Mama, they'll think I'm a sissy. They'll tease me."

"He won't hear the end of it for a good long time," Art promised her. "If you do anything so stupid."

"If those men—" Minnie said adamantly "—choose to behave like children because his mother took enough interest in his welfare to see what he was getting into, then I'm sorry for them. They haven't had a decent upbringing."

"I'm sorry for Arthur," Art said to her back.

She vanished into her bedroom, leaving the two males allied in their manhood by feminine unreasonableness. They stared thoughtfully at each other for a minute. Art grinned wryly.

"You'll just have to put up with it, I guess."

"We could go now. Before she's ready." Arthur swallowed hopefully, his eyes pleading.

"Wouldn't do a damn bit of good," his father said. "She'd be down there before you went if she had to fly."

The three left the house together in oppressive silence, Arthur walking a few paces behind his parents, feeling like a dragged puppy, his overnight bag of cheap canvas bumping against his reluctant knees. Minnie, aware of the displeasure of her men, bore it in silence. Wordlessly they climbed into the little Ford. As they turned out of the driveway, Arthur gave his mother a long look.

"*Please*, Mama," he said desperately.

Minnie shook her head firmly and Arthur subsided.

None of them gave a thought to Patty, alone and asleep in the empty house.

Art parked the car and went striding down the wharf without even a dis-owning glance for them. Minnie and Arthur straggled after him, both absorbed in their own personal misery. Arthur, completely reduced to a child again from the almost-man stature he had achieved momentarily at the breakfast table, was having all he could do to hold back tears of pure rage.

Minnie caught up with her husband just as he was going into his office.

"Art," she said pleadingly. "I wouldn't want him to get rough and coarse. He's a nice boy, now. He's a gentleman."

Art turned on her with a flash of teeth in his brown face.

"He'll be a namby-pamby if you don't let him get away from home and grow up!"

Minnie's first close-range look at Will Holmes, the skipper of the *Sally & Joe*, was reassuring. She found him lounging over the railing at the wharf head, waiting.

"Mr. Holmes," she said and Will turned his long, wrinkled, kind, brown face with its anxious eyes to her in astonishment. In all his years around the water, he had never been approached by the boss's wife at this hour in the morning. It simply wasn't the time for a woman to be kicking around, boss's wife or not, and his surprise was clear in his face.

"Yes, ma'am."

"I want to talk to you for just a minute." Minnie was relieved at the innate kindness she thought she found in his uncertain features.

"Yes, ma'am," Will said again and followed her obediently up the wharf. Will had been a man sadly down on his luck when the Swan brothers had bought the *Sally & Joe* and hired him to run her. He knew perfectly well he had been hired because he was willing to work for a smaller share of the take than another man would accept. But being on the way up for three or four years is not enough to give a man back what he's lost by being on the way down for ten.

Will was still insecure and anxious enough to wonder if he'd done anything wrong and what on earth Minnie Swan wanted with him.

"Mr. Holmes." Minnie finally turned to face him. "I wanted to talk to you. My boy is going with you this summer. He's going this morning."

"Well, I knew Art planned for him to go," Will agreed. "I never knew he was starting today, though."

"He is. I just wanted to ask you if you'd kind of keep watch over him. He's so young. He's only fourteen."

Will remembered wryly that he himself had started out at nine and thought himself lucky to be allowed to get so old before he had to go out and earn his living. He smiled.

"Fourteen's not so young, ma'am."

"It seems awfully young to me," Minnie said softly. "But, will you promise me to see that he doesn't—that there isn't any rough talk around where he can hear?"

Will's brow furrowed a little more. He thought wildly of Billy Ratcliffe and the stream of profanity that poured effortlessly out of him whenever the drag got hung down.

"Oh, my god, ma'am, excuse me! You're asking the impossible. I can't keep Billy from talking and if he can't swear he can't talk."

This was just the reaction Minnie had feared. But she threw herself on his mercies.

"I just want you to do the best you can. And please try to remember, he's only a little boy."

"Will," Art's voice said levelly behind them and they both jumped. "I want Arthur treated just like any other hand. He needs hardening up."

"Yessir." Will's relief was deep. He lifted his battered cap to Minnie and vanished down the wharf as fast as he could make his legs move.

SWAN'S HARBOR

He found young Arthur awaiting him on the *Sally & Joe's* deck and looked him over with dismay. It seemed to Will that Arthur looked only about half as big as he had yesterday. The boy stood there limply, his small bag at his feet, staring at the narrow planks beneath his feet.

Will started to say something about never having had a hand whose mother had come to him like a kindergarten teacher before; but another glance at Arthur's miserable face restrained him.

"Go on below," he said as gently as he could. "Stow your stuff away and then come back up."

Arthur went, stumbling over a coil of rope he apparently hadn't even seen. Watching him, Will shook his head dolefully. He didn't hold with this business of the boss's son going on the boat during the summer, anyway. It never worked out good. But he didn't feel secure enough in his position to protest the decision.

Half an hour later when the *Sally & Joe* passed out by the lighthouse and the bar into the blue choppy water of the tide-rip, Will took another look. Arthur was up on the bow with Will's big, yellow, coon cat, Peter, coiling around him. He looked like a different boy altogether. Will thought he could even make out a resemblance to the Swans in his eager face. He had never been able to see anything hopeful in the kid before—seeing him, as he had, hanging around the wharf without enough to do and with not enough native invention to find something. Well, he thought, better not decide he's a nuisance before we give him a chance. Maybe more to him than shows on top.

The dragger's blunt bow smashed into the chop, giving Arthur a fine drenching. Will saw the boy's astonished face, the mouth open as he gasped to get his breath back. Then Arthur turned and gave him a conspiratorial grin. Peter, Will saw, grinning back, had had the sense to get out of the way, knowing what might come bouncing up at him when those bows began to dip. Will nodded thoughtfully. He ain't as much of a sissy as his old lady would like to have him, he decided.

Minnie watched the *Sally & Joe* out of sight from the shadowy recesses of the big landing shed. The boys, hanging desultorily around waiting for the first load of fish to come in avoided her because there is something about the sight of a distraught woman that inspires men with deep horror. And they all felt it, glancing one by one through the open door, finding her there, dry-eyed and staring. They would withdraw in hasty silence. But Minnie didn't even see them.

She did know perfectly well that her behavior was going to make things difficult for Arthur. But she simply could not get out of her mind the look of disproportionate dismay on Steve's big ugly face last night when they had told him that Arthur was going with Will Holmes this summer.

In spite of her husband's reassurances, she couldn't make herself believe that look on Steve's face had been entirely the result of a simple superstition concerning a boat. The appeal he had made to her, that close association with the men on the dragger would be hard on a boy as young as Arthur, touched her much more strongly.

Arthur was big for his years and people tended to forget that he was only fourteen. The sense of relief she had felt when she looked closely at Will Holmes had been quickly dispelled by his reaction to her request that he and Billy try and refrain from their normal talk around the boy.

Taut, dry-eyed, and furious, she stood staring through the

dusty, spider-inhabited window after the *Sally & Joe*. This early in the morning there was no wind to disturb the Harbor and it stretched across to the other shore like a big saucer of molten gunmetal just beginning to take traces of color from the deepening sky.

Up alongshore the red buildings and long gray sheds of the boat yard were coming to life. She half-heard the scream of a power saw. Moored in front of the storage shed, perfectly reflected in the quiet water, were three tall-masted summer boats that had just been put into the water after the winter spent in canvas swaddling. Their masts, looking five times the length of the delicate hulls, reached gracefully into the neutral sky, their long reflections as solid as the tapering reality.

One of the dude boats from Camden, an old coasting schooner converted from a carrier of inanimate necessities which were no longer necessary, to the carrying of bright-shirted temporary sailors escaping from a life of regularity between Westport or White Plains and Manhattan to the illusion of piracy on the high seas, lay at anchor in the center of the Harbor. Aboard her, already, there was a sound of voices and the rattle of rigging. Across the hushed water the noises carried clearly to shore, like the beginning chatter of birds, sleepy at first, gaining a waking clarity and insistence as morning broadened from the east out across the water and over the islands.

Minnie came to with a slight start to find she had almost forgotten the *Sally & Joe*. She turned to stare once more and found the big dragger, reduced by distance to a toy boat, just rounding the point by the lighthouse.

Hastily she looked away, thinking: Unlucky to watch her out of sight.

When she passed in through the long buildings, Minnie glanced into the office and found Art already buried in his ledgers. He was alone and she was slightly surprised that he didn't have Miss Chick come to work at the same time he did.

He became aware of her hovering uncertainly in the doorway and glanced up.

"It's all right, Minnie." An impulse of rough kindliness touched him at the sight of her pale face. "He'll be all right."

"I know I've been foolish." Touched in her turn, she looked at him pleadingly. "I think Steve scared me. I suppose all mothers feel the same way the first time their children go off on their own."

"My god, Minnie," Art said. "I don't know whether they do or not. But if you'd only stop to think how hard it is on the kids. Arthur won't hear the end of this for a long time."

She glanced quickly over her shoulder, aware with an intuitive sense that she was being watched, and caught Pat Jellison peering in through the shed door at her. He disappeared like a jumping jack in reverse, his disappearance hailed by a burst of whispers from the invisible crew in the shed. He had been so obviously eavesdropping in hopes of further ammunition for the teasing to come that Minnie's heart forsook her.

"If it's any satisfaction to you, Art," she said hoarsely. "I wish now I'd never done it."

"I wish you hadn't, either," he agreed quietly. "But it's a little late to worry about that now. The damage's done. Why don't you go along home now, Minnie? You want me to drive you up to the house?"

He looked around at the books spread out on his desk with the harassed air of a man who has too much to do and too little time in which to do it.

"The walk will do me good," Minnie told him. At least she could remove that obligation from him in a minor attempt to make him think better of her after this morning's exhibition. He gave her a wide, relieved smile of surprising sweetness, his ugly face changing its entire expression.

If he would only do that more often, she thought, going slowly up the wharf to the white gravel road. Or if he could only see himself once when he relaxed enough to smile like that, he would know with certainty, she felt, why she had preferred him to Steve. On Steve's face, which was always on the verge of laughter, she had never yet seen an expression to rival that rare smile she had just received from her husband.

As she came up off the wharf, a dusty Ford roadster pulled to a stop and Frank Pierce, that friend of Steve's Minnie knew only to speak to, climbed out and stood staring thoughtfully down at the impersonal sheds.

"Morning, Mr. Pierce." She gave him a determinedly cheerful greeting.

Frank started and glanced at her, his deep-set dark eyes shadowed.

"Oh, good morning, Mrs. Swan."

"Steve hasn't come down yet," she offered gratuitously.

"Thanks." Frank nodded abruptly. "I'll wait. He ought to be along any minute."

Minnie passed him with the odd feeling that he had neither seen nor heard her. When she glanced curiously back at him, he was still standing there.

She shook her head, thinking vaguely: He acts funny; but he certainly has got lovely manners; and forget him. If she had looked back again she would have discovered what Frank was waiting for. Jacky Gott, his red hair shining in the sunlight, came loping up the wharf. He stood listening to Frank talk for a moment, and said something himself that involved a good deal of hand waving. Then they both got into the car, evidently to continue the conversation, because the little Ford didn't move.

Minnie walked up through the quiet, early-morning town, feeling as if she had passed from turmoil into calm, her thoughts already hurrying ahead to the house waiting with its chores, to Patty who must be her refuge now, who could never be torn away from her roughly as her son had been.

On the open unshaded road the sun was already hot, but when she passed into the cool green shadow of the great elms that lined the main street, it was like walking into water. She could almost feel her lungs adapt themselves to the intake of a different element. Her feet on the still damp sidewalk, made little sound and she felt invisible as a ghost, walking alone through the street where at ten o'clock there would such a jam of mail-getters, shoppers, and automobiles with their bright, out-of-state licenses.

She turned in at her own neat, white-picket gate, hearing with relief the familiar squeal of the unoiled hinges. As she stood there staring back along the hushed, shaded street, she was thinking idly of the terrible battle the Village Improvement Association had put up when the businessmen of the town wanted to widen that dangerously constricted section. It would have involved taking down the elms that had thrown their shade over the changes of more than a century. The VIA had won and the elms remained; but they stood so close to the macadam that the outer sides of their great rough-barked trunks were daily scourged and battered by drivers without the fine judgment necessary to park; or in winter by the snow-plow, forcing its big bow-wave of frozen snow away from the narrow driving lane.

Before she turned to go up the walk to the house, she saw

Steve's shining black car come down the street from the north and swing languidly around the corner by the traffic light. She drew back hastily, in case he should see her and come over. She was all right now; but if she had to listen to any more of his expostulation, worried as she had been, she knew she'd start to cry and she didn't want him, of all people, to see her in the ignominy of tears.

The wharf was still quiet when Steve got there. He had tried to be a little earlier this morning, wanting to get at Art again before he made any final decision. He had left the irritating white silk shirt at home and wore instead an old blue chambray one, fresh from Lizzie's mending. He felt that the large jib-shaped patch on one shoulder, its fresh cloth startlingly dark against the sun faded blue of the whole, pointed up the fact that he, too, could be economical. That should make an impression on Art.

It certainly had with Lizabetta. Steve grinned at the memory of the expression on her face when he had appeared before her with the just-laundered shirt, a great gaping hole in the back of it.

"For the lord sake, where'd you get that shirt?"

"Out of my drawer." Steve had tried to meet her eyes innocently.

"I never in my life put away a clean shirt with a hole like that in it!"

"I was surprised myself," Steve admitted. He didn't say that he had hunted all over the upstairs trying to find a corner sharp enough to inflict a three-cornered tear that would look natural.

"Give it to me." Lizzie stretched out an imperious hand. "And go get another one to wear. You've got plenty."

"No, I want to wear this one. Why don't you just mend it while I wait?"

"There's no need for you to go around looking like a sport one

75

day and a tramp the next," Lizzie had pointed out. But he won her over and, shaking her head at the utter foolishness of the procedure, she had taken the shirt over to the old Wheeler & Wilson, foot-treadle sewing machine and patched it. The result made a fine showing, Steve felt; you could see it a mile away.

He was craning back over his shoulder at the patch instead of looking where he was going, so he nearly ran into Frank Pierce's rear bumper. He stopped dead and, in the second before he could get around the car, he heard Jacky Gott's familiar voice; but the tone was unfamiliar. Jacky sounded driven and nervous.

"I don't want to go, Frank."

"You let me think you might." Frank's voice was trying to be reasonable over an undertone of disappointed anger. Hearing it, Steve felt his eyebrows draw together uncomfortably.

"I can't walk out on my job," Jacky protested tightly. "I got to make a living."

"Is that the only reason?" The coldness came to the surface this time.

"Well, you ought to know," Jacky said.

Steve, bothered for no reason he could put his finger on, and thoroughly ashamed of himself for standing here in silence, dealt the rear bumper a stout kick.

"Hey," he said into the immediate dismayed silence. He came quickly around to the driver's window and stared in at Frank. "Thought you'd gone." In spite of himself, his curious glance went past Frank to the younger man's surprised and somehow relieved face.

"I'm on my way," Frank said abruptly. He raked up the vestige of a grin and kicked the starter.

"Have fun," Steve said. He waved his hand casually and started down the wharf. Jacky got out of the car, said something in a low voice and came running after Steve. He caught him abreast the ice-house and they went down to the sheds in silence, both of them aware of the Ford rattling away.

Steve couldn't resist a glance at Jacky. He wanted to say: I didn't know you and Frank were that friendly. But he couldn't say it without admitting he'd been eavesdropping.

Still silent, Jacky left him at the entrance to the sheds and Steve took a quick turn out around the head of the wharf. There was no sign of the *Sally & Joe* here or anywhere else in the Harbor. Steve breathed a little easier. From the way Minnie had spoken last night, she had had no intention of letting Arthur leave this morning.

So the *Sally & Joe*'s absence meant there would be a few days' respite and would give him more time to marshal his forces. He was aware that the arguments he had used on the spur of the moment last night were ones that would put Art's back up. Art knew that the last thing that would ever worry Steve was the rough language the boy would hear.

He knew, since he was earlier than usual, that Chickie wouldn't be in the office to act as a buffer. If he went in now, he'd have to talk directly to Art. But he wasn't the one who had refused to speak in the first place. He'd just followed Art's precedent. When he got heated up about anything, he couldn't be bothered with all those confounded notes.

Turning, he strode purposefully over to the office door. As he had expected, Art was alone.

Art glanced up in surprise, let his gaze wander thoughtfully over the blue shirt, and then looked accusingly at Miss Chick's empty chair.

God amighty, Steve thought, he doesn't really have to talk. He can say all he wants to, just looking.

Art had obviously expressed his astounded dislike of Steve's intrusion when there was no third person present to whom they could both talk. He had also commented, unmistakably and cynically on that torn shirt.

"Art, are you still thinking of letting that kid go with the dragger?"

Art hesitated just long enough to make his brother wonder if the ban of silence was finally to be broken. Then he pulled a scratch pad toward him and wrote 'YES' on it in letters so large Steve could read them from the door, upside down.

Steve came over and leaned on the desk, looking down at Art's bent head, thinking: I'd like to let you have it, just once, you stubborn son of a sea cook. He found himself forced by Art's silence into a resumé of the reasons why he felt young Arthur should be kept off the boat. His argument got slower and slower until he finally lost his temper, more at himself because he had failed to provide the new and better arguments before he needed them than at Art.

Art refused to look up. Smiling slightly, he sat making an occasional note on the pad he had used to make clear his affirmative.

Steve stammered and subsided like a dying outboard motor. At last, wordless, he just leaned there waiting for some sign of response from that implacable bent head.

Only when the silence had become almost unbearable, Art looked up and the look said clearly: Are you finally through?

"That's all for now," Steve said, his voice thick with frustration and rage. Like trying to hit a feather pillow, he thought, waiting to see what Art would do.

Art began to write fast; but he didn't have much to say and it was only a minute or two that Steve stood watching the brown clenched hand race across the white paper before Art spun the sheet around for him to read.

"*If you had been down here at a decent hour you could have*

*wished him bon voyage. He just left. Your boat was tied up to
the car again this morning.*"

"Oh, you son of a bitch!" Steve said, snatched the paper, and
before Art could answer that, he was out of the office, letting
the door go behind him with an added force that made the slam
boom through the echoing sheds.

Steve found the *Eloise* just where Art said she was, tied up to
the lobster car at the foot of the runway. Where she had been
yesterday morning, drawing a reproach then. Devil take it, anyway, he thought furiously. I can't remember leaving her there
last night.

He started her up, cast off, and opened her to full throttle,
roaring out and away from the wharf in a great curving wave
of water. The *Eloise*'s lovely sheer bow with the force of the
heavy Gray engine behind it sheared through the limpid water
with as little effort as it would have through thin air.

During the night the wind had shifted and, although there was
barely more than a capful of it this morning, what there was
came from the southeast.

Once outside the Harbor he could see, far to the south, a large
boat drawing away from him. He recognized her because that
was where he had expected to see the *Sally & Joe*. He wrenched
at the throttle uselessly, knowing the *Eloise* was traveling at top
speed, knowing if it had been possible for him to overtake the
dragger there was absolutely nothing he could do. He couldn't
go storming after her and drag the kid off.

Art and Minnie had had no intention of letting that kid go this
morning. And if he could have kept his oar out of it, he might
have had another week or two to work on Minnie. As it was, he
had forced Art out of pig-headed stubbornness to send young
Arthur off before he'd meant to.

It wasn't necessary, either. The two men aboard the *Sally &
Joe* were all that was needed to work her. A boy would be so
much supercargo and more trouble than he was worth. It was
just a made job. Arthur wasn't old enough to work in the sardine
factory, and if Steve knew his Minnie, Arthur never would. She
would consider that degrading for a Swan.

He might have got a job caddying at the golf links. But Art
would put his foot down there. Caddying was all right for most
kids; but there was nothing certain about it. The good caddies
made perhaps enough to buy clothes for the next school year.
The others hung around the caddy house all day long, picking
up a round or two a day, not enough to keep a normal boy in
candy bars and cigarettes.

Steve shrugged, watching the dragger grow smaller in the
misty distance. He was probably being a fool about the whole
thing. But Hank had put it into words for him neatly when he
had gassed up the night before. "I heard she was a killer," Hank
had said flatly. "A boat don't get a reputation like that for nothing."

Yesterday, triumphant and at peace with the entire world,
Steve had worked slowly and shifted about a third of his string
of traps. Today, furious and chewing on the tag ends of his
anger, he had the other two thirds shifted by two o'clock in the
afternoon and was ready to go in.

Earlier in the day he had noticed, and smelled, the low gray
wall hanging along the horizon outside the islands. Now, pausing
for the first time since noon, to glance toward the east, he found
the fog nearly upon him. It always surprised him that anything
so opaque and solid looking should come silently.

On a quiet day like this it came in low, following the water
among the islands, covering the surface; and when that ground
was gained and held, sneaking up over the land, through the low

places. It was like some tremendously expandable stuff, contained in a small area at first, but, when liberated and exposed to the action of the air, able to fill the entire world from horizon to horizon with a dripping cottony silence.

A thick arm of it lay along the Sound, white and silent, blotting the hills from sight and obscuring the narrow entrance. The outer islands were invisible, and he watched the front of the fog coming slowly toward him over the quiet water. An arch of mist humped high over the obscured spruces on Brennan's Island, its rainbow shape glistening in sunlight.

On an impulse, he shut off his engine and stood listening.

He could hear the gruff roar of the fog-horn over the Devil's Pasture far to the east, the long, hoarse growl that ended in a sudden thud as if the sound had gone searching out until it reached a place where the fog now solid, halted its progress. The bell buoys were alive, too, bells that he never heard or noticed on a clear day now gave brazen tongue to danger.

He jogged slowly up along the shore and into the Harbor, hearing, as he went, what he thought was the distant echo of his own engine off to the east.

At the mouth of the Harbor the fog stopped and Steve knew it would sit there until sun-down; but then it would come in and by morning the Harbor would be buttoned down tight. He didn't bother to gas up but went straight to his mooring, retrieved his punt, and rowed in to the float, mooring her carefully around under the runway where she couldn't conceivably be in anyone's way.

Already there was a damp chill in the quiet air that made his shirt cling to his back with an unpleasantly clammy embrace.

"In for a good fog mull, Steve." Jacky thrust his red head over the railing above the float.

"Yes, hell take it! Probably last for a week."

"Suits me." Jacky gave him an impudently nervous grin. "Maybe a few of you eager beavers'll stay in."

"You're a lazy little devil."

He reached the wharf level in time to see Art come flashing out of the shed, across the wharf, and start down the ladder to where the *Pillbox* lay moored against the spiling. She was destined to spend the rest of her natural life right there. The transmitter of the radio-telephone was installed in her cramped cabin because the law said it must be aboard a boat.

Sometimes during the course of a day, Art would plunge, cursing, fifteen different times down that ladder. Now his voice floated back to them luridly begging to know why it was always low water around this thrice-blessed, spavined wharf.

"Anything wrong?" Steve jerked his head curiously toward the ladder.

Jacky's grin widened and got sure of itself.

"Just the *Sally & Joe*."

Steve's attention, which had been motivated by simple curiosity, sharpened to a focus.

"What about her?"

"Oh, Will called in about ten minutes ago. He's off Matinicus in the fog and he *says* he's broke down."

The emphasis on that word told Steve clearly that Jacky thought Will Holmes had simply let himself be scared by the fog into refusing to move.

Steve went silently over to the head of the ladder. Art's voice came up to him clearly:

"All right, Will, now calm down, dammit. Can you hear me? You called the Rockland Coast Guard, didn't you? They'll send the tug out, won't they? Just sit tight. Damnation, what's wrong with her? Ain't you tried anything? Ain't you looked her over? Might be some simple little thing you could fix yourself."

After a long snapping pause, Will's voice said cautiously: "I don't believe I could replace a shaft coupling, Art. I ain't got one."

Art waited; but that was all.

"All right," he yelled. "All right. They'll be out and get you. Go to Snow & Harmon's Yard. I'll call them up, let them know you're coming. Then get that damned crate back up here. And don't come in empty. I'll expect you in three days. You be here. Out."

"If he'd just poke his head out the window," Jacky said thoughtfully, "he wouldn't *have* to use the telephone."

He hesitated and then glanced slyly at Steve.

"You suppose Will's really lost a coupling?"

"If he says he has," Steve said coldly, his attitude telling Jacky he'd gone a little too far by putting his doubt in actual words.

Jacky moved quickly away, and when Steve glanced after him he saw just his red head vanishing through the wide shed door. That kid's getting pretty fresh, he thought. But he was right. It seemed like the sort of thing Will might pull if he felt the fog was too thick for him to navigate. In his younger days he would never have done it. Will had streaks of being a good man yet, but he was troublesome, because you had to kid-glove him along. Steve, superbly unaware of the meaning of apprehension, could dredge up little sympathy for a man whose whole life trembled on the edge of abject fear.

He glanced out toward the Harbor mouth. He could still hear what he'd thought at first was the echo of his own engine. Aware now that it was not, he found the engine sound much heavier than his own. It sounded like one of the Rockland draggers heading in and there was something sadly wrong with her.

She came looming up out of the fog. For a minute or two, in the dimness of her outline, he found nothing familiar, but when she limped into the sunshine he knew her and recognized by association the grizzled handsome head poking out the pilot-house window.

Anyone could tell the *Seventh Daughter* as far as he could see her. Her big, bluff-bowed hull had been painted green and black originally; but Joe Luccio, her captain and half-owner, didn't care what he used to patch her up with so long as it was paint. A long scrape low on her port side just above the waterline was laid over with bright red lead. Near the stern, on the same side, he had started to paint her thoroughly, using what resembled old-fashioned, tomato-red barn paint. During the course of the summer he would get the entire hull painted piecemeal, one coat, and within the year her original green and black would come wearing through.

As a result, since Joe went through this process annually, the *Seventh Daughter* looked like a rusty tramp. Actually she was one of the best boats out of Rockland. Joe wasn't colorblind when it came to hulls and engines.

Steve stood listening to her heavy diesel with a puzzled frown. He knew little about diesels; but anyone could tell there was something wrong with that one.

The *Seventh Daughter* came pounding and skipping in to the wharf, sounding like an old, wood-burning locomotive. Joe, after one wild enthusiastic wave, withdrew his head from the window, went aft, and became very busy doing nothing and anything that would keep him from having to speak to Steve for a moment or two.

Watching the stocky, broad-shouldered, surprisingly short man dashing busily around the heavy planked deck, Steve could feel his eyes narrow with suspicious amusement. He knew Joe well enough to know that this evasive action was out of character. Usually Joe's greeting was as hearty as a blast of hot wind from the northwest, and subtlety sat uneasily on his shoulders.

"Joseph." Steve grasped the bow hawser and made it fast to the nearest piling. "You having a little trouble?"

Joe gave him a quick sly glance out of sparkling black eyes, keeping his head bent so that his bushy eyebrows, as grizzled as his close-clipped hair, could act as a partial screen.

"Little," he said noncommittally.

"Engine sounds queer." Steve listened to the dying gasp of the big Gray.

"Started to act up on me outside the Pasture." Joe's natural volubility broke through. "Don't know what ails the damn thing. I'm going to get rid of it. This makes three times she's busted on me in the last two months. I'm going to use her for a mooring anchor. You see if I don't."

He sent a taut glance along the length of the deck to see that everything was according to Luccio, and came slowly up the ladder to the wharf. Steve looked down at the handsome, highly colored face. Joe was still successfully evading his eyes. If the head on an old Roman coin had had any color in it, the ageless impervious profile could have been the model. Joe couldn't have been forty and might have been eight years younger. He moved like a kid of twenty. But the wiry hair that lay in tight short curls over his long narrow head was as gray as the mane of an old lion.

"Art's going to be pleased to see you," Steve told him.

"I don't doubt." Joe pulled a cigarette from the pack in his shirt pocket without offering one to Steve. When he had a fine cloud of smoke going, he met Steve's eyes through it squarely. His shoulders moved in an infinitesimal shrug.

"What could I do?" One bushy eyebrow moved up. "I never would of made Rockland. I'll be here three, four days. A man can't go broke."

"Not if it's you."

Joe's mobile mouth curled. Before he could rally his forces against this unreasonable suspicion, Art came up behind them.

"Well, Joe!" In his voice there was no suspicion, only dismay.

"You boys got to help me out." Joe, who had apparently been gathering his resources for this meeting, spun on him with quick Latin gestures before which Art took a distasteful backward step. "I'm stuck here till the boys at the shop find out what the hell's gone wrong with my engine. I'll lose my load unless you take it. I'll go broke. If I can't get you to take this load of fish off my hands."

"Are you full?"

Art's haunted eyes considered how deep the *Seventh Daughter* was sitting.

Joe shook his head.

"I only got about eight thousand."

Art was silent, thinking. He spent the summer praying that this wouldn't happen to him. In the summer there were so many fish landed to the westward, and the price went so low, that the Swans were lucky if they broke even on what they shipped to Boston. The big Rockland draggers like the *Seventh Daughter* seldom appeared in the Harbor, preferring to land their fish in their home port. If poor weather or engine trouble forced them in, it behooved the Swans to take their load. If they refused, during the winter when the price was up and the big draggers the main source of supply, since they were the only boats able to fish offshore in rigorous weather, the Swans might whistle for fish and get none.

Steve could see all these facts turning over and over behind Art's stolid face. Joe saw it, too, and watched craftily.

Joe was a high-line man and it was safe to say that the *Seventh Daughter* was responsible for an eighth of the fish shipped off the Swan wharf during the winter months. They couldn't afford to lose him for reluctance to do him a favor when he needed it.

"Are they any good?" Art growled, admitting defeat. "How long you had them aboard? I don't want to buy at fresh fish prices and find out I've got fish hash."

Joe drew himself up indignantly, his honor impugned in the one spot it was vulnerable.

"I never cheated you yet."

"Oh, all right." Art glanced down at the fighting cock stance with a faint grin. "I'll lose money on you, though. Dammit, I'll have to give you half a cent less than I'm giving the other boys."

Joe screamed his protest and, Greek meeting Greek, they moved into the shed toward the office, still arguing. Steve, his hands in his pockets, lounged after them listening, his face tight with amusement he tried not to show.

"Well, all right, then," Joe was saying quietly when Steve reached the office door. "But give me twenty now, will you, and hold it out when you tell me what she weighs out."

Steve's amusement vanished in distaste. This trick was one Joe usually played and it always set Steve's teeth on edge. He watched without comment while Art peeled two tens from the wad in his pocket and handed it over. Satisfied, giving up more easily than either Steve or Art had expected him to do, Joe tucked the money away in the pouch he hauled from the bulging pocket of his khaki trousers.

"What they don't know won't hurt them." Joe gave them a fleeting glimpse of his strong yellow teeth. For a second, to Steve, he looked more like a jackal than a lion. A captain that would hold out on his crew to the extent of twenty dollars, was pretty low. It meant simply that there would be twenty dollars less to go into the shares when Joe paid off. In the summer time, it wasn't so bad. But in winter, when that crew worked like devils in a hell of ice, the captain who held out on his men was a creature with little or no conscience.

Steve stared thoughtfully, wondering how you could still like a man when you knew he was cheap enough to do a thing like that. Joe did it apparently feeling this little rake-off was his right and something to be so accepted by everyone concerned. Art's sly companionable grin of admiring approbation upheld this attitude.

Turning, Steve went rapidly out through the buildings to get away as quickly as possible from that atmosphere of penny-pinching.

Joe came pounding after him.

"You don't think much of that, hanh?"

Steve didn't bother to hide his distaste; but he was still surprised that Joe had been observant enough to see it.

"Cheap skate stuff."

"Not out of your pocket." Joe grinned, unabashed. "You get your value for the money."

"Yeah; but it's still pretty small potatoes. My gosh, if you're going to gyp your crew, why don't you do it in a big way?"

"In the long run," Joe pointed out, "I make just as much out of it and they don't get excited because they never know. You got to play it smart."

"If they ever did find out, I wouldn't blame them if they towed you on behind at the end of a line for ten, fifteen minutes."

"*That*'d finish me off, all right. It's what I'd do myself; but I'm too smart for them. That's where you'd slip up, Steve, taking a lot to once and letting them find out. You'd end up at the end of the line. Me, I stay alive."

"Hey, Joe," Jacky yelled after them. "You going to the Pioneers Ball?"

"Bet your life." Joe waved his hand. "Wouldn't miss it."

He met Steve's suddenly understanding eyes with a wide smile.
"You going, Steve?"

"So that's it. I'd forgot all about the ball. I might have known."

"Well, why not?" Joe spread his hands widely. "Tell you
what," —he turned confidential— "I got my eye on a pretty little
girl last time I was in here. Thought I'd see if she was still
around."

"So *that's* it," Steve repeated. "Why, you old stallion! That
was the most convenient breakdown a man ever had, wasn't it?"

"Just my good luck." Joe accepted the good luck unquestion-
ingly. "Might's well take advantage of it. This is a real pretty
little girl. Don't even know her name."

"It would serve you right if I wrote Marie a letter," Steve told
him and was pleased to see Joe's high color fade at the mere idea.

"If you never want to see me again, you do that," Joe said, his
eyes deadly serious. "If she thought I ever looked at another
woman, she'd put a knife between my ribs so easy—like slicing
butter. That Marie, she is a handful and I need a rest now and
then. Something easy, to calm me down."

Steve had never seen Joe's wife who kept his house and the
five children they had back home in Rockland; but Joe's graphic
and sometimes indecent descriptions of her made him feel as if
he knew her personally. By Joe's tell, she was an extraordinary
woman—six feet tall, he would say, describing with his voluble
hands the way Marie towered over him; and every inch of her
as feminine and unpredictable as a good boat.

"I won't do it; but by the judas, I ought to."

"My pal!" Joe reached up to give him a companionable pat on
the shoulder. "I love that Marie like no man ever loved a woman
before. But I just spent a week to home and I tell you, Steve, a
week's long enough. Why, if we had to live together the way
most husbands and wives do, we'd kill each other by the end of

the first month. Nobody but a fisherman could live with her."

"What do you suppose—" Steve said musingly "—she does when *you're* away?"

Joe's face went even paler and his eyes slitted. His expression gave Steve a quick vicarious chill.

"She waits for me to come home," Joe said, leaving no room for doubt and putting a full stop to that line of conversation. Steve, recognizing the warning signals, let it drop. Funny, no matter how well you got to know this guy, well enough so you could say outrageous things to him about his business methods without offending him, there were still places you couldn't tread.

"You going uptown, Steve?" Smiling as if he had never done anything else, Joe thrust his arm through Steve's. "Take me up. I got to have a glass of beer and my supper. I ain't eaten since the engine let go."

Steve motioned him toward the Cadillac.

"New car," Joe said admiringly, his eyes widening. He walked around her twice, approvingly. But he shook his head when he climbed in. "Little quiet for my taste," he explained. "I like some red on them somewheres. Red or yellow. Something cheerful. This black's too damn much like a hearse."

Steve let Joe out at the beer parlor, and Joe crossed the street assuring Steve at the top of his leathery lungs that he would see him tomorrow night at the dance.

"You'll see my pretty little girl," Joe roared, disappearing into the shadowy restaurant. "I'm sure she'll be there," his voice floated back. "You can introduce me."

Steve grinned, wondering idly who Joe's pretty little girl could be. He doubted very much if she would be there. The little girls the men off the Rockland draggers picked up weren't usually present at the Pioneers Ball, which was one of the big social events of the summer season. He was a little surprised that Joe had managed to get a ticket. They were hard to come by, and Steve was pretty sure the Old Settlers Club, which was responsible for the dance, would have seen to it that the Guinea Fleet men stayed in their proper place.

He forgot all about Joe as he thought suddenly that he should have mentioned the dance to Ann before this. Judas, what a time to invite a girl to the Pioneers Ball, the night before! He realized sheepishly that the reason he had put it all out of his mind was simply because he didn't want to invite Ann. He wanted to go stag just in case his own pretty little girl should be there. The parallel between himself and Joe amused him at first and then disgusted him slightly. He liked Joe; but to find that he himself worked the same way, when he had been so superior and amused about Joe's machinations, made him angry with himself.

Well, he didn't feel like seeing Ann tonight. She knew him well enough not to be disappointed if they didn't even go. Of course, he *had* told her weeks ago that he had the tickets and maybe she would consider that invitation enough.

With the sun's setting, the fog was drifting in high over the town, covering the bright sky with a flying scud of gray. Already it was wet enough to lay the dust on the gravel road shoulders and put a slick sheen of dampness over the macadam crown. He could sleep in the morning, and, if he decided to he would have all day tomorrow to see Ann.

Happily, with the feeling that he had solved his problem, he put the whole thing out of his head and swung into the lilac-crowded dooryard wondering hungrily what Lizzie would have for his supper.

The next morning the fog was so thick that Steve could barely make out the bulky end of the barn thirty feet away when he glanced out the window. The Bay itself might have passed right out of existence. The only sign of the sea was the mournful regular bellow of a tug and barge coming down through the Narrows.

He spent the morning cheerfully doing nothing, and after he'd eaten his dinner he drove downtown under the cavernous old elms, their upper branches, one hundred and twenty feet overhead, diaphanous and veiled with fog. When he passed Ann's house, set far back from the road in its low green field, he felt a slight pang of conscience. He ought to decide what he was going to do tonight and let her know. She wouldn't be home now, though, which took care of any impulse he might have had about stopping in.

The wharf was a bustle of activity. He had met the ice truck up at the traffic light and he found five or six tons of it in three hundred pound cakes blocking his way to the float. Two of the boys were sliding the big cakes up the shallow ramp to the ice house. The ice looked extremely valuable, like tremendous, clear, blue-white jewels, if anything that valuable could ever have been that big.

Steve picked his way cautiously over the treacherous, clear, melting splinters of ice, along the buildings to the door of the loafers' shack. The Harbor, beyond the wharf head, was a woolly mystery, peopled from the noise, by large, hoarse-voiced animals, all dying. There were moans, toots, whistles, blats, every conceivable noise that could be made by a boat in a fog. The *Seventh Daughter* was gone and Steve thought he could make her out moored to the piling over at the boat yard.

When he shoved the door open and went in, the noise from outside faded slightly; but the noise within, although different, was as deafening. The radio-telephone receiver sat on its shelf making a sound like eggs frying too fast in a too-hot spider. At a rickety table in the far corner, the permanent bad-weather poker game was going on to the accompaniment of terse and monosyllabic insults.

In the shed next door the boys were busy packing the fish Joe Luccio had landed last night. They were iced down, two hundred pounds to a barrel, and then headed with a thick, strong, insulated paper on which the contents of the barrel were described in heavy black crayon.

As Steve poked his head through the door, Jacky had just discovered one with no marking on its neat top. His language added an almost visible sulphur-blue tinge to the pall of tobacco smoke wreathing through the open rooms.

"Who headed up this barrel and didn't mark it?" Jacky yelled. "What's in it?"

Pat Jellison thrust his thin, worried, pimply young face around the door frame.

"I guess I did that," he said weakly. "Rushing so, I forgot."

"You forgot!" Jacky mocked Pat's harried voice in a tremulous falsetto. "Well, all right, what's in here?"

"Hake," Pat said with a sort of dying, but still hopeful, gasp.

"You sure?" Jacky thrust out his jaw and glared.

"Yes, I am." Pat's voice firmed. "It's hake."

Jacky grabbed his sheath knife and slit the neat head. Getting his fingers under the flap, he ripped it off, still swearing, and started burrowing through the top layer of ice.

"Hanh," he said scornfully, coming upon his quarry. "Maybe to you, that's hake."

"Warn't, was it?" Pat asked.

"Oh, get to work," Jacky yelled. "And for pete sake see if you can keep your mind off the women long enough to tell a hake from a haddock, will you?"

Pat vanished and Jacky started re-heading the barrel. When it was done, he wrote 'haddock' across the top, firmly, and under-lined it.

Steve smothered a snicker and dodged back so Jacky wouldn't see him and find an excuse for conversation. He refused an invitation to join the poker game, fiddled without success for a moment with the dials of the receiver, stepped idly outside into the dampness again, and stood looking thoughtfully over at the dim bulk of what he took to be the *Seventh Daughter.*

Not quite sure what he was going to do, he went down and untied his punt and started sculling slowly up along the wharves. The wind was quiet, and the oily swell rolling slowly in from under the curtain of fog was nothing more than a suggestion of motion.

He could hear the roar of water from Jim's Gut, far up the Harbor. That was a funny thing, he thought idly, seeing in his mind's eye the tortuous, narrow channel of the Gut, winding in to the serenely sheltered salt water pool. At flood tide the Gut was quiet as a mill-pond and you could row in through safely; but at the beginning of the flood, water glissaded into the pool as if it were pouring down a bottomless hole. It slid with great strength and noise through the twisting Gut, and was torn to shreds on the ledges guarding the entrance to the pool before it passed on to the serenity of the sheltered saucer and waited the turn of the tide to go through the same procedure on the way out again.

Years ago, when Frank Pierce had first taken over the "Chronicle" he had been deeply interested in the story of the Gut. He'd made quite an article out of it.

Steve remembered taking Frank there one day at half-tide. They had prodded around in the ashes of Jim Connor's cabin that had once stood on the nipple of land that formed half the wall of the Gut. Jim had turned up out of nowhere, built himself a little shack, and tried for years to convince other people of his own conviction that the Gut could be harnessed somehow to provide enough cheap electrical power for the entire town. Eventually, growing incautious with growing familiarity, he had drowned there on a changing tide, leaving the Gut still unharnessed. Ten years later, one Fourth of July night, a bunch of big boys looking for excitement had set the shack on fire.

Frank worked up a two-column story out of that. He'd made a good deal out of misunderstood genius, seeing with his own eyes the possibilities of that water power once leashed.

The water under Steve's punt was opaque and deep green. As he rowed he could look up in under the long-legged wharves and hear the steady querulous clicking from the barnacles and other anchored shell fish anticipating the flood tide with its load of food.

Nearing the boat yard, he glanced up to verify his identification of the big dragger. The gleam of gold leaf told him he'd been right. Joe kept that name and port of call bright and new no matter what color he painted the heavy hull. There was dead silence aboard the boat. Obviously no work was being done on her engine at the moment.

Steve tied his punt to the float and went up along the launching shed in search of Kelsey Farrell. He saw him two minutes before he could catch him. Kelsey was a little stooped man, permanently twisted out of shape by chronic arthritis. He moved like a crab, sideways, with his arms curved widely out from his body to provide balance. But he moved twice as fast as any normal man could.

"Kelsey," Steve yelled. "You got a minute?"

Kelsey turned and came rushing back instead of waiting for Steve to come up with him.

"All the time anyone else has," he announced, the words snapping out of his tiny pursed mouth. "Twenty-four hours a day."

"I just wanted to ask you what was wrong with Luccio's engine."

Kelsey gave him a quick upward glance, sly and bright as the look of a gnome, and dropped it to the fragment of wood he was turning rapidly in his claw-like hands.

"You and Art really interested in that boat, ain't you," he said. "Art's been up here already this morning trying to find out what was wrong with her."

"You tell him?"

"I told him it was the wrist pin gave out."

"That the truth?"

"Nope."

Steve snorted.

"That Luccio." Kelsey's mouth twisted upward into a reluctant grin. "He's a pretty sharp cooky. Trouble is, he can't enjoy being sharp unless he tells the whole world about it. I swore to him I wouldn't say anything. Then, fifteen minutes later I hear him giving the whole business away to some goof he picked up down on the float."

"You've gone that far," Steve prompted. "You might's well let me in on it."

"I suppose so. Though I'm getting a day's pay for nothing not to. I wouldn't want it to get back to Art from me. I'm afraid he'd split a gusset or two and I wouldn't want to be responsible for that. Art takes great comfort in making a nickel, and if he ever found out Joe Luccio worked him into taking them fish when there warn't no need for it, I don't know what he'd do."

"I do," Steve said firmly. "He'd be quite likely to dream up some awful way of getting back. You wouldn't know anything about it until it happened, either, and then you couldn't be sure he was responsible."

Kelsey laughed.

"Well, that Joe, see, he wanted to go to that dance they're having tonight. Real bad. And he had them fish and didn't want to go back to Rockland with them. So he takes a screw driver and messes around with one of the injectors on the fuel rack control adjustment. Gets the mixture too rich. Makes that big deisel sound like somebody was playing tunes on her with a five pound maul. It only took me fifteen minutes to fix it. But Joe made a bargain with me. He says he'll give me a full day's pay if I'll send somebody down every hour or so to pound around and make out like they were working on her, see? And not say anything to anyone. Then, the damn fool goes to work and starts spilling the whole thing to the first half wit he can find willing to listen to him."

Kelsey paused for breath, considering Steve's expression to see how he was taking the information. Reassured by the amused quirk at the corners of Steve's wide mouth, he went on:

"That's the trouble with most smart boys like that. They just can't stand not being appreciated, see? That lad's going to get himself in a real bad pickle someday, just because he can't keep his big mouth from flapping."

Kelsey left abruptly, having answered the question and having nothing more to say. Steve watched him go with wry amusement, not too bothered because he himself was losing money on Joe Luccio's whimsical yen for a pretty little girl. He did wonder what Art would say if word of Joe's trick got back to him. It would probably make him so mad he'd go shooting his mouth off to Joe and lose a darn good source of winter supply.

The story didn't surprise him because he had suspected something like it ever since he'd watched Joe tie up at the wharf last night. What did take him aback was the fact that Kelsey Farrell would tell a yarn like that for an extra day's pay. He'd always thought Kelsey came as close to being an honest man as anyone he knew.

"From them that have," Steve said aloud, going back down to his punt, "take what you can get." Not dishonest. Just smart.

Steve was through his supper at six thirty and was loitering aimlessly around the living room staring out into the fog. Thick as wet cotton batting it pushed up against his windows.

At quarter of seven Lizzie thrust an agitated head through the door and looked at him curiously.

"Well, what is it?" After a minute of her scrutiny, Steve couldn't bear it in silence.

"Aren't you going to the dance?"

"For pete sake, doesn't anyone ever think about anything but that damn dance?"

"Lord sake, I never knew you to miss a Pioneers Ball since they started having them!" Her agitation changed to concern. "Steve! You aren't sick?"

"Do I look sick?"

"Can't say you do; but you certainly look like a tramp. If you're going you've got to make some changes fast. You look like a porcupine."

Steve ran a thoughtful hand over the two-day growth of beard.

"Yes," he said firmly. "I'm going." He spun around and started up the stairs two at a time. Her implication that, if he wasn't sick he must be getting old, stung him and taking those stairs two at a clip would show her how old he was.

He decided he'd get ready and then go down and stop at Ann's. She would hardly be expecting him, and, chances were, she might not feel like getting dressed and going with him at the last minute. Sheepishly he regarded himself in the bathroom mirror over the frothing white mask of shaving lather.

SWAN'S HARBOR

Poor Ann, he thought. She really deserves better than that of me. Out of conscience, he did not go so far as to think actively: I hope she won't go. He thought only: Perhaps she won't feel like it.

Fifteen minutes later, shaved, showered and half-dressed, he stood bending from the waist to see his head in the mirror, working over his short, intransigent, tawny hair with two military brushes. The mirror had been set for his father who had been a short man and Steve had never taken the trouble to move it up the inch or two that would have made the difference between strain and comfort.

After he had done all he could with it, he stood staring at his own face. He accepted the fact that he was anything but handsome. He took considerable pride and satisfaction from his over-all appearance, though, and the excellent physical condition that underlay it. He had discovered, with the years, that his face didn't matter so much.

Pleased but not complacent about what he saw, he straightened up with a slight sigh. Having lived through a war unscathed, he had learned that the amazing strength of the human body was nothing to the ungodly strength of the forces outside it that conspired at times to destroy physical perfection. During those years from 1941 to 1946 he had seen enough human wreckage to last a man a lifetime. He had often wondered what he would do if it happened to him, and had decided that about the only thing a man could do, would be to find some place down on the flats and let the tide come in over him. He would have, too; but he'd been lucky. The body of which he was so vain, had come out of the mess of war as untouched as it went in. The only thing he had sacrificed to the experience was his complacent acceptance of that body.

As he went out the bedroom door, quick, excited anticipation

99

for the evening welled up in him. He knew now that he had never really hesitated about whether or not he'd go to the dance. He had just been playing a childish game to make the anticipation greater when he was ready to admit it.

Lord amighty, he thought, running down the stairs, wouldn't it be awful if she wasn't even there! He wasn't thinking about Ann.

He was thinking of her, though, when he went swiftly up the herring-bone brick walk to the wide front door with its fan light of convoluted glass. He opened it without knocking and stepped into the hall.

"Annie?"

Her answering voice from the kitchen drew him to the half-open door where he stood waiting until she turned from the sink. He liked to look at her back, enjoyed the way the long curves of her body joined one another, the way she moved.

Her shining, brown hair was brushed up from the back of her neck into the beginning of the smooth braids that encircled her sweetly shaped head. His hands knew the feel of that head, the smooth-sliding warmth of her heavy hair when it wasn't so neatly braided.

He was surprised at himself that he could feel this spreading warmth in his stomach looking at her, when he had been just thinking so busily and with deep excitement about another and totally different girl.

Ann turned, giving his finery a deeply quizzical look.

"Well, *you're* certainly dressed to the nines."

Steve met her hazel eyes with an ingenuous grin.

"Can't take my girl to the Pioneers Ball looking like a tramp, can I? Lizzie said I did, so I repaired the damage."

"Oh, Steve!"

"What's the matter?" Completely innocent and astonished at

her dismay, he nevertheless had difficulty in holding her steady gaze.

"Am I supposed to read your mind, darling? I had no idea whether you wanted to go or not. And I'm not ready."

She glanced down at her old slacks, fingering the limp blue chambray shirt.

"It would take me an hour," she protested.

"Why, Annie, I told you I had the tickets two weeks ago."

"Yes," she said. "I know, baby; but that's not an invitation."

"I meant it to be." He looked at her steadily and felt that he was telling her the absolute truth. "I'm sorry, Ann. You ought to know me by now."

"You're always saying that to me." She showed a brief flash of anger. "And I don't suppose I ever will know you until we're both old and gray and then I won't give a damn." Her voice broke slightly and Steve, hearing that betraying catch, went quickly over and put his arms around her.

"I'm a son of a sea-cook," he said, his lips against her ear. "I'm a low—"

"You're all of that," Ann said firmly and turned her head to meet his mouth, stopping effectively what he would have said. Two minutes later Steve put his hands caressingly on either side of her warm face and bent her head back to feel with his lips the rapid pulse in the hollow of her throat.

"Darling, look," she said, and he recognized the quick, husky sound of her voice, feeling in himself the answer to it. "Either we're going to the dance or we aren't. Which?"

"We could go later."

"You know the old saying."

"You can't have your cake and eat it, too." His voice was an amused mincing falsetto. "All right." He opened his arms wide and Ann backed away from him laughing, her eyes deep now as they had been the morning they'd had breakfast together in the big room looking out over the Bay.

He followed her in through the little house to the foot of the stairs, smiling as he saw her hesitate at the top and then go on without turning to look at him.

The impulse to which Ann had nearly yielded wasn't the one Steve so complacently suspected. For a second, removed from his vital warm immediate presence, she was furious with him. It was so like him to wait until the last minute this way and then arrive astonished that she wasn't dressed and ready to go. He had done it to her so often. Each time it happened she was infuriated, but never before to the point of thinking she might not go at all.

She dressed hastily, still angry, and her hand holding the lipstick shook so that she had to wipe off what she'd already done and start over. The action was a habitual one.

Surprised at memory's tenacity for small things, Ann could remember the night she had first gone through that same uncomplicated set of motions for the same complicated reason. Five years, she thought, startled into a wry amusement at herself that such small things associated with Steve could be so important to her.

That summer their relationship had changed from the purely casual one of two people who have known each other all their lives. The instantaneous and inexplicable attraction that rarely takes place between any but strangers had sprung up between them. They both knew what they had was important. They were together as though they were the only two people left in the world. The one thing lacking was the word, the touch, the moment, and they waited for it, not quietly but with the tense assurance that when it came they would both recognize it.

Steve had been an hour late that night and when he finally arrived, he was maddeningly sure that she would be waiting for him. The most infuriating part of it all was that she had been.

SWAN'S HARBOR

Rather than let him be so sure of himself, she made him sit down in the living room while she went hastily upstairs. Once up there, aware that there was nothing more she had to do, she hastily removed her already perfect lipstick and started to reapply it. But the thought of Steve down there waiting for her, strange and new in that glassed-in world of familiar things, made her hand shake slightly.

Presently, unable to continue her delaying action any longer, she had come to the head of the stairs.

Steve was standing beside the newel post, looking up at her. The dim light from the upstairs hall fell directly on his face. He said nothing, but his intent steady eyes told Ann that she faced the moment of decision from which she would never turn back and that the decision rested with her.

Slowly, feeling as if her knees had suddenly refused to behave, she came down the stairs, wading into his waiting silence as if she waded into deep water. Still wordless, he took her into his arms. They had no need for words. The time for words had been earlier, would be later. Not now.

When they finally left the house, they had met her father coming in the gate. He'd leaned on his cane and stared, his eyes narrow.

"Thought you'd gone."

Ann realized how easily Steve had laughed and lied.

"I was late getting in tonight, Sam. I only got here ten minutes ago."

Downstairs, now, Steve was not remembering that night. As he went over to the Boston rocker and sat down, he found he was breathing faster than he had been.

This room, which was what he would have called unhesitatingly and scornfully a woman's room, wasn't at all like Ann. He thought she had probably spent so much time here she never noticed it now. But he was surprised that she had never reacted against vanished tyranny enough to put some of the breakables away. It must take her hours to dust the place.

The room was so small it made him feel that an unguarded gesture would bring something crashing down with a breaking chatter of glass.

He was staring defensively at the mantel with its frescoed march of small fragile objects and beginning to feel stifled when Ann finally came downstairs. It had taken her only half an hour; but to Steve it felt like the full hour she had promised.

He forgot about the room when he looked at her. She wore a long, plain, green dress he had never seen before, and at each step the skirt flared slightly, giving a quick glimpse of vivid color that was repeated in the flame-colored cape she'd thrown over her shoulders. Against the stiff, stand-up collar of the cape her head looked like some exotic and untouchable flower.

Steve got up silently and stood looking at her in wordless astonished admiration.

"Do you like it?"

He swallowed and nodded his head.

"I—I never saw that dress before."

"It's new. I couldn't resist it." She didn't tell him she had got it especially for this dance and had nearly given up thinking she'd get a chance to wear it.

"By rights—" she looked at him steadily "—I should have said I was going with somebody else and let you think that over."

"I'm glad you didn't."

"Well, I couldn't," she said honestly, evaded his arms with a practiced swing of her hips, and was out the door.

"Snap that light off, Steve." Her voice floated back to him.

It was only quarter of nine when Steve parked the Cadillac in front of the hall. Already a lot of cars were nosed every which way into the parking space and, thinking of his fenders, he decided he'd prefer to take a chance on leaving her beside the road. At this, you counted on getting a dented fender or losing a bumper if you stuck with the dance until intermission. By that time few of the celebrants were still capable of judging distance by a foot or two, and that made all the difference to a fender.

"Want a drink before we go in?" Steve felt for the bottle he'd thrust down under the seat.

Ann shook her head.

"Let's wait a while. I'd rather dance a little first."

Steve surrendered his tickets at the booth and received in return two small tags, one of which he gave to Ann who slid away along the wall saying: "I'll be back in a minute."

He stood there in the crowd around the door waiting for her and watching the couples already circling the floor to the best efforts of Sid Bower's Sidewinder Six. Usually a thing like this didn't really get going until nine-thirty or ten; but now it was already in full swing. He smiled to see that some of the men had stuck firmly to the idea of a costume ball. He could make out a coonskin cap with a red, already perspiring face under it; and a tricorne with a stiff white pigtail sticking shortly out behind.

Later on there would be a prize awarded for the most original costume; some god-awful thing like a dozen screaming White Leghorns or a hogshead of salt fish or a bag of corn, something that would have pioneer connotations and be extremely difficult to use. By that time everybody would be so high that it would seem very funny. Two years ago, it had been the Leghorns and the winner had liberated them in the hall. The Leghorns had been inspired to think they were partridges. When Steve had left at twelve-thirty, they were roosting on the collar beams among streamers of crepe paper and unlit kerosene lanterns, behaving with all the incontinence of sea gulls around a wharf.

SWAN'S HARBOR

Steve searched the moving crowd eagerly for the sight of a honey-colored head, but there was none whose owner wore her hair in a short straight bob. She couldn't have come yet, he decided patiently.

"Steve!"

At the delighted roar, he turned to face a Joe Luccio unimaginably arrayed. He wore a beige gabardine suit, white shirt and soft, gray, suede shoes. His tie was most admirable. It was a deep burnt orange with hand-painted mermaids climbing an invisible Jacob's Ladder up his broad flat chest.

"You found her yet, Joe?"

"No." Joe shook his head; but there was confidence in his handsome face. "She ain't come yet. She will, though. She looked stylish to me, and them stylish ones, they never get anywhere like this till ten, eleven o'clock. I been right here by the door, though, and I'm going to stay here till she turns up."

"I wish you luck."

Joe's glance slid by Steve and he smiled widely.

"If that girl you come with was anyone's but yourn, Steve, I'd forget all about my pretty little girl and take her instead. By judas, she's really a looker, ain't she?"

Ann was working her way back to find him. She had left her cape in the cloak room and her warm brown back and shoulders were bare. Looking at her, he could feel his eyes widen. He glanced grinning at Joe and shook his head.

"Unh-unh," he said and went to meet her.

When he looked back from the safety of the dance floor, Joe was gazing wistfully after them. "I don't blame you," he mouthed before Steve lost him.

For the space of the first two waltzes Steve managed to fend off the stags by a system of grimaces; but he lost her then and it took him fifteen minutes to get her back, only to have her snatched away almost as soon as they'd been once around the floor. It went that way until intermission when he recovered her and they went out to the car to have a drink.

The foggy blackness was alive with the rustling of couples, the clink of bottles, the startled sudden yelps of disembodied and uncanny laughter.

Steve was beginning to feel let down. Here it was intermission already and he hadn't set eyes on the girl he'd been looking for. It occurred to him for the first time that she might not be staying here in the Harbor. Whoever she was, he knew she was somebody he'd seen before.

When he and Ann stepped back inside the hall, after the music started, it was suddenly all right. He looked across the crowded hall right into her eyes and, finding a recognizing light in them, instantly he was startlingly alive again.

It seemed to Ann she could feel the sudden change from flaccidity to excitement in him through the rough cloth of his sleeve where it brushed her bare arm. She glanced at him in astonishment, met his suddenly sparkling eyes, and looked with a familiar sense of dismay around the hall searching without success for the reason.

He let the first stag that approached them cut in. As he vanished, Ann watched him go over her new partner's shoulder with puzzled attention. She knew all the signs, having seen them before. Facing them again, she felt slightly sick to her stomach.

Near the door Steve paused to see if his quarry was still on the floor. Jacky brushed past him, splendid in tweed jacket and gray slacks, his red hair damp and shining.

"Jacky!" Steve grabbed his arm. "Who's the blond girl over there with that Benson kid?"

Jacky's eyes searched for the couple. His face turned slightly stiff looking when he found them.

"Perley Washburn's girl," he said.

That's why she looks so familiar, Steve thought, amazed. Why, she's lived here all her life. But who'd ever think she'd grow up to look like that! The last time he'd consciously noticed her she had been nothing but a bumpy-kneed little kid playing down around the wharf with the boys.

"What's her first name?"

"Hilda." Jacky gave him a look from the corners of his red-brown eyes. Man-to-man, he added: "She's no good. She just plays a guy for what he's got and then holds out on the sweet stuff."

"Maybe she needs a little understanding," Steve said. He looked at Jacky with the good natured contempt a man feels for a boy, and Jacky faded into the crowd, flushing at the unintended insult which was all the more cutting.

Out of conscience, Steve danced once more with Ann before he could bring himself to approach what he felt would be the peak of his evening. For Ann, it was five minutes of misery. His attention wasn't on her, he barely seemed to hear her when she spoke to him, his eyes were always looking beyond her. Leaving her finally to the cocked hat and pigtail, feeling that he had done his duty, Steve turned to find Hilda and she was gone.

At first he couldn't believe it. She'd just come and a moment before he'd seen her dancing near the door. Disappointment, almost strong enough to make him feel weak, welled up through his body.

"Damnation!" he said loudly and started shoving his way along the edge of the crowded dance floor. Angry at himself for not having cut in on her when he had the chance, he went slowly over to the door and glanced outside, wondering where she could have gone so suddenly.

She hadn't gone far. She was leaning against the rough, fog

damp shingles of the old building, her clenched hands covering her mouth, staring widely at the crowd of struggling men who were filling the night with noise that resembled in miniature the sound in Madison Square Garden on Golden Gloves night.

Looking down on the mass from above, Steve could see that it centered around two grunting figures who seemed to be trying hard to kill each other. Around the outside of the swarm which consisted mainly of other men trying to get inside to see what was going on, Jasper Brown, resplendent in a new uniform, moved cautiously, stick in hand. He was trying to get inside, too; but not very hard. As Steve stared, Jasper managed to penetrate the outer circle and in the moment he stood with his stick poised to strike, Steve recognized the head that would receive the blow.

"Joe," he yelled. "Joe, look out!"

Apparently Joe felt rather than heard the warning. He jerked his head aside just in time and took the stick on his heavily padded shoulder. Then the crowd closed in on the two battlers before Steve could see who the other one was.

He hesitated, wondering whether to join in the fun. He glanced at Hilda and found her watching him with a sustained dismayed horror.

"What goes on?" he said.

"That—that Italian! We came out the door and he—he— I want to go home."

The opportunity was too good to be missed. Steve thrust his hand under her elbow and hurried her across the yard to his car. Nobody noticed their departure.

The Cadillac slid easily away into the fog before Steve really looked at the girl huddled away from him in the far corner of the seat.

"So *you're* his pretty little girl, are you?" he said softly.

"I don't know what you mean." Her voice was strangled and

rough. "I think you men are all crazy. I was coming out the door, minding my own business and that—that Wop came up and grabbed my arm. That old man. He'd been drinking, too. He was drunk. He—" Her voice faded and died.

"Never mind it now," Steve said soothingly. "You're all right. I've got you safe now. No need to worry."

She made no answer and when they passed with a swish of slow power under the next street light, Steve glanced at her again. Instantly his heart was pierced with an emotion so sweet and new that for a moment he thought he couldn't contain it in silence. She was sitting very straight in the seat, her back just touching the firm cushion lightly. Her hands were folded in her lap and she looked straight ahead, exactly like a small girl in Sunday School who had been told to sit up straight and behave herself. He wanted to laugh for pure pleasure, but that would have startled her, and he couldn't have explained.

"What shall I do with you?" he asked softly.

"*Do* with me?" He heard her startled motion, her head turning, like the secret sound of a bird stirring in a full-leaved lilac bush in the silent night. "Why, take me home. What else?"

"You should never have been at that brawl," he said shortly. "What're your people thinking of to let you go to a wrangle like that, anyhow?"

"I was twenty-two my last birthday."

Steve really did laugh then.

"I don't believe it." He didn't, either, because she looked so young to him. He decided she was probably seventeen masquerading. But her reaction to his disbelief made him rejudge. Her voice was indifferent and completely casual.

"You can believe whatever you want to," she said. "I don't really care."

"You will." He put as much meaning as he dared to into the two words and knew immediately that she resented it.

"Look," she said stiffly. "I don't know what you think I am. I suppose you're so used to having women throw themselves at you you can't believe I haven't. I would have gone with anyone who came along just then. I don't like fights. They make me sick to my stomach. All I want to do is go home and forget it."

"Right-o." At least, he thought grinning to himself in the safety of the dark, I'm not going to have to pretend to introduce myself to her. She not only knows me for sure, but she's also been listening to all the gossip that comes along.

In her father's big rambling old house on Main Street a dim light burned in the front room.

"They don't wait up for you," he said.

"Why should they?"

"Hilda." Steve sat searching frantically for something to hold her a second longer. She got out of the car quickly and was on the verge of going up the walk without another word for him. Now she turned and stood waiting impatiently.

"That boy you were with. You left him in a pretty tough spot. Won't he wonder what happened? Don't you want me to tell him where you went?"

"I *am* sorry." Instantly she stepped back to the car and looked in at him. "I guess I was pretty upset by the whole thing. Anyhow, I was forgetting my manners. Yes. Please tell him I went home. That's all. It was Carl Benson. And tell him," she hesitated slightly, "that I hope he's not too badly hurt."

"I'll do that." Steve wondered idly what young Benson's reaction would be when he found out who had taken his girl home. "That all?"

"That's all you need to tell Carl."

He winced at the implication that Carl would understand everything else it was necessary for him to understand.

"But I do want to thank you, too."

"Skip that," he said roughly.

"No, really. It was very nice of you to take the trouble and I'm an ungrateful creature. But I really am a little upset."

"Perhaps," Steve said lightly, "you'll give me a chance to see what you're like when you're *not* upset."

For a moment he thought he'd overstepped his advantage again, she was silent so long before she answered him. When she did, relief at her tone made him catch his breath. It was completely different, light, happy, slightly coquettish.

"Perhaps I will. If you'd like to, Mr. Swan."

"Try Steve. It's a lot easier. And I'll call you in a day or two, if I may."

"Yes." She turned hastily away. "Do that."

"Goodnight, Hilda," he called after her, wanting greatly to get out and walk up to the door with her; but feeling it would be pushing his luck too far. He'd have to remember that she wasn't anything but a child and children are suspicious.

He turned the car there in the street, and when he drove away he was positive he hadn't seen the big front door open. That meant she was still standing on the shadowy verandah, watching.

"Steve, old boy," he said aloud. "What a knight in shining armor *you* are!"

Back at the hall the excitement was over and the combatants had disappeared. Only Jasper, triumphant and strutting like a rooster, paced the parking space grandly twirling his whistle, ready to tell all and sundry about the battle he'd won.

Steve ran lightly across to the steps to stand in the open door looking around the hall at the stream of overheated dancers circling past him. It was getting malodorous now and would be worse by one o'clock when the dance would begin to break up. He could see no sign of Carl Benson. He worked his way slowly along the wall to the door of the men's room. He bent his head under the lintel, not because it was necessary in this case, but because the few daily times when it was essential had turned it into a habit.

He was looking at the floor, expecting nothing, and saw nothing to warn him. He heard only a solid-sounding thud. Everything circled and dissolved into a brilliant painful splash of gory color and turned black so quickly he was unaware he had fallen.

If the circumstances had been different in the slightest degree, Carl Benson knew he would never have done it. He had simply followed the first impulse that came into his slightly fuddled brain when he glanced up and saw that tawny unsuspecting head. Fortunately for him, he was alone in the washroom.

He wasn't drunk, simply feeling a little above himself, and mad enough to chew the heads off brass nails. It didn't help a man's pride to get a thorough hiding in front of his girl. And then have the girl walk off with somebody else.

He stood staring down at Steve's prostrate body, thinking: My god, he's big! Steve looked twice his size sprawled on the tiled floor. His eyes were shut and he breathed heavily. His nose had begun to bleed and the spreading pool edged out slowly toward Carl's foot. Seeing it coming, he hastily drew away.

He glanced thoughtfully at the half-full wine bottle in his hand wondering whether or not to leave it here and run. Then he decided he'd better take it with him. He thrust it firmly between his arm and his ribs under his suit coat, leaving the coat unbuttoned so the bulge wouldn't be so apparent. Hastily, before somebody should come in and find him standing over the body, he slunk out of the room and along to the door. If anybody noticed him they would think he went with his face averted because of the split lip, the big bruise on his cheek-bone, and the beginning-to-turn-yellow circle around his left eye.

It was too much! That damn Wop beating him up like that and Steve Swan walking off with his girl!

I'll show them, he thought, climbing carefully into his old roadster. When he swirled out of the parking space, he came dangerously close to the fish-tail on the black Cadillac. For an insane moment he toyed with the idea of going back and ripping it off. It would serve that Swan bastard right. But he decided he'd already done enough and kept going.

He was beginning to feel nervous now that he'd done it and got away. Perhaps he should have told somebody there was something wrong with Steve. Carl was sure nobody had seen him and he could have given the alarm without getting into trouble. But what if he'd killed the big devil. There had been, it seemed to him in his present state, an awful lot of blood. Covered the whole floor in there. If he went back it would make him sick to see it.

Back at the hall somebody had discovered Steve immediately; but it was a full half hour before he opened his eyes. When he did it was to see Ann and Jasper Brown doing an intricate and disembodied dance over him. All he could see were their heads, attached to nothing, floating in interweaving circles about two feet above his face.

"What?" he said weakly. "Oh, my head!"

He discovered with relief that both those circling heads were attached to bodies and, when he'd found them, the faces stopped whirling.

"Who did it, Steve?" Jasper bent over him pleadingly. "Just tell me who did it. I'll see he's taken care of."

"I don't know. I don't know what it was." His head felt like a pumpkin with the seeds possessed of an active life of their own. He tried to push himself up off the floor, seeing the excited gang staring through the door.

Somebody put a firm arm behind his shoulders. He sat up and the nosebleed started again, gushing in a red sheet down over his white shirt front.

"Steve," Ann said tightly. "Lie down till that stops."

"Got to—" Steve began, thinking there was something he had to go and do but unable to think what it was.

"Here." When he refused to subside, Ann thrust his handkerchief into his hand and he sat holding it to his face. He couldn't think. He shook his head experimentally and knew instantly that was a terrible mistake. Everything began to go around in circles again.

"He won't lie down," Ann said brusquely to the jittering policeman. "Get some men to help me get him out to the car. I'll take him home."

Steve never knew how he got out of the hall and into the car. The motion of the machine beneath him was no greater than the heaving of that solid floor had been.

Ann parked in the yard and without a word to him got out and went quickly up the hill to the back door. Steve heard her go with confusion. Was she going to leave him sitting here alone and hurt? He got one hand on the door handle and opened the door; but he couldn't make his legs move. It was a slight relief to him that he actually knew what he wanted to do even if he was unable to do it.

It seemed like an hour before he heard her coming back. Lizzie was with her, saying little and saying that in a hard, acrimonious, old-sounding voice.

Together the two women got his tottering bulk out of the car, up the hill, and up the stairs into his bedroom. He could help a little once they had him upright between them; but if one of them had removed her support, he would have gone down like a sack of sand.

For chrissake, he thought, utterly bewildered, what happened to me, anyhow?

They sat him on the edge of the bed and all he wanted to do was lie down and go to sleep; but Lizzie wouldn't let him.

"No, you sit right there," she said harshly. "We've got to stop that nosebleed or you'll choke to death."

An hour later, after something cold and wet had lain on the back of his neck for an eternity, they let him lie down and he started to float off somewhere on a fat pink cloud. He roused to spasmodic protest when urgent hands unbuckled his belt and he tried to push them away.

"Oh, stop!" Lizzie said. "You won't be any surprise to either of us."

Half an hour later, when the two women left the bedroom, he was deeply asleep.

"Now," Lizzie said firmly, turning to face an exhausted Ann. "You can tell me what happened to him."

Ann shook her head.

"No. I can't. And neither can he. We found him lying on the floor in the men's room, unconscious. He was out for half an hour. When he came to, he didn't even know what had hit him."

"Brawling in dance halls!" Lizzie's sharp eyes were contained but furious. "What kind of a way to act is that—for a man like him?"

"Lizzie." Ann put her hands wearily to her forehead. "I can't argue tonight. Let's not. Please try to understand how I feel and don't resent me so. I love him. I don't think any more of the way we live than you do. It's just that I'd do anything he wanted. If he told me to lie down in front of his door and let him use me for a door mat, I think I'd do it."

Lizzie put out her hand and laid it lightly on Ann's shoulder; but the touch, light as it was, established a communication between them that had never existed before.

"All right. You go home. If anything happens, I'll get the doctor, then I'll call you."

"You don't think we should call the doctor anyhow?"

"He'll be all right. I'll watch him."

She would, too, Ann thought, going alone down the stairs and letting herself out. Lizzie wouldn't go five feet away from that bed until Steve woke up. And she herself could do no good if she insisted on staying.

She climbed wearily into the Cadillac. Parking it before her own front door, she thought with a weak upsurge of mirth: This is really having the name without the game.

She was weary to the point of death; but it was hard to go to sleep, lying there in the hushed house remembering Steve's face, white under its tan, against the pillow. When she finally dropped off she slept solidly until the phone woke her at eleven the next morning. Lizzie's voice, still harsh but with a new undertone of companionship in it, said in her ear:

"Ann, he's awake and eating his breakfast. He feels better and he wants to know if you know what happened to his car."

"You can tell him I came home from the buggy-ride in style in his damned Cadillac." Ann's relief made her brusque. "I'll bring it up as soon as I can haul myself together."

By the time she had leisurely finished breakfast and was ready to take Steve's car home, Ann's relief had existed long enough to turn sour. Sometimes she thought her entire life had been spent coping with difficult men.

An only child, her mother died when Ann was in high school, leaving Ann and her father to each other's mercies. Samuel Harris had been one of those men who spend their lives formulating great schemes which, in their minds, could result only in tremendous success. His schemes had always come, curiously enough, close to the success he constantly dreamed of. So close that their successive failures left him a frustrated and bitter old man who could, with justice, blame his final failure on fate or somebody else's blunder.

During his last years he had been bitter about everything: his own penniless old age which kept him dependent on his daughter; his daughter for being a daughter, not a son; the memory of his dead wife who had failed him when he most needed her; bitterest of all against Steve Swan who was nothing better than a common woman-chaser and who was bringing him down to his grave with shame.

Ann, seeing the likenesses between the two men who ruled her life during the last year her father lived, thought she might easily be the fool Samuel told her she was, to let another, domineering, careless, thoroughly selfish male take over when she was just beginning to escape from the domination of the first one. Her father didn't put it on quite that footing; but Ann did, when she let herself slip into the habit of bitterness that Samuel had made the common atmosphere in this house.

When he died, it was as if a thundercloud that had influenced her mental weather for thirty years had been dispelled by a northwest wind. Freedom from that brooding presence was so heady that, for a long time, she had not wanted anything else, any more than Steve had. There was no doubt in her mind that she loved him. What she'd told Lizzie last night had been true for so long she no longer needed to think about it.

She wasn't sure whether Steve loved her. When she had to think about that, she knew that if he did, he himself was unwilling to admit it. It *had* to be something like that to let him treat her as he did. The four years since Samuel's death had been a series of peaks and valleys for his daughter. For months things would go smoothly. Steve would be around every other night, until it seemed as if they might as well be married and living in one house instead of two. Then, suddenly Ann would realize she hadn't seen him for a week. Finally she would catch sight of the reason, some vacant-faced, pretty, little thing, useless and cute as a kitten.

A month or so later, Steve would turn up one night, unannounced, sheepish and completely silent about his absence. He would take either the jealous silence or the jealous tirade with which she met him and which she couldn't restrain. But it always ended the same way, and they went on together for months until he vanished once more.

Ann had prayed she would be able to tell him sometime, on his sheepish return, to get out. She had so far lacked the pride and stamina. Walking up the hill she thought she might be able to do it now, if it were about to happen again, as she had suspected last night.

"He's still in bed." Lizzie met her at the door. "Don't you want to go up and see him a minute?"

"No," Ann said thoughtfully. "I don't believe I do."

She laid the car keys in Lizzie's hand and left the older woman staring after her, her brows drawn together in a puzzled frown.

I'm so tired, Ann thought defensively, knowing she should at least have said good morning to him. I'm just too tired to face him. As long as he's all right—

Besides, it was twelve o'clock and Peter would be wondering if she were dead. She forced herself to walk briskly and by the time she got downtown she had managed to work off the lassitude that had been like a chain hobbling her ankles.

The office door stood open to the warm dampness of the street. Ann went in quietly, hoping that Peter might be out and unaware of the time of her arrival. He was, however, leaning against her desk and he looked up at her with a hint of a sympathetic grin on his round good-natured face.

"I wasn't expecting you till Monday."

"I wish to god you'd called me, then." Ann pulled a long face. "I could have slept for the rest of the day."

"I would have if I hadn't been so selfish." Peter shoved his rotund body into an upright position and gave her the steady regard she had learned how to meet with un-understanding equanimity. "But, you know, I miss you when you're not here for a day."

"I'll have to teach you how to type," Ann said levelly.

"Guess you will." Peter was instantly business-like; but he couldn't resist one more prod. "Good thing for business there's only one Pioneers Ball during the year."

"Isn't it?" Ann agreed equably, sitting down behind the desk and immersing herself so completely in the heap of papers that she was apparently unaware of his departure when he finally turned and went into the inner office.

Part Three

*O*N MONDAY THE fog that had been hanging over the Harbor like a wet wool blanket for four days seemed, incredibly, to get thicker.

Steve had stayed gratefully away from the wharf all week end and on Monday he didn't go down until afternoon. On Sunday morning he had decided that his head would never be the same again. He was so unaccustomed to having any part of his body hurt enough to make him aware of its individual existence that carrying around a wash-tub-sized head on his normal and inadequate neck was a burden.

He sat around the house all day Sunday, doing nothing, just waiting for it to feel better with the patient lack of understanding of an animal. Like a hurt animal, he growled when approached.

Two or three times, Lizzie, coming with offerings of soup or toast and tea, had been sent flouncing back to the kitchen in a dudgeon.

Finally she had stood her ground, tears of outrage runneling the furrows on her powdered cheeks.

"Well, all right," she'd said. "I don't say it doesn't serve you right for brawling in dance halls. A man of your age! Because it does. Why don't you go to the doctor if it hurts so?"

Steve had put back his cotton-filled head and howled. Regretting the rash action sadly, he yelled at her:

"What in hell do you mean, a man of my age? For chrissake, Lizzie, are you trying to make an old man of me before my time? I'm thirty five. *Thirty five years old*, Lizzie!"

His ugly face distorted by a rage so deep she was amazed at it, Steve got up and came over to where she stood trembling in the hall door, ready to dodge back into her kitchen like a rabbit into a brier patch if he once took his hypnotically outraged eyes off her face long enough.

"I was not brawling, Lizzie." He hadn't moderated his voice and the blast of it at close range sent Lizzie backward a protesting step.

"Will you two silly women get that through your thick heads once and for all? *I do not know what happened to me.* I went in through that door and something hit me and that's all there was to it."

"Steve, wait—don't—it's not good for you."

"Nobody knows that better than I do." His anger cooled enough to let him feel the echo of it throbbing behind his forehead. He put up one hand and touched the space between his eyes tenderly.

"But thirty five is not old, Lizzie. I don't want any soup, nor yet any calves foot jelly. I am not an invalid and this headache will go away as soon as I can crawl in a hole somewhere where you and Ann can't find me."

"I was just—"

"I don't give three damns in the blue hollow of hell what you were just. All I want is to be left alone. Will you try to do that?"

"I certainly will," Lizzie snapped. "As long as you're behaving like a bear with a sore head."

"Well, that description is very apt," he told her, quieting.

"That's exactly what I am. So git, before I really lose my temper."

Wordlessly Lizzie turned and fled back down the hall to her kitchen where, presently, Steve could hear her protesting wordlessly but noisily through the medium of banged kettles, slammed stove lids, and fiercely operated water faucets.

His out-of-proportion anger that Lizzie had borne was actually directed at three women. Lizzie got it because she was the only one present and for the ferocious moment she represented all her sex. Only one-third of it was rightfully hers for her solicitous but infuriating attitude of ministering to the deathly ill. But all three of them were conspiring to make him feel like an octogenarian. Lizzie with her reiterated 'a man of your age'; Ann with her wordless but equally apparent disapproval of his behavior; Hilda simply by being so terribly young herself.

And he, the innocent, was so completely misunderstood that he couldn't bear it without yelling at somebody. If he really had dived into that fight, as he had wanted to, and, as a result, had come home with this tender screaming head, there might have been a little justice in the way Ann and Lizzie were behaving. As it was, he was that most injured of all, the innocent bystander who didn't know what hit him.

He did know that there had been a human agency behind it, and when he found out what that agency was there would either be somebody else with a head that felt exactly like his, or he would feel twice as bad as he did now.

When his fury had faded slightly, he found that he felt distinctly better and that he was half starved. Sheepishly he went out to the kitchen and spent half an hour cajoling a silently enraged Lizzie into making another offer of the previously resented soup, toast and tea.

By Monday morning he was feeling so much better that inactivity worked him up into a fretting rage of boredom. He paced the living room furiously until eleven thirty, when he ate his dinner. After that, no longer able to face the same four walls, he went down to the shore.

The fog was thicker than ever; but when Steve got out of his car he heard, far off to the northwest, a faint rumble of thunder among the hills and knew that the change was coming. The distant growl sounded like an artillery barrage, so far away that it was as yet nothing but a shudder of sound.

He could barely make out the shadowy forms of boats at their moorings as he went slowly down the wharf. There wouldn't be many of them out today. No one would go out in this pea souper unless he had to.

When he thrust his head in through the office door there were glistening beads of dampness in his thick short hair. Art wasn't at his desk; but Miss Chick was scuttering around in her papers so much like her namesake in a thick litter that Steve had to grin.

She looked up, saw him, and took a long, sibilant, startled breath, her eyes rounding with apprehension.

"What's the matter with you, Chickie?"

"Oh, my goodness, I heard you were awfully sick! I heard you'd been in a terrible brawl and got half killed down there to the Pioneers Ball! I've always said they shouldn't allow the things that go on down there. Why, nobody in town is fit to do anything the whole week end after one of those dances!"

"Well, do I look half killed?" Impatiently he considered her worried foolish face.

"No. No, you don't. No, I can't say you do." The measure of Chickie's astonishment lay in the number of times she repeated herself.

"Where's Art?" Still miffed enough to be short with her, Steve glared at the empty chair. He didn't want to see Art; but he couldn't think of anything else to ask her.

"He's down in the *Pillbox* talking to Will Holmes."

"Will still in Rockland?"

"Yes, and he says he's going to lay up there until the fog lifts. Arthur is furious with him." Chickie was the only person Steve knew who used Art's full name. "Arthur is trying to get him to come home and Will won't."

"Well, I don't know as I blame him much. Art won't have any luck at long distance bullying, I'm afraid."

"He's been working on Will now for the whole morning and Will won't stir." She glanced thoughtfully at her desk, saw there a memorandum, and said: "Oh," in a startled voice.

"Matter?"

"There was a phone call for you about fifteen minutes ago."

Steve gave her averted pink face an amused look. Chickie never admitted that she might have heard any of the gossip Steve knew was rampant about him; but he could always tell when the message she had to relay was from a woman. There was a certain timbre in Chickie's voice, an embarrassed evasion about her usually straight glance.

"Was she old or young?" he asked playfully and Chickie was surprised enough to stare at him.

"How did you know it was a woman?"

"I can tell just from the way you look."

Chickie made a dismayed clicking sound with her tongue against her upper plate.

"Sounded kind of thirtyish to me," she said tartly. "I said you were sick and she said she'd try the house. She didn't leave any name."

Her last sentence put the seal of her disapproval on all his amorous escapades; but the first one made him lose his quickened interest. For an instant he had thought wildly that Hilda might have called him. But Chickie was usually right about the age of the caller. Nobody, no matter how obtuse—which Chickie was not—would have mistaken Hilda's voice for that of a woman of thirty.

"Wonder who it was." He stared a moment, puzzled, knowing that Ann would never call him at the wharf. She wouldn't call him for a while anyhow. He had known, when Lizzie told him Ann had refused to come in Saturday morning, that she was put out with him and felt the way Lizzie did about his story of getting hit on the head when he wasn't looking.

"Well, she'll call again if it's anything important."

He pushed himself upright, away from the support of the door frame, and wandered out into the shed.

Jennie Chick nearly got up and went to the door to call him back. She had made a disquieting discovery Saturday and it was riding her thin shoulders like the old man of the sea. She couldn't have felt any more guilty if she herself had been doing what Art Swan was. And Steve should know. After all, Art ran the business; but Steve's interest in it was as great as his and Jennie felt strongly that somebody should protect that interest since Steve apparently had no idea of distrusting his brother.

It would never have entered Jennie's head to distrust him either, until Saturday when she found the second set of books.

The books on the Swan business were stacked on a shelf behind Jennie's desk where she could reach them simply by spinning her swivel chair around. Everything was there. Cash Receipts, Disbursements, the thick, blue fabric-covered ledgers. Art had told her firmly that they were open to Steve whenever he wanted to look at them; but Steve had never shown the slightest interest. So Art and Jennie had got into the habit of making out a simplified analysis every few months and giving it to him.

The figures Jennie used to make it out were those she took from the ledgers behind her desk.

Art's desk was sacred and she seldom went near it, certainly never to open the usually locked drawers. On Saturday he left the office at three saying he'd promised to take Minnie to the movies and he wanted to make the early show at Centerville. After he'd gone Jennie, looking for the stamp pad, had gone over to his desk. The top was bare and automatically she reached for the handle of the first drawer.

It opened easily before she had time to realize and be surprised that it was unlocked. Then a greater surprise drowned the lesser. She was staring down at another ledger exactly like the one that lay on the shelf behind her own desk. Puzzled and unaware that she had no business to look at it, she lifted it out, and it fell open easily to the balance sheet headed May. She took in the figures, thinking at first they must be for another year. She knew those books as she knew her own face in the mirror, and the figures under Receipts were certainly not the ones she had in her own ledger.

Puzzled, she leafed back through the book, recognizing Art's stubby writing, until she found the year. There it was, unquestionably, 1952.

Subconsciously she was beginning to understand. She almost shut the book and shoved it out of sight as if that would make her forget it. Then, instead, shaking with apprehension, she took it over to her own desk and laid the two ledgers side by side.

She had been right. The figures weren't the same. There was a difference of—her brows knit thoughtfully—exactly ten per cent. Art's private ledger showed a profit of ten per cent more than Jennie's.

Feeling sick to her stomach, Jennie had put both ledgers carefully away. She left the office early herself Saturday night.

She didn't know what to do with her knowledge; but she felt that something should be done. She had been so silent and bad tempered Sunday her mother had thought she was sick. She had still reached no conclusion by Monday morning.

If she told Steve he would go roaring to his brother and Art, knowing immediately where the source of Steve's information lay, would fire her. Jennie couldn't afford to lose this job. She had been lucky to get it, at her age, and she had to keep it.

So she sat in silence and let Steve go, knowing that he was being cheated every day of his life; but lacking the courage to tell him because of what might happen to her. She was ashamed of herself and sorry for Steve. But she consoled herself, thinking: He has plenty without it. It needn't concern me. It would be a long time, though, before she would be able to look Arthur Swan in the eye again.

Steve found the shed jammed and the boys cleaning fish for the peddlers. They had to have fifteen hundred pounds, some merely dressed, others filleted, packed in labeled boxes and ready by early Tuesday morning when the door to door men arrived with their small trucks.

Feeling useless and, as he did once in a great while, conscience stricken about the way the business went along without a word from him, Steve wandered down to the float and stared off into the fog. He could hear Art's voice raised in a vocal maelstrom of rage, issuing from the *Pillbox*'s cabin. He could also tell by the rising timbre of that voice that Art had come up against a stone wall in his usually biddable captain.

The thunder had come closer since he'd gone into the office. It would be on them in force in less than an hour, he judged. A cloud bank from the west was climbing the sky behind the fog, turning things a queer dark yellow. A strange gusty wind had come up, from no one point of the compass but all points, and was lashing the fog in eerie wisps around the corners of the buildings.

He stood wondering whether he'd have time to row out and pump out the *Eloise*'s bilge before the storm hit. He had nearly made up his mind to do it when there was a scrabble of hasty feet on the ramp behind him.

Jacky Gott, his face queerly white and tense under the flame of his hair, was coming quickly down to the float.

"Steve!" he said urgently.

"Matter, Jacky?" Steve stared. "You sick?"

Jacky shook his head.

"Lady up there to see you," he said. He wasn't stuttering; but his voice sounded as if he might.

"Who?"

"Oh, why, it's that Mrs. Pierce, you know. That—oh—that newspaper—Frank's wife."

"Well, what did she do, bite you?"

Jacky had the super-ego that sometimes goes with red hair; but in the five minute interval between Steve's sight of him in the shed and this moment, he had lost it all.

He shook his head sharply, not even offering a grin.

"Steve," he said quickly, his voice low. "I never—it wasn't me. Whatever she tells you. He was the one."

"Are you crazy, kid?" Steve's eyes narrowed intently on the young man's stricken face. "What in hell are you trying to say?"

Jacky took a deep breath that rattled somewhere in his chest. Whatever he would have said died in his throat. Martha Pierce's voice from the head of the way seemed to strangle him.

"Oh, Steve, there you are."

Steve looked at her with real pleasure. Martha was one of the few women he had liked from the first moment they'd set eyes on each other. There wasn't a coquettish bone in her plump sensible body. She was good-looking, not pretty, and so completely in love with her own husband and satisfied with her own family, that it left no room for that expectancy of flirtation he found in most women. So they had met on a level plain of impersonal liking which had developed into a strong foundation of mutual confidence.

Their friendship grew like the unexpectant friendship between two men. But when Steve looked at her distraught face now he remembered that she was a woman and saw that she was a deeply troubled one.

"Come on down," he called. "Only take it easy on that ramp. It's slippery."

Jacky waited wordlessly at the foot of the runway until she had reached the bottom; then he went haring up it. Looking after him, completely bewildered, Steve saw him hesitate at the top as if he wanted to stay and listen to them. Steve stared, coldly, until Jacky moved reluctantly out of sight.

"That kid!" He turned to her. "He's getting so nosy it isn't even funny any more. How are you, Martha? I haven't seen you for weeks."

"Oh, dear!" She gave him a wry mirthless smile. "I don't really know how I am, Steve."

"What's the trouble? If there's anything wrong and I can help, you know you only have to say."

"That's why I'm here. I don't have many in this town I can turn to for help, Steve. I mean, not many I'd *want* to. And I've simply got to talk to somebody about Frank."

A little trickle of apprehension that felt like fog turned liquid rolled down Steve's spine. He had an instinctive feeling that he wasn't going to care for this, whatever it might turn out to be. He didn't like to be forced into a position where he would have to decide who was his friend, Frank or Martha, and hoped she wasn't going to push him into it now.

At his silence, which neither invited nor repelled confidence, Martha said:

"Frank's got a new hobby horse lately. He's decided something ought to be done about the way the whole coast exists through the winter just for summer coming. He says the entire state battens on the summer people. Look." She started wrestling furiously with her coat pocket. When she brought out the folded paper, the torn lining came with it, Steve saw with a pang of amusement. If that wasn't like her! The last time he'd seen her wearing this coat a month ago, she'd had the same trouble with the lining of the pocket. But it was still unmended.

"Look at this thing he's written." She thrust the paper into his lax hand. "Read it, please. Read it."

Steve bent a reluctant head over the cheap sheet of newsprint, following the poor typing with increasing amusement:

"New England people are insular. We sit here on our tired weary man-handled coast and refuse to admit that a great empire has widened out to the west. The backbone of a continent is something to go and see and come back to say: The Sierras disappointed me. They're nothing to the Berkshires.

"The wave of the past mourns against our rocks, broken in chaos—while we ignore in its decadent roar of frustration the tremendous surge and re-surge of the shining combers of the future screaming in from the seas of promise in the west.

"The known, the sailed-over, the behind-us-forever. Let somebody else discover and enjoy the thin-oxygened heady wind of the future. We will let our lungs grow flaccid in the dioxide saturated air our fathers breathed.

"You will say that this new empire is based upon a vile commercialism; but we do not want that here. And that is a lie. We had it here. We mourned its passing. We wish it back. But the old, not the new.

"We are used and tired before we're born. We prate of the horror of amassing money by the crass necessary methods used by other men.

"Commercialism we must accept if we would live. It is the fore-runner of Armageddon and few of us are privileged to recognize that."

When he had finished, Steve stood with the paper loose in his fingers, not wanting to let her see his amusement.

Suddenly he put his head back, and let out his laughter.

"Very fine sophomore editorializing." He handed the paper back to her. Then he looked at her face and was astonished to find it stonily controlled against the turmoil of misery. In a minute, unless he did something, she was going to cry. At their backs the coming thunder storm let out a threatening long-drawn roar.

"Martha, what *is* it? Not this silly damn thing. What's wrong?"

"Turn it over," she said.

Steve did, and read in Frank's hard, blunt hand: *The mass of men lead lives of quiet desperation.*

"Is that sophomoric?"

"Not the original. But so many people have used it to describe so many things it was never intended to mean."

"Steve, you're trying to put me off. You're treating me like a child. And you know I'm not."

"I'm sorry." He met her eyes squarely. "I guess I was thinking more of myself. And Frank. Once you talk about the part of a friend he's chosen to keep from you, somehow you don't feel the same easiness with him again. Whether he knows it or not."

"All right. Perhaps I should have just asked if I could talk to you."

Overhead the heavens split. The lightning, diffused behind the fog, was a livid lavender, lasting for dazzling seconds and coming from no specific area of the sky. The surface of the float was instantly mottled by large, irregular, dark spots, each the size of half a dollar.

Steve took her arm hurriedly.

"We'll be drowned if we stay here a minute longer. Come on up to the office. No." Instantly he saw that wouldn't work. "We better go sit in the car."

They hurried up the wharf, pursued by the hurrying sound of the rain, beneath the pyrotechnics that tumbled and roared overhead. Thudding along, with her heels tapping twice to his once, Steve found that the pounding set up an echo in his still tender head. But action gave him a moment's respite. There was more behind her coming to him than she had been able to bring herself to tell him and he wasn't sure he would want to hear it. He thought fleetingly of Jacky, who apparently thought he knew what it was all about.

Reluctant and puzzled, Steve thrust her bodily into the car and ran around to the other side to get in himself. The back of his blue shirt was a leopard skin of wet and dry, and when he leaned back in the seat he could feel each separate drop of rain in a small cold patch against his skin.

The moment they reached haven the rain broke and fell as if from an upturned bottomless bucket invisibly but directly above them. The sound of it hitting the metal roof was the sound of solidity. Instantly the few outlines still visible in the yellow fog vanished and they were walled in by steel and glass against a world of water.

"Something terrible is happening to Frank," Martha said

quickly, wanting to get the words out and recognized before she changed her mind. "I don't know what it is. I don't want—" Steve knew she had been going to say she didn't want to know.

"He's gone again," she said.

"Yes, I know."

"Then he told you." She considered him impersonally. "I wish he'd thought to tell me. What makes him do it, Steve? I wake up one day to find him gone and I never know whether it's Alaska or Atlantic City until I get a post card maybe a week later."

Steve shrugged, thinking blankly what it must be like for a woman living with Frank Pierce, if she really loved him, and Martha did. That vanishing act must have been horrifying the first time it happened.

"I'm sorry," he said helplessly, mankind apologizing to womankind for the vagaries of his half of the race but unable to explain.

"There's been a new thing. This summer he's been coming home late. He'll say he wants to be alone in the house and tell me to take the kids and go to the movies or something. I always do."

She gave him a broken imitation of a smile that touched him deeply.

"The only thing I can think of—Frank's in kind of a difficult position for a man, Martha."

"You mean my money, don't you."

Steve nodded. Frank Pierce was the product of a little, bony-pastured, unproductive farm in the western uplands of Massachusetts. He seldom mentioned the fact; but he never tried to hide it. And Steve, remembering the four years in Brunswick, remembered too that Frank had always been broke. He would spend money on some handsome, expensive, useless object, possession of which meant he would eat two meals a day instead of three, and consider the expenditure well worth it.

"But we talked that all over the night we decided to get married," Martha said doubtfully. "He never felt funny about it. The money was there. We could enjoy it together. That's only sensible. And it let us live where he wanted to and do what he wanted to do. That's what it's for. We've never even bothered to mention it since."

"Maybe that's not it then." Still unconvinced, Steve stared thoughtfully at the curtain of water streaming down over the windshield. He knew that he himself in Frank's position aware that he was supported and subsidized by his wife's money, would never have an easy moment. But then, he and Frank were like black and white.

He came to to find that Martha had been talking and he had missed the first of it.

"—won't give the children any time. He's drinking much too much. I honestly think he's losing his mind." Her eyes met Steve's honestly. "The worst thing of all is that he won't have anything to do with me, either. It's been nearly six months now, Steve. Does he think I'm made of wood? No woman can stand that!"

Steve said the only thing that entered his head, the only thing that would explain Frank's behavior to him.

"Well—is it another woman, do you think?"

"I did think so, at first. You see things whether you want to or not. There were lipstick marked cigarettes in the car ashtray once or twice. I didn't give it too much importance. There were any number of ways they might have got there; but I know now how they did. It's more than that—"

Apparently she had come to the point. He saw the pupils of her eyes widen slightly, heard the long breath she took. She started to speak, hesitated, and went on and he knew this was what he wasn't going to want to hear.

"I went into the bedroom the other night and Frank was standing there in front of my vanity table." Her voice was low, monotonous, as if she had to work to control it and found a monotone easiest. "He didn't know I'd come home. He had my lipstick open in his hands. I had the feeling if I hadn't come in when I did, he would have used it."

"Martha, *are you crazy?*" Completely shocked and ravaged by what she was trying to tell him without putting it into actual words, Steve was horrified. She nodded her head.

"Yes," she said firmly. "I am. I really think I am."

"What—did he do?"

"He just put it down when he saw me."

Listening to her steady voice, Steve thought of Frank sitting here in his car, probably near where they sat right now, watching the boys diving off the spiling, their young bodies brown and lithe, glistening with water, strong in the sunlight. The cold trickle along his spine now was pity for his friend. Then, blindingly, he remembered Frank leaning over Jacky on the lobster car, saying something in a low voice and whatever he was saying had made Jacky stare after them with that unpleasantly heavy look on his handsome young face. He recalled the partial conversation he had overheard against his will the morning Frank left.

"He looked at me," she was saying, the words coming on an involuntary sighing breath, "and said: 'Martha, I'm getting old. I don't want to get old.'

"He looked down at all my truck, you know, lipstick, cream, stuff like that. For a minute I thought he was going to shove it all onto the floor. He said: 'You have help. All this stuff helps you keep up the illusion of being young. Men don't have any help.'

He lifted his hand and that's when I thought he was going to push it off the table. But he just picked up his brush and we both pretended he was intending to brush his hair all the time. But he looked at me in the mirror as if he hated me."

Thunder shook the car, lightning made a purple cage outside, barred with rain. Steve sat thinking: My god, what'll I say to her? I don't know what to do.

"Steve," she said and he had never heard anyone say his name with that intonation before. "If he ever leaves me for anyone, no matter who, I don't know what I'll do. I've loved him ever since we were children. When he's away from me I feel as if everything just stood still, even my blood, until he comes back and things can start going again."

Steve knew what she meant because this was an exact description of something that was beginning to take place in him. He thought of Hilda with relief. At least, whatever was happening to Frank, whatever crazy thing it was, didn't happen to everyone. He wanted immediately to leave Martha, to get rid of her somehow, and go rushing uptown to find his girl, to reassure himself that the sight of her would make him feel the same way it had the other night, as if his circulatory system had turned to a spring-leaved tree and all the leaves were moving in a warm wind.

"Well, my god, Martha," he said into her expectant silence, "what do you want? What can I *do?*"

"I don't know. If I could make him see how I felt about him. If *you* could—"

Steve's face stopped her and she gave a peculiar little laugh. "Oh, that's silly, I know."

"I can't help thinking you must be wrong." He protested against the conclusion she had drawn. "I've known Frank for years, Martha. If there'd ever been anything like that, I'm sure I'd have seen signs. In the Army, sure. Maybe before."

"*I've* known him since he was four years old." Not bothering to refute him, she merely offered the information for him to consider.

"Well," she said. "I guess we'll get along, Steve. We have so far. It's been good to be able to get it out of my system though. It seems to get worse if you don't talk. I'm sorry I couldn't think of anyone but you."

Steve knew he had failed her and was ashamed; but he couldn't have offered to speak to Frank. That would rob him of any usefulness he might have for either of them. You *couldn't!* What could he say?

The wind had hauled into the northwest as they sat talking and now it poured down across the Harbor, blackening the water and tearing the fog to shreds. The rain slackened enough to let them see the boats nosing around to the pull of the wind.

"The rain seems to have let up a little," Martha said dully. "I guess I'll—no, Steve, don't get out. Just let me go alone, will you?"

Before he could move she was out of his car and splashing unheeding through the puddles. He watched her cross to her own car, get in, and pull quickly out of the parking space without bothering to look either way.

He was ashamed again, this time of his relief. Her going was as if somebody had taken a great weight off his chest. He felt a breath go all the way down for the first time since she had evoked for him that insane picture of Frank standing motionless in front of the vanity mirror with the lipstick in his hand.

Steve shook his head, trying by simple physical means to banish the image; but it stuck in his mind stubbornly.

Twice more as he sat there the great deluge of water closed him into physical isolation as desolate as the mental isolation Martha had created for him.

Women! he thought, not for the first time. But if there were no truth in her story, why had Jacky behaved as he had? The proof of Martha's revelation lay there before him if he wanted to examine it. Jacky was scared enough now to spill the whole thing. But Steve had no need to question him. Martha had not been hysterical; neither was she unsophisticated.

He knew as surely as he wanted to know that she had been telling him the truth, because all the disjointed, unexplained pieces fell so easily into place once he'd been handed the key.

"Oh, dammit," he said loudly and struck himself hard on the knee with his clenched fist.

Gradually the saffron and lavender world around him lightened. The thunder rolled over and away to the southeast. Presently he looked up and saw for the first time in five days blue sky in the west and the Harbor, already churned by the rough wind into small whitecaps, free of fog except for a few lingering wisps in the shadow of the lee shore.

At least he could be grateful that the weight of sodden weather had lightened.

With a strange uncertain feeling that he must immediately affirm his own virility, Steve went at a gallop down the wharf to the office. He snatched the phone off Art's deserted desk and under Chickie's curious eyes gave the operator the number he had already looked up twice and would always remember.

"Hilda?" he said tentatively to the bodiless voice that finally answered. "Are you busy tonight?"

He forgot to say his own name in his hurry; but she knew and was sure enough of herself not to have to pretend she didn't.

"I'm sorry. I'd given you up."

"Tomorrow night, then."

"Yes, all right."

"I'll come for you at seven."

"Yes, all right," she said again and hung up, leaving him staring at the dead phone in astonishment.

"Humph!" He hung up and looked accusingly at Chickie. "When you want a woman to talk, she won't. When you don't, she won't do anything else!"

Before she had time to fire up and defend herself against the unjust accusation, he was gone. The day was as blue and gold around him when he went out as if fog and rain had never existed. Only the planks underfoot, black instead of dry silver-gray, betrayed the weight of water that had just fallen. They looked and felt spongy as if water would squeeze out of them under his weight like water out of swamp moss.

Hurriedly so that Jacky wouldn't see him, Steve ghosted along the shelter of the buildings to the bait shed and in through the door as silently as a wisp of that vanished fog.

He hauled two tubs of trawl from under the bench and started baiting them. It gave him something to do with his hands and something to think about while he was trying not to think about anything else. Usually he scorned to do this himself. There were always three or four boys hanging around who'd bait a tub for a dollar or two.

He could make a couple of sets tomorrow between hauling his traps. Maybe pick up a halibut. There wouldn't be any lobsters to speak of for a while now. Busily he planned the next few days, ignoring forcibly the thoughts that kept tapping for admittance far back in his mind.

Once he found himself wondering where Martha had gone.

Where Frank could be. Then he managed to force them back into the willful oblivion he had created for them.

The sky that arched over the Harbor in the morning was like the iridescent inside of an inverted luster bowl. It stayed that way nearly all day. There was no wind, and the combination of warmth and lack of air motion sucked color out of things that would otherwise have been brilliant with reflected light. It was hard to tell, when Steve came out past the bar, where water ended and sky began. The rough-backed islands floated halfway between sea and air.

It looked to Steve as if there wouldn't be a breath of air stirring all day long. Art would be glad of that for two reasons. The calm clear weather would bring Will Holmes back from Rockland in the *Sally & Joe.* And on the high water, Arnold Black could get his big old pile driver down the Sound and into the Harbor to start work on the wharf. If, by any chance, Arnold had no intention of moving the driver today, Steve had a suspicion something would inspire him to change his mind by the time the tide reached flood.

He set his course to pass the southern end of Flying Sister Island and in three quarters of an hour he was in under the bluff red rocks. The water in the narrow channel between the Flying Sister and her near neighbor to the south, the Black Sister, was deep and green, shadowed by the great cliffs that rose perpendicularly from the surface. At certain times of the tide the sea sluiced through the gut as smooth and hard looking as metal, green and still molten from the crucible. The tide running in now was against him and when the *Eloise* set her bow into it the force of water cut her speed so that Steve had to open the throttle to hold his headway.

He stared up dreamily at the cliffs glooming above him with

their crown of black-green spruces. There were five of the Sisters altogether, counting the two tiny almost accidental Twins off the northeast point of the Haunted Sister. The Twins, either one of them, could have been covered at high water with an extra large bed quilt.

He shot out of the shadowed gut and the push of water slacked against the bow of his boat. She lurched forward and steadied at a speed three or four knots faster than she'd been making before with no touch of Steve's hand on the throttle.

He stared back at the narrow water-way, marveling at the sleek hidden strength of that tide surging in through to flatten and spread out across the sheltered Bay and into the saucer of the Harbor. If you ever stopped to think about anything like the strength of the implacable water it would scare you to death, like any danger that didn't actually show and which you recognized only when it was past.

He held his course southeast until he could see all his marks; the end of Black Mountain edging out past the woods on the northern end of the Flying Sister, the sharp white finger of Bartlett's Narrows Light bisecting the serrated low back of Long Island to the southeast. He knew then the water under him had shoaled rapidly and that he lay over the end of the Mitchell Shoal which ran from this point easterly for half a mile toward the indistinguishable horizon.

In season the Mitchell Shoal was an impossible place to set a trawl because every lobsterman in the Harbor had traps down there. But now, with the lobsters going inshore to the rocks to shed, there wasn't a buoy showing.

Steve set his trawl, watching the baited hooks flip out over the stern, expecting cod and haddock and hoping for halibut. When it was set, with the water-tight, brilliantly painted trawl kegs marking its presence, he headed back inshore to haul his traps. Once that was done, he would return and take up his set.

The shedders were just beginning to move. He would find one or two in a trap, a third of what he would normally have taken in traps untended for nearly a week of calm weather. He didn't like to handle the shedders. They yielded softly under his fingers when he took them out of the traps and slapped the measure against their shells. In at the wharf a little later, Jacky would try to persuade the summer trade that the shedders were better flavored than the hard lobsters; that the fishermen themselves preferred them for eating.

His entire string of traps yielded about fifty pounds, with perhaps ten of them hard shelled. Disgusted, he shoved the last trap off the gunwale with a splash that sent water cascading coldly down the front of his barvil, the long yellow oilskin apron he wore to keep his clothes dry. He pointed the *Eloise* once more for the Sisters and slouched beside the wheel eating his lunch and letting her make her own way over the glassy water toward the slowly looming Islands.

He was thinking moodily that he wished the life he led on solid land could be as direct and uncomplicated as the one he led with the scarcely less solid hull of the boat between him and the unknown depths out of which he made his living.

He had been trying not to think of Frank and Martha Pierce all morning. Now he deliberately set himself to think about Hilda Washburn. As the day grew closer to evening, he began to feel a combination of apprehension and excitement that he thought he had outgrown years ago. Where would they go? What did she like to do? Above all, what would they talk about?

He was beginning to wonder with real concern if he could get back to that naive level of polite flirtation that he could remember from the time when he himself had been twenty-two. After the heady peaks of exhilarated companionship he had known with Ann.

Ann, he thought guiltily, and felt resentfully as if somebody had laid a heavy hand on his shoulder. He felt something else, too, less easy to identify than his guilt, something bereft and forsaken in the deep cavity under his ribs that seemed to be completely hollow at the thought of her.

Hauling his traps had taken Steve so far to the south along the shore that his course back to the trawl lay this time south of the Black Sister. If he had gone through the gut again with the tide flowing strongly at the beginning of the ebb, it would have been like coasting down a tremendous green hill of ice.

He rounded the Sister and went out past her seaward side, watching the ospreys circle worriedly above the cliff-bound shore. There must be three pairs of them nesting there this year. He could make out two nests, half a mile apart, looking like nothing but a bunch of sea worn sticks dropped carelessly in the tops of the big cat spruces.

There had always been at least one nest there; he could remember it from when he had been a boy and gone mackereling off the eastern shore. The nest had served as a marker and a good-luck token. He always caught mackerel about fifty yards straight offshore from it when he could find them nowhere else. He remembered the exciting quick tug at the jig, the beautiful striped fish zig-zagging in to the skiff through the chum-streaked water, and the piping squeal of the circling fish-hawks.

Steve got lazily to his feet and squinted out through the windshield for his trawl marker. It should be showing any minute now. He didn't bother with the marks for the fishing ground. He knew approximately where it was, and the bright yellow kegs with the wide metallic blue band around them were easy to spot.

If he had been attending to business, Steve would have realized something was wrong five minutes earlier than he did. He glanced over his shoulder in astonishment and found the Sisters much farther away than they should have been.

"What the devil?" he said aloud.

Depending on his trawl buoys, he had overshot the Shoal by a quarter of a mile, simply because the buoys were nowhere in sight.

"Pete sake," he said, swinging the *Eloise* into a wide turn. "I didn't think there'd ever be tide enough out here to tow them under."

Lobstering at high water on a high run tide was a nuisance. If the warp happened to be a little short for the depth of the water, the buoy, extended to the maximum length of its rope, failed to stay above the race of tide. He had found some buoys, on a high tide, towed just under the surface, their colors bubbling up at him through the swiftly-moving green water, where they would offer the greatest possible hazard to an incautious propeller.

But even as he turned and jogged back in, watching his marks this time, Steve knew what had happened. It had nothing to do with the tide. Some cussed fool of a dragger had towed the Shoal right across his trawl set and taken the whole rig off across the Bay. Sometimes it happened accidentally; sometimes not. The big Rockland draggers were the worst offenders. Once Steve had seen one of them change her course slightly to be sure and get a trawl set at an angle to her line of drag.

Cursing to himself, he reached the spot where he had put over his first buoy early this morning. There was no sign of it. He set a course out along the Shoal, staring overside into the quiet, opaque greenness for some sign of his gear.

Those draggers could make a good job of it without even trying. Damn them, anyway. There was his day's work shot to the devil. A whole week's work, when he stopped to think what it would cost him to replace the lost trawl.

Steve shrugged and headed for the Harbor. No point in wasting any more time. The trawl was gone for good; but the dragger that got it must have been a ghost.

Doesn't that beat the old devil, he thought angrily. Apparently there was only one dragger in the whole Gulf of Maine this morning and that one had decided to drag along the Mitchell Shoal.

He was still pondering profanely when he passed the Sisters on the way in; but by the time he made the bar and went curving into the shelter of the Harbor, he had reached the 'what can't be cured must be endured' stage. If somebody had made a mistake the offender would recognize the trawl buoys and come around sooner or later offering to pay for the lost gear. If there had been no mistake, Steve would never hear any more about it. In either case, he could only wait and see.

He glanced in at the wharf and saw with relief that Art should be in a pretty good temper tonight. The *Sally & Joe* lay docilely at her mooring. Up on the widening flats between the wharf and the Coast Guard Station, the pile-driver's un-nautical rigging pointed at a crazy slant to the sky.

That meant that everything Art had been stewing about had resolved itself in this day of calm. It would be kind of a relief to have Art placid again. It made no change whatsoever in their personal contacts; but it did mean that Art wouldn't be careening around the wharf screaming his head off.

However, when Steve had unloaded his lobsters, picked up his mooring, and sculled rapidly in to the float, Art was doing just that. His infuriated voice, raised to a sort of howl, came floating down through the quiet air. Steve sighed, unable to distinguish words, but recognizing tone. Now, what's set him off, he wondered dispiritedly, not wanting to wade through the thick impersonal atmosphere of his brother's wrath.

Steve's head came above the level of the floor-boards and his eyes met the straight, amused gaze of the boy who squatted on his heels outside the door waiting. For a split second Steve didn't even recognize him. Then, with astonishment, he considered the change that had taken place in those familiar features in a week.

When Steve had last seen his nephew, that face had been as pale as the underside of a cod fish. Now it was as red as an overboiled lobster and the tender skin along the hair line had begun to peel. The greatest change of all was more than skin deep and to Steve it seemed impossible that it could have taken place in so short a time.

Arthur's eyes met his steadily. The amusement in them was quiet and not the snickering enjoyment of a kid hearing a man being thoroughly told off. There was a tinge of something not quite so definite as pity, that tempered the amusement.

Steve lifted his eyebrow questioningly, still hardly believing what his eyes told him. Arthur jerked his head toward the office from which came the spouting shower of words.

"Will Holmes," he said laconically.

"What's the matter now?" Steve stared. "He was raving yesterday because Will wasn't here. Now he's raving because he is?"

"I guess he's just getting it out of his system," Arthur said mildly. "We had a little trouble on the way up."

"Anything serious?"

"No-o-o. Not to us. He decided to make a drag for flatfish and hauled up somebody's trawl. He told Daddy about it and said it ought to be paid for."

"Well, I'll be damned!" Steve saw light. "You dragged on the Mitchell Shoal, didn't you?"

Arthur nodded.

"Be damned!" Steve said again. "Get anything?"

"Not enough to pay for the trawl."

"Well, then, you had a kind of a dry run on your first trip, didn't you?"

Arthur got to his feet, pushing himself stiffly up by his hands against the warm siding. He moved slowly like an old man, and Steve recognized his expression as a protest against the screeching objection of unprepared muscles that had been hardly used.

"Yeah; but things didn't break right at all. Will is going again tomorrow."

"Er—you going, too?"

"Sure." Arthur's protest was against the implication rather than the actual words. "I'm going all summer."

"You must be kind of broke now, though." Steve reached slowly for his hip pocket, waiting to see what Arthur's reaction to the known preamble would be. He knew a moment's disappointment when Arthur's eyes slid secretively away from his.

"Well, I am a little short. But I was going to see if you'd *lend* me five until we get back from this next trip."

That at least was an advance, Steve thought, fumbling a five dollar bill out of his bill-fold. He supposed he shouldn't expect miracles in too short a time. Wait until the kid got his first share and discovered the mature satisfaction of earning his own money. At least there had never even been a pretense between them before that the money Steve handed out would ever be paid back.

Steve watched him tuck the bill away in the completely empty pocket-book.

"Well," Arthur said. "I guess there's nothing for me to wait around for. That sounds like it's going on for hours."

He nodded again toward the pounding voice, grinned, and started up the wharf, walking slowly but without a sign of a limp. Watching him go, Steve recognized what that effort cost him. He had evidently been waiting here quite a while and got thoroughly stiffened and now that the soft young body was set in motion, every muscle in Arthur's back and legs must have been pleading for the relief of a limp or a twinge.

He wondered if it would be a comfort to the kid to tell him that the second time wouldn't be so bad and after the third trip he wouldn't even know he'd been working. No, if Arthur could get himself past the first great abyss of weariness and ache without assistance or reassurance, he really had guts. It was doubt of his guts that had been worrying his uncle.

The office door flew open and Will Holmes came out. His anxious face looked as usual, except for his nose. The nostrils were widened and at the base of his nose, on each side, there was a small round white spot as big as the head of an eight penny nail.

Steve opened his mouth to say something. Then, looking at those white spots, decided not to. He had a feeling that Will didn't even see him. Art's voice started up again inside the little office and Will stopped to listen without turning around.

"And farthermore, if you don't learn how to take care of that engine, I'll have a diesel put in her. You don't know how to run a diesel, Will. That would leave you out of luck, wouldn't it? I'm not going to put up with this crawling much longer. If you're scared, say so, and I'll get somebody who don't jump every time he sees his shadow."

Will moved as if somebody had thrust a stout pin into him.

"Art, that ain't fair," he protested. "You know damn well I ain't scared of anything that's within reason. Anyone says he wants to run a strange course in a pea-soup fog and won't be scared, is either a damn fool or a liar."

Art's accusation was unjust, Steve knew, remembering with a chill along his own spine, Will's first trip in the *Sally & Joe*.

They had got her late in the season and all summer long there had been few signs of herring along the coast. The factories had worked only spasmodically and in October there were no herring at all for the lobstermen to salt down for winter bait. Then Jackson Harper, whose weir out on Simpkins Island had been fishing for nothing all summer, came up with a full pocket one morning. Will had taken the *Sally & Joe* out in record time and had put a load aboard her that would have made another man shudder.

Fortunately it had been a windless day. Jackson himself had called in to the wharf and told Art he had a crazy man running his dragger. The *Sally & Joe*, according to Jackson, had four inches of freeboard when she left the weir. Will had let them load her forty-five feet with three hundred bushels of herring which amounted, Steve had figured, to twenty-one thousand pounds, over ten tons.

When the *Sally & Joe*, only her bow and shelter house showing above water, her big Chrysler Crown throttled as low as it would go and still push that tremendous weight through the water, had come in sight off the bar, even Art was holding his breath. A capful of wind, an unexpected wake, a sign of a roller would have filled her.

Will turned her wide and easy for the channel; but at the shortest part of the turn, solid green water came in over her port side and Art made a heavy, unconscious gulping sound deep in his throat.

When she finally lay at the wharf, they could see that Will had his kidboards in—those wide boards that extended from side to side of the dragger, dividing her big well into four smaller containing spaces. Without those, his cargo might have shifted on him and flipped the big boat over like a canoe. Will grinned up with proud amusement at their tight faces.

Art said only: "Get them fish out of her, quick."

He turned on his heel and went into the office without another word, and Will had favored Steve with a pleased wink.

In view of Art's well-controlled feelings then, Steve thought he had a nerve to accuse Will now of being a coward. Will was simply a man who knew his own limitations and those of his boat. He wasn't afraid to push her when it seemed all right to him to do so. But the devil himself wouldn't make him when it didn't.

"I've said all I intend to," Art said, still invisible.

Will went unseeingly past Steve and down the ramp to where his punt nuzzled against the float.

"Will." Steve leaned over the rail above him. "Don't give that trawl another thought. It was mine and an old one."

Will looked directly at him; but his expression didn't change and Steve realized with a sense of shock that he represented Swan brothers as well as Art did, and that the bawling out Will had just taken came by implication from him too.

"I'll see you get paid for it," Will said levelly and shoved off. He glanced up to find the boys lining the head of the wharf watching him. Realizing that they had heard the whole exchange, he looked away stiffly.

Peter, his great tawny coon cat, appeared squalling on the stern of the dragger. Will stopped rowing, glanced once more at his expectant audience, and had to grin in spite of himself. He whistled three high clear notes and Peter jumped. He came up, still squalling, swimming for dear life. Will waited, letting Peter do all the work, but when the triangular yelling head came alongside the punt he reached over and grabbed the big cat by the scruff and pulled him in.

Peter's purr was deep as a growl. He shook himself like a dog, scattering drops of water, and settled calmly on the stern seat to lick himself dry.

A yell of delighted laughter went up from the wharf; it did Will more good than anything else he could have heard. Thanks to Peter, the laughter was on his side. He reached over and patted the big yellow head. When he took up his short oars again, his shoulders were no longer rounded, and he was smiling.

At seven o'clock that evening on the dot, Steve drove slowly down the street through town, past the red light, past his brother's house, under the glooming tunnel of the great elms.

He felt funny. He was more nervous tonight than he had been the first time he had ever gone on a date with a girl. At least, as he remembered that earlier nervousness, this was stronger. He felt for no specific reason that whatever he did tonight would be decisive. His lips were dry, as if they had been sunburned, and the palms of his hands, closed tightly on the steering wheel, were damp.

The evening was young enough so that the heat from the day still shimmered off the pavement and the square, cream-colored cement front of the Post Office where the gaily-dressed knots of summer people dawdled and gossiped waiting for the night mail to be sorted.

When he passed Ann's house, gray, small and inviting, in its stand of elms and maples, still with that feeling of impending decision upon him, he slowed the car. He was not enjoying his nervousness, and if he stopped here tonight, he knew there would be no possibility of renewing the strange sensation by the same means. Hilda had been reluctant enough to say she would see him. If he stood her up this first time, there would never be a second.

Before he could quite make up his mind, the car slid on down the street and he knew he had never really intended to stop. The only thing bothering him, Steve told himself shame-facedly, was conscience; and a man couldn't let his conscience ruin his entire life.

He stiffened and felt the familiar premonitory trickle of cold along his spine that always preceded decisive action with him. He examined the possibility of his whole life, that had just occurred to him and realized beyond a doubt what he intended to do about Hilda Washburn sooner or later. He was thirty-five, and everybody had been telling him either directly or by implication that it was time for him to settle down and stop tomcatting around. He found he was telling himself the same thing.

Once he had identified the basic reason for his nervousness, Steve felt slightly better. Judas priest, he thought with a sheepish grin, Lizzie'll have a fit! He didn't think about Ann again. Neither did he consider Hilda. That would all come out right with time. Once she found out he was serious, that his intentions were highly honorable, she'd forget that defensive suspicion he had sensed in her.

Of course he mustn't rush things. He'd have to plan his campaign carefully. She was only a kid, and girls that young liked things nice and romantic. Well, he could do that. He could be as romantic as the next one.

Unconsciously his fingers traveled up to his tie and adjusted the perfectly aligned knot. He glanced quickly into the rear view mirror and smoothed his short hair unnecessarily.

He had stopped the big car in front of the Washburn house and started to get out when he caught sight of a light dress nearly a hundred yards away from the gate. He settled back into his seat and stared blankly, recognizing Hilda with an instant certainty; wondering if she had forgotten all about him. Thoughtfully he put the car in gear and ghosted slowly along to stop beside her.

"Going somewhere?" he asked politely, leaning over to look at her through the rolled down window.

She didn't turn until she heard his voice; then she came directly to the car and stood with her hands on the door looking in at him. Steve saw with surprise that her eyes looked dark now and he had been positive they were blue.

"I—I was just strolling along, waiting for you," she said. "I wasn't sure you'd—"

Wordlessly he swung the door open and she got in, settling herself demurely in the seat, hard up against the door and as far from him as she could get. He watched her serious face intently, feeling laughter deep inside his chest but afraid to let it out for fear he couldn't explain to her that it wasn't amusement, simply pleasure at seeing her and having her sit there with him.

"You knew I'd come didn't you, really?" He was still watching her. She met his eyes fleetingly and looked away.

"I suppose I must have." Reluctantly she made the admission, gazing carefully now at her folded hands.

"When I first saw you way down here, I thought for a minute you'd forgotten all about me and were headed somewhere else."

"Did you care?" Steve thought her tone was distinctly flirtatious, and he did laugh now.

"I wouldn't dare tell you how much," he said and sensed her instant withdrawal at his response. My lord, he thought, it's like sitting alongside a winkle, remembering the small sea animals that would extend themselves boldly if left alone, but once touched they were back in their shell in the twinkling of an eye. It wasn't the easiest thing in the world to know how to talk to her. It seemed to him that she invited frankness and when she got it, was inordinately horrified.

He could see that she was going to be a constant source of

surprise to him; and he would have been even more astonished to know why he had found her where he had. It was simply because she didn't want her mother to see him and know that she was going to spend her evening in his company.

Her parents' knowledge of her companion would not have stopped her; but all through that evening she would have carried with her the inevitable remarks her mother would have made, seconded by her father's weak: 'That's right, Hilda.'

She thought she would have been unable to spend an hour with Steve Swan holding in her memory the:

"Now, Hilda, you're old enough to know what you're doing; but I want you to remember you're our daughter—"

"Now, Hilda, you know what his reputation is—"

"Now, Hilda, he's much older than the boys you know. Do you think—"

It seemed to her sometimes she had never gone anywhere, with her mother's knowledge, that her departure had not been preceded by a series of highly suggestive remarks all beginning 'Now, Hilda—'. It tended to make her nervous and suspicious and she knew it made her hard to talk to.

Tonight her escape and the absence of the 'Now, Hilda's' was almost as oppressive as if they had all actually been said.

Steve couldn't know that and she had no intention of telling him. She realized that she must seem terribly young to him. To reveal that preamble she had to bear would make her appear much younger. She wanted him to think her sophisticated beyond her years. She didn't want him to find her dull.

Steve put his hands firmly on the wheel and glanced questioningly at her.

"All right," he said. "This is your evening. Where'll we go and what'll we do?"

"There's an awfully good movie in Centerville," Hilda said wistfully. "Walter Pidgeon's in it, so it won't be silly, you know. If—if you like movies."

The hesitancy in the last sentence choked Steve's horrified protest in his throat. He sat wondering dazedly when he had last seen a movie and couldn't remember.

"Let's go then," he said bravely. Once through town he let out the big engine and the car settled down to the road like a rabbit in a hurry. He found Hilda's face rapt and delighted with the smooth speed. At least, they seemed to have that much in common.

"I could do this all night long." She looked at him completely without self-consciousness, her face relaxed, her honey-colored hair streaming back smoothly in the breeze.

"Let's."

"Never, never stop. Just keep going forever."

"I couldn't even consider that," Steve said with firm jollity. "I get awfully hungry and when I'm not fed it makes me ugly."

"Well, I'd let you have a hamburger now and then."

"In that case I agree without a reservation."

But when they reached Centerville, he turned the car docilely through the entrance to the macadam parking place behind the garish neon sign that yelled its message of pain and passion up and down the hot wide street, and Hilda made no protest against stopping.

The feature hadn't started when they went into the theater and Hilda sighed happily.

"I *do* hate to come in in the middle," she said softly. "I get so mixed up and I always feel as if I ought to get my money back."

Steve grimaced stiffly, as he guided her down the plush aisle to the first empty seats he could find.

During the next hour and forty minutes he sat numbly staring at the screen, acutely conscious of Hilda beside him. But she was engrossed in the tremendous message being vicariously relayed to her through the medium of the falsely rounded figures moving before her. Thoughtfully he glanced at her face which he could see clearly in the reflected silver light and found her intent and fascinated. At one point, unable to bear her proximity without physical contact Steve reached out and captured one of her hands and held it tightly. She made no move to retrieve it letting her hand stay in his as unconsciously confiding as a child clinging to a grown-up when it crosses the street.

When the picture ended and the lights came up, he turned to find her eyes shining with pleasure.

"Now, wasn't that a good movie?" she asked, giving his hand a final pat and handing it back to him firmly. "And you thought in the beginning you weren't going to like it, didn't you?"

"It sure was a good show, honey." He found that the easiest lie.

"It was so real, so—sort of mature. If they only made more like that people wouldn't get so bored with the silly musicals, would they?"

Steve, who preferred a good, simple, plotless musical or a rousing old horse opera to the thickened psychological batter they'd just sat through, found himself capable of agreeing with her simply because her eyes were shining.

"I always wonder just what I'd do myself in a situation like that." Steve had to lean forward to hear her as they made their way up the aisle. He found she was living personally through the heroine's recent dewey-eyed crisis when, confronted by the fact that her hero might die with a brain tumor, she had managed to snatch him back from the jaws of death by holding her head high and persuading him that it wasn't a tumor at all, that the greatest medical brains of the country were mistaken, that he must live—for her. And, by god, he had, Steve recalled mistily.

"Well," he temporized, "you can't really tell what you'd do in any situation until you're faced with it, can you?"

"I know; but I just wonder."

"All right, Hilda. You look at me the way she looked at him and I'll forget all about my brain tumor."

She gave him a swift, startled, half-believing glance over her shoulder, found him smiling, and flushed pinkly.

"You're making fun of me, aren't you."

"I wouldn't," he said quickly, realizing he had under-estimated her in his own revolt against Hollywood.

Silently she went out through the lobby and stood hesitantly on the sidewalk.

"Hungry?" He took her arm and started her across the street to the nearest restaurant. Once they had ordered and were settled in their booth, she began to talk again easily, but not about the movie. Only once did she hesitate in her light chatter that amused him so and kept him listening closely. She stopped when the waitress came with their orders and glanced thoughtfully from her own beautifully decorated sundae to his coffee and sandwich.

"I must seem like a baby to you," she said; but her smile was unrepentant. "But I *like* sundaes."

"I want you to have anything you like and I assure you you don't seem like a baby." He laid his hand firmly over hers and held her eyes just as firmly with his own. "If there is ever anything you want, Hilda, tell me what it is and if it's humanly possible, I will get it for you."

"I believe you would."

"I mean it. I won't promise you the moon because I don't ever want to break my word to you and we'd both find out later I couldn't possibly give you that. But any of the lesser satellites I'd make a good try for."

She gave him a curiously sober questioning look that made him feel as if she had closed her hand warmly on his heart instead of his fingers.

For the rest of that evening, with Hilda relaxed, happy, and chattering beside him, Steve felt as if he floated on air. He had managed somehow to give her enough confidence in him to make her relax; and when they drove back through town that night and stopped before her door, he was dazed with his own exalted tenderness.

He got out of the car, walking on air, and went around to open her door. Hilda slipped out past him and in the deep blue dusk under the big trees, she looked ethereal. He was torn between the desire to stay where he was and watch her walk away or to go with her to have every possible moment of her company.

He decided to go with her, and they walked in silence up to the door of the dark house. At the step she hesitated, then said softly:

"Thank you. I've had a lovely time."

"We'll do it again soon."

"I'd like to."

She turned away and Steve put his hand on her shoulder, knowing that she expected it and was hoping he wouldn't. Exercising more restraint than he thought he could, he did something he couldn't remember ever doing before in his life. He lifted her hand to his lips and kissed it gently.

"Goodnight, sweetheart," he said and before she could move, he had turned and run down the steps. When he reached the car, he found that she had stood watching him because, only then, the big door opened and shut again. He sat there until a light came on in an upstairs front room.

Hilda would have been less than human if she hadn't been aware that Steve's car stood there before the house until her light came on. And she would have been a lot older than twenty-two if she could have heard it start and drive away without going to the window to watch it out of sight. She saw the sparking red of the tail-lights diminish up the street and when the car slid into the puddle of light from a street lamp, she saw the back of Steve's head catch the light, hold it a moment, and dissolve into anonymity.

What a lovely car that was, she thought, remembering the rush of speed, the road rolling smoothly back beneath them, the roar of power under the hood. He had surprising taste for a lobster-man. Perhaps it was because he was a little older. If any of the boys she knew, Carl, for instance, could have afforded a car like that, it would not have been a black one.

Thoughtfully, feeling completely alone since she was the only one awake in the sleeping house, she went over to her dressing table. Reaching for the cold cream, she caught sight of her face in the mirror and stayed as she was, arm extended, examining that face for what Steve might have seen in it.

He didn't make any bones about liking her and he said so, directly, in a way that left no room for doubt. It had embarrassed her at first; but, when she began to feel that she really knew him, he was much easier to talk to than a younger man would have been on a first date.

He was terribly homely, though. She looked at her own face, perfect in physical detail except for that slight heaviness around the chin that made it into a rectangle rather than a triangle. That particular shape had been made so desirable by certain of the younger Hollywood starlets that she no longer considered it a defect.

Steve now, he was really ugly. She shivered slightly, recalling the harsh blocky lines of his face, relieved from the possibility of brutality only by the network of good temper wrinkles around his eyes and mouth.

He wasn't so old either, when you stopped to think of it. He couldn't be more than thirty-five, and he didn't look that. It was just that he had been away so much when she was growing up that she had lost track of his age and had consigned him to another generation forgetting that he was much closer to her own.

She thought, idly and without actual intention, that he must be quite well-to-do. He had to be to run that tremendous car and live in that beautiful old house. The life he apparently led would have appealed to her in its feminine counterpart. Free to do whatever he wanted to and with money to let him do it. That must be fun—to live like that without a worry in the world.

Hilda's main reaction to the entire evening, and one she had managed to hide from herself even, until this minute, was a half-disappointed surprise at the way he had behaved. Everything she had ever heard about him, all the idle gossip and inarticulate innuendo, had prepared her for anything but Steve's actual manner.

Raised in the generation that thrived on the double date, Hilda had become accustomed to that final wrestling match just before the last goodnight. She hadn't known quite what to expect from Steve; but what had happened left her astounded.

Why, he hadn't even tried to kiss her and it wasn't because he hadn't wanted to. She smiled secretly and lifting her hand looked at it thoughtfully. She had never had her hand kissed before. It was fun, having it done for the first time. Different. It had really been cute, the way he did it, too. Reverent; but leaving her with the same breathless feeling she would have had if he had kissed her lips.

She tried to visualize Carl kissing her hand and the resulting picture made her giggle suddenly.

If Steve Swan was really as nice as he seemed to be it might be fun to run around with him this summer. Then Carl would see that he couldn't be so sure of her. Lately he had started to be a little overbearing and nobody was going to order her around.

Perley Washburn was in a quandary. In the first place, Dolly had been driving him crazy for the last week. In the second, he was fonder of his only child, Hilda, than he was of anyone else in the world. And if Dolly was right and Hilda was heading for bad trouble, the way Dolly said, Perl thought he might possibly kill himself.

Dolly and Hilda, between them had driven him to the verge on which he hesitated now. And the prospect of his action scared him to death.

It had taken Dolly a week to talk him into it. Even then, he wouldn't have let her drive him if he hadn't been horrified himself. Ordinarily it was simpler to give in to Dolly right away; but in this case, where it involved an unforseeable encounter with Steve Swan, Perl had let a week go by before he'd agreed.

It had been a horrible week. Either Dolly would be icily silent and refuse to see him when she looked at him, or she would nag, nag, nag constantly.

He wasn't a courageous man. He wasn't as big as a horse either, the way Steve Swan was. Nor was he any longer young enough to defend himself against an infuriated onslaught. Somehow he had the impression that Steve Swan was a man who liked to settle things with his fists.

Perley looked thoughtfully and with a quivering stomach at his own hand clutching the steering wheel. It was pale and blue veins stood up on the back and the fingers were thin, the hand of a man who works under cover and gets little exercise. He made a tentative fist out of it and the result was so pitiful he couldn't contemplate it without another shudder.

He got out of his car, staring miserably down the wharf, and walked along until he came to the arrogant black fishtail that told him Steve Swan was either still out fishing, or somewhere around the wharf.

Damn him, anyway, he thought. Why can't he leave my girl alone? There's plenty of others for him to play around with. And why did Dolly ever have to find out that it was Steve Swan with whom Hilda was going out every other night or so?

In the first place, Perley didn't like Steve Swan. A law-abiding monogamous man himself, he couldn't like, much less approve, of the way Steve Swan swashbuckled around as if the law wasn't made for him, just for others. And, besides all the incidental woods-colts he had sowed around town, there was that girl of old Sam Harris's, that Ann. By all accounts they were living openly together and should have been married for the last five years.

He moved forward with reluctant feet down the long wharf. The rancid smell of oiled and rotten fish came out in a wave at him from the bait shed. Under the eaves great colonies of barn spiders had set up housekeeping in a series of large interlocking webs. Some of them looked to Perl to be as big as half a dollar. He looked away from their heavy pursy bodies, feeling his already nervous stomach give a lurch at the smell.

Then it lurched again and he made an involuntary sound of

dismay, deep in his throat. Steve was standing in the open door of the room from which the radio-telephone spit and crackled. He wasn't going or coming. He was simply standing there, leaning negligently against the casing. Perl decided that Steve's face was reasonably friendly, and took a deep breath.

"Hello, Steve."

"Hi, Perl."

There was a long thoughtful silence during which Perl had time to begin to be dismayed again and Steve began to look quizzically amused.

"Is there something I can do for you, Perl?"

What Perl wanted to be able to say was: Yes. You can leave my Hilda alone! What he did say was:

"Steve, I've got to have a word or two with you!"

Steve inclined his head silently, ready to listen. The silence was not reassuring to Perl. He began to feel like a Pekinese approaching a Great Dane with warlike intentions. He also was aware that Steve knew exactly what he was going to say and didn't intend to help him begin.

Steve did know and was playing for time himself, though not as obviously as Perl. Perl was really upset, he saw with a pang of pity for the small man facing up to him, apparently scared to death; but still courageous enough to do what he had come to do.

Steve was tall enough to be able to examine dispassionately the top of Perl's head. Perl was completely bald except for an ear-level fringe, and he combed a few long wisps of gray-black hair up from the left side across his bald spot, plastering it in place with some kind of stuff that gave a high polish to skin and hair alike. At the moment, he was beginning to sweat and the shining dome was ornamented with beads of clear glistening water.

Steve took his fascinated eyes away from that betraying moisture with an effort. Poor little bugger, he thought. Well, I might's well declare myself now as later and take a load off his mind. He didn't make the decision without a wrench, knowing once the committing words were said, enjoyable, pleasant, complete freedom would lie behind him forever. He had known freedom too long to accept the first shadow of a fetter lightly although the fetter was self chosen.

I'll make him ask for it, anyway, he thought. He might's well do a little work.

"Well, have the words then, if you've got to, Perl," he said with simulated impatience.

Perl jumped, stuttered something and settled into a babble of talk.

"It's about my girl, Steve. I don't know nothing about it, myself, just what Dolly—that's my wife, you know—says. But she says Hilda's been going out with you lately. She's been running around with you, ain't she?"

"Why, we've been to the movies a few times. Maybe three or four. I don't know. That what you mean by running around, Perl?"

"Yes. I guess so."

"So what? I don't see much wrong with that."

"Well, well, I don't say there is," Perl said hastily, placatingly. "For all I know, like I say, it's perfectly all right. The only thing is, Steve, like Dolly says, Hilda's a lot younger than you. See? She's not used to— Well, she might misunderstand. She might think you was serious, you know, and that could easily lead to trouble. What I mean, Steve, I don't know what I'd do if anything ever happened to Hilda, if she ever got in the family way, or anything like that."

He petered out piteously, having said exactly what he meant and finding no answering flicker of expression in Steve's stony face.

"Is that all?" Steve asked.

Perl nodded miserably.

"Okay." Steve gave him a tight grin. "Let's take it one by one. Hilda's twenty—?" he waited.

"Two," Perl furnished limply.

"I'm thirty-five. That's thirteen years. I guess you win on the first point, Perl. I'm older. Let's take the next. You say she might misunderstand, might think I was serious. Well, she couldn't possibly think I was any more serious than I am."

"Hanh?"

"I'd like to ask her to marry me."

Perl's lower lip fell loosely away from the upper one, leaving him staring and blank with astonishment. Well, Steve thought, eyeing him with distasteful scorn, I won't have much trouble with my father-in-law.

"Hilda?" Perl gasped.

"I just been telling you," Steve said impatiently. "Hilda."

Perl closed his gaping mouth, opened it, closed it again. No sound came from him.

"Well?" Steve tried to prod him into comment, one way or the other.

"You're saying you want to marry Hilda?" Perl blurted.

"Look." With exaggerated patience Steve leaned forward until their faces were level. "Concentrate, will you. You've got only one daughter, haven't you? Hilda? I would like to marry her if she'll have me."

Perl's immense surprised relief made his knees feel liquid.

"You got any objections, Perl? You think I'm too old for her?"

"Why, judast," Perl said, "you ain't any more than a kid!"

"I'm thirteen years older than Hilda," Steve pointed out again with what he felt was devastating honesty.

"Wha—what does *she* say to it?" Perl hadn't even heard.

"Who, Hilda? I haven't mentioned it to her yet."

"Well!" Perl's honesty was just as devastating as Steve's but less calculated, and it pointed up the weakness of his status as master in his own house. "It don't really matter what *I* say, Steve." He hesitated and Steve saw the idea with all its implications hit him for the first time. A wide delighted grin spread over his worried face. "But as far as I'm concerned, I can't think of anything that would please me more."

"Okay." Steve straightened up and gave his belt an unconscious hitch of triumph. "That's all I want to know."

He started to turn away. Then he looked back at the still-astonished Perl and said flatly:

"Of course, on the practical side, Perl, I can give her a lot another man couldn't. I'm pretty well-off."

Perl nodded and collected his thoughts enough to be coherent. Brother, he thought, it's lucky for you, you can.

He stood watching the big muscular back move gracefully away from him and he saw it through a rosy haze. He still felt as if somebody had poured a bucket of water down over his head; but he was triumphant, too.

Dismissed, he went thoughtfully back up the wharf to his car.

Well, well well! Just think of that! Wouldn't *that* be a feather in their caps if Hilda managed to catch Steve Swan for a husband! Then maybe Dolly would give over her constant yammering about the money they had wasted educating their daughter unnecessarily. Maybe there'd be an end to the yickering about how ungrateful Hilda was for everything they had done for her. Because, of course, if she married Steve Swan she would be in a position to return many times every cent they had ever put out on her.

Perl's eyes narrowed thoughtfully. Perhaps it would be best

to warn her, prepare her beforehand for the possibility, and point out to her quite firmly that this was her golden opportunity to repay them for making her into the kind of a girl a man like Steve Swan would want to marry.

He could leave that to Dolly and she'd tend to it nicely. By nicely, he meant definitely. Of course, Dolly had always had a good deal to say about Steve. For the first time Perl left off the 'Swan' in his thoughts. But this would change everything. Dolly was too sensible not to see the new light Perl's news would throw over Steve's little outside activities.

Any man, Perl told himself, with a worldly acceptance of masculine nature and forgetting that he himself certainly had not, likes to sow a few wild oats before he settles down. That kind makes the best husbands because they get it all out of their systems first.

He was so pleasant around the drugstore for the rest of the afternoon that his four clerks went about their work in terror, wondering if he planned to fire anyone and, if so, which one.

Hilda and Carl were sitting in the hammock on the Washburns' deep front porch behind the lush curtain of the Dutchman's Pipe vine that spread itself thickly across the front of the old house every summer. They had been sitting there all evening, since seven o'clock when Carl, unheralded and unexpected, had presented himself at the front door. Hilda was beginning to get tired of just sitting listening to him talk about himself. She couldn't have said why she suddenly found herself bored by his detailed relay of his future plans when she had always joined in so happily before in his discussions of how many traps he planned to set by fall when he was going to give up his steady job and go fishing for a living.

Fortunately on this evening when she found Carl dull for the first time, she had something else to think about. Last night, when she had turned her light out and gone to bed, she had heard a sound in the quiet house that was completely unfamiliar and startling. It had taken her quite a while to identify it beyond doubt and when she did, commonplace as it seemed, she still found it amazing.

In their own bedroom, two doors away down the long hall, her mother and father were discussing something with apparent amicability. They often carried on discussions after they had closed their door and retired into whatever privacy the thin-walled old house afforded. Usually, though, the discussion led to raised acrimonious monologues carried on for a long time in Dolly Washburn's hard faded voice and when that voice ended, all sound did as well.

Tonight, though, the entire tone of the exchange was different, so much so that Hilda could hardly make herself believe those muffled voices belonged to the same two people she had listened to on so many other nights, shivering with distaste and wishing there were some way she could shut out the sound of matrimonial bickering.

Unable to believe her ears and curious beyond caution, she had got out of bed and padded quietly down the hall, her bare feet making only a little scuffing sound on the worn, hard surface of the carpet. There was no light under her parents' door which meant they were already in bed. She hesitated and, driven to worried activity, set her ear against the thin door.

She was rewarded by words and a tone in her mother's voice she had never heard before.

"Well, Perl," Dolly said quietly. "Perhaps you're right. I'd like to think you were, for once."

"I don't see how I could be anything else in this case. It was straight enough. He wouldn't have talked the way he did if there was anything underhanded about it."

"It certainly don't seem so."

Hilda could feel a furrow of puzzled wonder crease in between her own eyes. Now what on earth were they talking about? She felt a momentary twinge of shame for eavesdropping; but it wasn't strong enough to send her back to her own bedroom.

"It would mean a big change for all of us," Perl said thoughtfully. "If only she'll—" His voice faded off and stopped.

"Biggest of all for her," Dolly amended.

"I suppose so." Her father's voice grew slightly impatient; but not enough to institute argument from his wife. "It would be the best possible thing for everyone. I never dreamed!"

"Nor did I," Dolly agreed. "Why, when you come home and told me, you could have knocked me over with a feather."

Perl chuckled and the unaccustomed sound made his daughter, crouched tensely outside the door, jump and start away.

"You can imagine how *I* felt today then."

He gave another chuckle, a fat and satisfied sound.

"Well, g'night, Dolly."

There was a resounding clang from the old fashioned coiled springs as Perl turned over and settled himself to sleep. Hilda waited hopefully; but there was no further sound from the closed room in which her parents had obviously finished a conversation they both found eminently satisfactory.

She went slowly back along the hall to her own room and crawled into bed to lie staring through darkness at a ceiling she couldn't see.

Now what were those two cooking up for her? She hadn't an instant's doubt that the 'she' involved in that remarkable conversation was herself. When her father used the pronoun with the particular inflection he had given it tonight, he might just as well have spoken her name. She didn't care at all for the sound of things; but she couldn't interpret what she had heard, and she fell asleep wishing she hadn't gone and listened at all.

The next morning her suspicion that she might consider that 'she' as referring to herself was confirmed in a curious way. It was all of nine-thirty, not the usual seven, when her mother's imperious voice summoned her from the foot of the stairs. And when she went down, her breakfast was ready and waiting on a clean table, not one cluttered as it normally was, with the used and empty dishes and other detritus of two previous breakfasts. Hilda couldn't understand it; but she took full advantage of the lightened atmosphere.

She spent the afternoon lounging in the hammock with the latest romance from the lending library at the drugstore, which she didn't pay for because Perl felt it was pretty silly to pay himself for renting books to his own daughter.

Dolly had let the morning pass peacefully. Not once had she found fault with anything. But occasionally Hilda would feel the oppressed sensation of being stared at and would look up to find her mother's gaze following her like something with feet.

Reading Dolly's strange new expression rightly as a mixture of admiration and curiosity, and unable to bear it without knowing the reason for it, Hilda had retired to that cool cave under the Pipe vine as soon as she could and had stayed there, for the rest of the afternoon.

It had been a distinct relief from tension when she had heard Carl coming up the front walk that evening. She realized suddenly that his voice had been going on beside her like a brook and she hadn't heard a word he'd been saying.

"—so-o, I took the bottle and let him have it." His young voice was trying to sound tough and succeeded only in still sounding scared at his own temerity.

"You did *what?*" Startled, Hilda gave him her undivided attention.

"Hilda! You ain't been listening to a word I said!"

"Well, I have only—who did you say you hit?"

"That s.o.b. of a Steve Swan. After that mix-up I had with the Wop down to the dance the other night. See, I found out where you went, that he took you home, and it made me kind of mad. Oh, not at you."

"I should hope not!" Hilda stared angrily. "Let me tell you, Carl Benson, I would have gone home with any gentleman that offered to take me."

"Gentleman!" Carl stiffened. "I suppose you mean it wasn't very gentlemanly of me to resent it when that old Eyetie made a pass at you. What'd you have me do? Say: Thank you very much; but not this time?"

"There would have been other ways to take care of it besides getting into a common fistfight."

"Well, dear, dear, dear!" Carl's voice minced in her ear. "Since when have we become such a lady?"

"Look, Carl, I don't have to take that kind of talk from you. You've never seen me when I wasn't behaving like a lady and I don't intend you will."

"Excuse me for living," Carl said coldly and settled into silence.

"And then, on top of that, to half kill him when he came back! You behave like a—a—" She searched for the epithet that would be most scarifying and found it unerringly. "Two-year-old."

Carl bristled.

"Well, queenie," he said crudely. "Don't flatter yourself for a minute he took you home because you were a bee-yoo-ti-ful damsel in distress, will you? I'll tell you why he did it. That so and so's out to get his knife into me, see? And he'll do anything to do it, too. So you can get right out of your mind any idea that Steve Swan would be interested in a baby like you. He likes *his* women warmer than *you* could ever be. And what's more, he's got his hands full right now with a good one. He don't need anyone like you."

"If that's true—" Infuriated, Hilda got up and stood staring down at him. Inside the house the telephone rang shrilly. "If what you say is true, then perhaps you can tell me why he called me up the next day practically and asked me to go out with him."

"He never did!"

"And what's more," she said coolly. "I went. I had a very nice time. And certainly nothing happened to make me think he was anything but a perfect gentleman, just as I had thought in the beginning."

Carl's jaw dropped and he took a deep furious breath. He was on the verge of retorting unforgivably, when the voice from the front door saved him from the pitfall of whatever his hot, young, jealous rage would have made him say.

"Hilda." Dolly's voice came firmly from the haven of the screen door. "There's a phone call for you."

Hilda turned and went without another word, hearing behind her as she crossed the hall to the telephone, Carl's feet go plunging down the verandah steps and out the walk. The gate squealed protestingly under his hand, heavy with anger, then gave a final click, definite and expressive as a pistol shot.

She picked up the receiver, glanced thoughtfully at the unusual sight of her mother's back retreating tactfully into the living room, and said "Hello," tentatively.

"I hope it's not too late to call you." Steve's voice, warm and attractive, was as familiar to her now as if she had been hearing it over this wire all her life. "If you're not busy tomorrow night, I thought we might have dinner somewhere and maybe go for a ride afterward. Might even find a dance, somewhere."

175

Out of her anger at Carl, Hilda was more outgoing than she would have been, aware as she was of the two people sitting silently in the front room.

"I'd like that very much," she said. "What time shall I be ready?"

"Well, I've got to haul my traps tomorrow. I should say about six-thirty or seven. Okay?"

"That'll be fine."

"See you then," Steve said. "Goodnight, dear."

Before she could either answer that or refute it, he had hung up, leaving her with the dead receiver still at her ear. She put it quietly back in the cradle and turned to the stairs, hoping to escape before the barrage of questions began. That it had been a vain hope, she knew from its inception.

"Hilda, who was *that* young man?" Dolly called from her invisible listening post. Hilda went reluctantly to the door and glanced in. Her mother was sitting bolt upright in the straight chair under the bridge lamp, its yellow shade decorated with a full rigged ship, threw a sallow light on her bony, discontented face.

"He has a very nice voice over the telephone," she said. "Was it anyone we know?"

"Why, uh—" Hilda groped for a name, knowing the right one would bring the 'Now, Hilda' recriminations of vulgar suspicion. Perley saved her from the inept lie. He lowered the Bangor paper and peered at her across its accordioned top.

"Steve Swan, wan't it."

It was a statement and Hilda, recognizing its tone, realized that both her parents had known whose voice it had been. She stared at them, thoroughly puzzled, intercepting a warning glance from Dolly to her husband.

"Why, yes, it was," she said helplessly, recognizing the im-

176

possibility of putting off the coming storm but thinking its fore-runners the strangest she had ever seen. She was looking at her mother when she admitted Steve's identity and the unchanged bland smile, so unaccustomed on those familiar features, scared her as much as the expected thunderous protest would have done. "Is—is anything wrong?" she asked weakly.

"Come and sit down, dear," Perley said gently, looking at his surprising daughter with new eyes, but with an affection completely unchanged. He loved his only child deeply and always had since he'd first set eyes on her as an unattractive, red, squirming mass twenty-two years ago. Nothing that happened could ever change that; but now he could see clearly that she was a pretty girl, too, and some of his surprise at developments vanished as he acknowledged her attractiveness.

Hilda went slowly to the nearest chair, sat down primly, and waited, looking curiously from one unpredictable parent to the other.

"Hilda," Dolly began; but Perl interrupted her firmly.

"Please, Dolly, let me, will you?"

Astoundingly, she was silent.

"Hilda, how well do you know Steve Swan?" Her father's voice was excited, but gentle.

"Not very well." Hilda felt as if she wanted to cry. She just couldn't understand these two people. Half the fun of going out with Steve this past week had been in the knowledge that her parents would be deeply disturbed if they had known about it. Now they were taking that excitement away from her and she wanted to cry from unexpected fright.

"I just, well, I went to Centerville to the movies with him first a week ago. We've been a couple of times since. And that's all." She closed her mouth abruptly, determined that they wouldn't get the story of that brawl involving Carl and the Italian drag-german out of her.

"Do you—well, like him?"

"Oh, Papa!" Her voice began to shake. "How can I tell? I—just don't know him well enough to say."

"You're scaring her, Perl," Dolly announced.

"Well, lord, I don't mean to."

"I don't understand," Hilda protested. "I thought you'd be mad if you found out about it and now, look. I don't know what this is all about."

Her mother got to her feet and, in the movement, took her face from light into shadowy dimness. Hilda found the action a startling one.

"I think," Dolly said firmly to her husband, "you've gone this far, Perl, you should tell her right out what you're talking about."

"If it's anything bad about Steve," Hilda said hesitantly, "I won't believe it. He never—he didn't—all the time we've been out together, he never even tried to kiss me."

Her parents exchanged another puzzling look, puzzling to Hilda, but clear as day to the two of them who had done much of their marital communicating by looks. It said simply and with relief: That bears out the whole business. That's the way a man like that might act if he meant what he said.

"I see him the other day." Perl had the sense not to say he had sought Steve out for the purpose. He seemed to grow bigger without moving in his chair. The self importance of the admittedly ineffectual man, made him swell. "We had a long talk about you." The passing of two days had let him transform the incident into a 'long talk.' "He talked real straight."

"I don't understand what you mean, Papa."

"Oh, Perl," Dolly said. "For heaven sake, come out with it!"

"He asked me if he could marry you," Perl blurted and sat back in his chair, beaming with satisfaction that lasted only a second.

Hilda's eyes got big and dark.

"I wish you hadn't told me," she said loudly. "I wish you'd kept quiet. He hasn't said anything to me. I've just seen him those few times. Now I won't be able to face him."

She burst into tears.

"What did you say to him, Papa? Oh, dear!"

Perl, his mouth open blankly, swallowed hard. Feminine tears always reduced him to jelly, and tears where he had expected happiness, left his mind a complete, horrified vacuum.

"Why, good god amighty, Hildy," he used his baby name for her without knowing he'd done it. "I never intended any harm, baby. I told him it was all right with me, if it was with you."

"Well," Hilda stopped to let out an uninhibited hiccup of combined rage, bewilderment, and tears. "At least, you've left me that."

She raced up the stairs to the safety of her own room, leaving Perl sitting there numbly listening to the sound of her fading protest.

He turned outraged and innocent eyes on his wife.

"Now, what on earth made her act like that?" he said, demanding explanation of inexplicable female behavior from the only source of information he had. Dolly shook her head.

"Girls that age sometimes do," she said dryly. "Especially when you hit them over the head with a hammer. Let her sleep on it, Perl. She's just scared."

He stared, shook out his paper with force, and retired behind it, the picture of misunderstood well-meaning. He supposed, returning to his approved editorial extolling the foreign policy virtues of the G.O.P., that he would live the rest of his life—

if it were fifty more years—without being able to figure out the workings of the feminine mind. If such a thing existed, he added sourly but silently.

Well, there went all the new-found hopes that had greened in his mind the last two days. If she reacted the same way when Steve asked her as she had tonight, he could forget about having a well-to-do son-in-law.

Part
Four

*S*TEVE CAME UP the runway from the slip on the double. He had decided, coming in the Harbor, that he'd call Hilda as soon as he got ashore. He wanted to make sure she hadn't forgotten he'd be along tonight to take her out to dinner. Above all he wanted simply to hear her voice and he had invented this unnecessary excuse to do so.

With his hand on the closed office door, he hesitated, hearing the low voices inside. He'd been hoping Art wouldn't be in there; but he was and there was somebody with him. Steve glanced questioningly at Pat Jellison.

"Who's in there with him?"

"Carl Benson," Pat said. His pimply long face twisted into a sly grin. "I'd stay away from him if I was you, Steve."

The tone of his voice, knowing and amused, made Steve jerk around to face him.

"What's *that* mean?" he asked.

"Well." Pat's grin faded but he couldn't resist displaying his knowledge. "Carl's an awful good hand with a bottle."

"So what?"

"Just, if he happened to have one handy, he might conk you again."

Pat started to move away; but before he could escape, Steve had him by the shirt front. Pat turned white and started to stammer.

"Don't, Steve! Now, don't, Steve. Stop, will you? *I* never done anything."

Steve had a good firm handful of the kid's shirt and he gave it a stout twist, straightening Pat's lanky body.

"Tell me," he said harshly. "If you know what you're talking about and what's good for you."

"All right." Pat made a gargling noise. "Only you're choking me. Leggo."

Steve slacked up slightly. Pat's skinny fingers worked nervelessly on Steve's fist, achieving nothing.

"That night you got knocked out at the dance," Pat said quickly, in a half-whisper. "Carl done it. With a wine bottle. Now that's all I know. Now let me go, Steve."

"Is that straight?" Steve gave him a ferocious scowl and Pat choked again.

"So help me God. He done it."

Steve let go so suddenly that Pat, who had been leaning away from the pull, staggered backward through the open bait shed door. There was a muffled thud as he sat down solidly on the planks, a scrabble, as he got up, wordlessly, a scutter of booted feet as he ran.

Steve stood panting with sheer rage, waiting for the office door to open. That cussed kid, he thought. So that's who's responsible for my three day headache!

Inside the office, Art's clear voice was saying:

"Well, you better get her out of the way, son. I'm going to start work in the morning and I wouldn't want anything to happen to her."

"I'm darned if I know where I'm going to put her." The other voice, not familiar, but which Steve knew now, sounded dispirited.

"Look," Art said. "I'm sorry. Because I am, I'll tell you what *I'd* do. I wouldn't bother trying to get a mooring permit out of Bill Theriault. In the first place, he won't give you one. I'd just go ahead and move it. Put it down the best place I could find and not say anything to anybody till it was done."

"I suppose I might's well." Carl sounded slightly more hopeful.

"But," Art continued definitely. "If you ever say to anyone I suggested your doing it, I'll haul out your liver and make lobster bait out of it."

Carl laughed. He opened the door and stepped out to find Steve waiting for him. He turned three shades lighter and looked cautiously over his shoulder for a possible way to retreat and found none.

"You going to move your mooring?" Steve said tautly.

Carl's jaw worked. He nodded his head.

"I suppose I've got to," he said, suspicious, not sure what was coming.

"Well, how about doing it right now, instead of talking about it." Steve jerked his head toward the slip. "The tide's just right and there's two dories down there."

"I can't do it alone," Carl pointed out.

"Nobody said you had to. I'm here. Come on."

He went into the supply shed and came back with a coil of rope over his shoulder and a twenty foot length of two inch galvanized pipe.

"Latch on," he said, shoving the pipe at Carl who took it nervously.

Steve led the way down the runway with Carl, too astonished to do anything else, right behind him. Looking from above down at the big tawny head, Carl was reminded vividly of the last time he had seen it. The palms of his hands started to get moist. His mouth, on the contrary, when he tried to swallow, was dry. The tide was at low water slack and if they were going to catch it, they had to move fast. Carl worked cautiously at first, trying to give full attention to what he was doing and watch Steve at the same time. He wouldn't have been surprised at any minute to find himself going overboard with his leg in a bight of chain that had a rock on the other end of it. By the time they had the two dories out over his mooring rock, with the length of pipe lashed between them stiffly, and the mooring chain hauled tight over the pipe, Carl had relaxed enough to stop watching. You couldn't, not and work like that.

"All right." Not even breathing hard Steve straightened up. "It'll be all of an hour before the tide comes enough to float it. You stay here, keep an eye on things. When she stirs give me a shout and we'll take it about fifty yards up the Harbor. I was noticing just the other day, there's space enough in there for your boat to swing as long as you don't add five or six feet onto her stern."

He swung his feet into the punt that nuzzled one of the dories and sculled over to the *Eloise*. Carl could do only what he was told, left there with no way to get ashore unless he walked.

He sat down limply on the thwart, lighted a cigarette, and stared after the punt. Steve climbed aboard the *Eloise* and disappeared into her cabin, coming back up with his bilge pump. Presently he had a stream of oil tinged water sucking overside. He seemed to be completely engrossed in his pumping, to the extent that he didn't have a glance to spare for Carl.

Carl sat squinting through smoke, thoughtfully, trying to figure this out. The only conclusion he could reach was that Steve had no idea who had knocked him out the night of the Pioneers Ball. But it was funny for him to help anyone out like this. It wasn't what Carl would have expected of him. As a matter of fact, neither of the Swans were behaving as he would have expected. First Art had gone out of his way to suggest what to do about the mooring; and now Steve was going more than out of his way to get it done. Maybe he'd been wrong about them all along.

Carl gave a thin, tough, young grin, thinking: Well, somebody might's well get something out of them for nothing. There's got to be a first time.

Almost an hour later to the minute, he felt the first movement under the dory. Looking down he saw a cloud of mud rising from the bottom where the great square stone had shifted slightly in its mushy bed.

"Hoy," he said urgently.

Steve's instant attention told Carl that he hadn't been as unaware as he had seemed.

"She moving?" he called across the quiet water.

"Stirring up the mud," Carl yelled. "I can't even see the rock now."

By the time the rock was suspended clear of bottom, Steve had the two dories firmly in tow. The odd procession moved slowly up the Harbor, the *Eloise* straining hard against her load.

Working in complete silence, they set the mooring and brought Carl's little *Puffer* up to her new position. Back aboard the *Eloise*, they both stood watching to see how she'd ride. Her neat small stern cleared nicely when she had taken out her mooring chain.

"Bill will be surprised," Steve said.

He worked his boat back to her own mooring and rowed ashore with Carl in the stern of the punt. Carl got out first, moored the punt, and straightened up, hands on his narrow hips, to give the *Puffer* a last considering glance.

187

"Well," he said sheepishly. "I guess I owe you a vote of thanks."

"You don't owe me a damned thing," Steve said musingly. "But just answer me one question, will you?"

"Why, sure." Carl turned, relaxed to meet Steve's level gaze. "What is it?" Then he realized what the question might be and swallowed noisily.

"Can you swim?" Steve asked and Carl's astonishment reflected itself in his puzzled voice.

"As well as most," he said. "Why?"

"Idle curiosity," Steve gritted. He reached out and spun Carl around easily. When Carl felt the hands close on his shirt collar and the seat of his dungarees, it was too late. Steve picked him up bodily, gave him one full swing, and let go. Carl hit the water spraddled like a frog and went under. When he came up gasping from the icy shock, Steve was waiting for him, down on one knee on the float.

"That," he said, "was for knocking me out. This is for the headache I had."

He set the flat of his hand on top of Carl's head and pushed. Carl's mouth was open when he went under the second time and what felt like a gallon of salt water went down his throat. He came up blind and choking and would have sunk again without help; but Steve got his hands ungently under the thin armpits, lifted him out of the water, and set him down on the edge of the float with a thud. Carl's legs trailed loosely overboard and he didn't lift his head.

"Next time you feel inclined to sock anybody with a bottle," Steve suggested, "pick someone you can handle. If I hadn't had a job to do fast, I'd have killed you."

He strode up the runway and, glancing back from the top, saw that Carl would be there for some time. He was bent over, retching miserably, getting rid of the water he'd swallowed. Steve's pity was only momentary. He went away thinking: Serves the little devil right.

Hilda, sitting shrinking in the wide seat of the Cadillac beside the total stranger, was thinking in complete despair: What will I do if I have to get to know him all over again every time I see him?

It seemed hardly possible that the silent man driving the big car could be the same smiling light-hearted Steve she thought she had come to know these last days. When she looked over at him now, his glance was unamused and intent and thoughtful.

Tonight he had been different from the beginning. When he'd first arrived at the door, he was grinning and above himself. He'd said something about giving free swimming lessons; but Hilda, immersed in her own troubles, hadn't bothered to find out what he was talking about.

Later, after they had eaten at the big openair seafood restaurant in Centerville, Steve absolutely refused to suggest going to the movies. He had been with her three times in the last week and a half and he didn't intend to sit through another such ordeal for months to come.

He drove slowly down through the main street, under the bare light bulbs strung across from building to building, to the lower road that curved along the coast toward the Harbor. He was thinking, with amusement at himself, that he was still hungry. He'd been too nervous to eat. He was so deeply engrossed in his own reactions he was only foggily aware that Hilda was unusually silent. The old brick and frame faces of the water front buildings became farther apart. After the road drew out past the final one, the tremendous shell of wood that housed the Centerville Yacht Storage Yard, it narrowed and the surface got bumpier. Trees and fields grew in on it until the car lights closed them into an endless green tunnel with infrequent openings to the west through which they caught fleeting glimpses of moonlight on quiet water.

At last Steve turned sharply right and jockeyed the big car down the narrow grass grown track. They plunged into a steep little valley, up the other side and out onto a bluff so high and sudden that Hilda gasped. He stopped there and sat in silence staring out across the great glistening surface of Black Mountain Bay to where the lights of Talent's Quarry gleamed on the opposite shore, so far away they looked like a string of electric colored beads.

"Isn't that beautiful," Hilda said softly.

"Umm."

She was silent a moment. Then she said, in that lightly flirtatious tone he always misunderstood:

"I wonder how many other girls you've brought here to look at the moonlight."

"Oh, Hilda!" Impatient with nervousness, he moved in restless protest. "Don't be naive. I'm thirty-five and I'm not a eunuch. If I said I hadn't ever brought anyone, you'd think I was a fool and a liar."

Her instant stillness made him soften his voice.

"But I could promise you, if you like, that you'll be the last," he added.

Hilda sensed the approach of what she had been dreading. Unable to change the subject quickly enough to give herself time to think, she said stupidly:

"What?"

"As you say," he pointed out. "I brought the others to look at the moonlight. I never brought a girl here before to ask her to marry me."

His abruptness drove every coherent thought out of her head.

"You're in such a hurry, Steve," she protested in honest dismay. "I've only—we—how do you—"

"How do I what?"

His deep voice sounded amused and tender at the same time. The tenderness touched her; but the amusement made her remember what he had just said. He was thirty-five. Thirteen years older than she was. If she married him, her whole life would be a constant strain to seem mature, to be old enough to keep him interested. It didn't occur to her that it might be her youth that had attracted him. She didn't know what had. She wound her hands tightly together, in a gesture that was becoming habitual, to keep them from shaking.

"You've never even kissed me."

She mumbled the words with her head down, praying that he wouldn't laugh at her.

"You're awfully inconsistent," Steve said gently; but he didn't laugh and no longer sounded as if he wanted to. "You say I've hurried you and then you say I've never kissed you. One of your objections to my proposal is easily remedied, Hilda."

He tilted her face up and kissed her, lightly at first. The tremor of nervousness that had started in Hilda's hands, grew until she knew Steve must feel it; but after the first few minutes, it was no longer nervousness.

Astonished, grateful, shaken, and feeling like a stranger to herself, Hilda found herself leaning against his shoulder staring into moonlight spangled darkness.

"That would be all right, wouldn't it?" Steve said, his voice a low murmur of sound in her ear. Hilda was silent, feeling the deep intake of his breath, the steady beating of his heart, as regular as the sound of the sea.

"Will you marry me, Hilda?"

Her bemused eyes looked blind in the moonlight.

"If you're really sure you want me to."

"Sure!" Steve repeated the word as if it were obscene. "Let me tell you," he said. "Let me show you."

A deep starting, rapidly growing weightlessness under his gentle firm hands made her forget everything but herself and Steve. They might have been alone together in a vacuum.

Later when they were driving home, Hilda could remember thinking only: It will be all right. Anything like this would have to be. She must be in love with him if he could make her feel the way she did. She no longer sat in the far corner of the seat. Instead, she was so close to Steve, imprisoned willingly by his arm around her, that she was constantly aware of his body, as strong and hard to lean against as the trunk of a tree.

She knew that it was late when they stopped in front of the house and Steve let her go reluctantly. They went up the moonlight-dappled walk to the door and it took him five minutes to say goodnight to her.

He was halfway back down the walk again when she heard him exclaim.

"Hilda!" He came back at a run and up the steps two at a time.

"What's the matter?"

"I nearly forgot this." He was fumbling hastily in his coat pocket. "I got it yesterday and I've been thinking about it all day today, and then, by judas, I nearly forgot it."

He grabbed her hand roughly and thrust the ring on her finger. It hurt her when it went over the knuckle.

"That's a No Trespassing sign," he told her. "So everyone will know you're mine."

For the first time since she had begun to know him, Hilda felt that she could be amused at Steve. After a minute, he stopped being surprised and laughed, too.

"Well, after all," he said. "It's important to other people, if it doesn't matter to us."

She stood soberly watching him go down the walk again, soberly because they had not been laughing at the same thing and she wondered if it would always turn out that way.

Steve didn't look back, and when he had driven away, Hilda opened the door and slipped into the dimly lighted hall. She couldn't resist glancing down at the ring immediately, any more than she could have resisted her pang of disappointment when she first felt the size of the stone. Being that big, it couldn't be a diamond and she had always wanted a diamond engagement ring.

The great, square, green stone flashed ominous fire at her and, even to her, looked ostentatious and out-of-place on her short pink fingered hand. She had never seen an emerald before; but it left her no doubt what it was.

She didn't really like it. It made her feel cold. It didn't look to her like an engagement ring; but if Steve wanted it that way, she could wait. Undoubtedly, later on—she still couldn't think consciously 'when we're married'—he would get her a diamond.

Jennie Chick sat at her desk watching her hands curiously. They lay loosely on the desk-top; but the fingers seemed to have a life of their own. They were quivering slightly and no matter how much will power she exerted, she couldn't seem to stop them. And she couldn't decide what emotion was making her tremble like that: Relief, anger, what was it? Certainly a large amount of it was the blank astonishment of anti-climax.

Well, she thought, that will teach me to mind my own business.

She had borne her unwanted knowledge of Art's ten per cent as long as she could. That morning when Steve had raced past the door, she happened to be alone in the office and she had got up, without knowing she intended to do it, and called after him.

Steve, glancing back at her from the runway, shook his head.

"No directives this morning, Chickie. I feel too good. Save it till I get in, will you?"

With the knowledge she had intended to impart to him for his own good turned back upon itself, Jennie had felt flat and sorry she ever followed the impulse to call to him. But, all through the day, she kept remembering that tremendous surge of relief that had filled her entire consciousness when she found she had decided to tell him. The instant's relief made the eventual total relief look too sweet to her. It was the only thing to do. So she was waiting her chance when the *Eloise* came racing into the Harbor that night.

As she watched Steve rowing in to the float and coming up the way she thought, puzzled: But how young he looks. He moved and looked ten years younger than he had yesterday, and yesterday he had looked anything but old.

She waited for him at the door and saw with a pang the look of dismay on his face when he spotted her. Well—she took a deep breath and drew her shoulders back—it was for his own good she intended to tell him. She had forgotten by this time that it was for her good as well, that she could stand no more sleepless nights, no more tense unhappy days, aware of that other ledger in Art's desk as if it were written in letters of fire. If anyone had chosen to pronounce the words 'ten per cent' in her hearing at this point, she thought she might possibly faint.

"I'm in a hurry, Chickie," Steve said hopelessly.

"I'll walk up the wharf with you," she announced, falling into step and Steve, to avoid being impolite, had to shorten his stride for her.

Unable to think how to do it subtly, once she'd started, Jennie had blurted the whole thing out into his vacuum of unreceptive silence. When she finished, she waited in stricken quiet for his reaction, knowing that it would decide her own future and was more important to her than it could ever be to him. She waited a long time, until Steve said in a peculiar voice:

"Jennie." His use of that name rather than the nickname made her start nervously. "Why don't you take a nice long vacation?"

"*What?*"

"I mean it. Why don't you take a few days off? You haven't since you went on that trip three years ago. You're working too hard."

Looking at him while he was studiously avoiding looking at her, Jennie found that he simply hadn't believed her. That was the last thing she had expected. He thought she had made this whole business up out of whole cloth. The simplest thing would have been to drop it there, having once told him. If he refused to believe her that was none of her business. Her conscience, for the first time in a week, was clear. But, in honesty, she couldn't without another effort.

"I saw the book, Steve. I'm not blind!"

"No, my dear," he said easily. "I don't say you are. But it must have been something else altogether. I'm sorry, Chickie. That's the way it is. I don't believe Art would hold out on me."

"Well, all right," Jennie said weakly, unable to see what else she could do. She might have shown him the ledger; but the idea of trying to explain those figures to him when he knew nothing whatever about bookkeeping and didn't intend to believe her from the beginning, was too daunting.

She felt let-down and flat, having expected fireworks and achieved not even a weak fizzle. But she felt relieved as well. She had done her best and the responsibility was no longer heavy on her shoulders.

"That's right." Steve took her hand and patted it soothingly. "Forget it, Jen. Now I'll tell you something nobody else knows yet." His whole face seemed to break up before her eyes into little twinkling pieces. She thought she had never seen a man look so happy. "I'm going to be married," he said. "I'm going to marry Perl Washburn's girl."

"Oh, Steve!" Her stiff lips moved into a smile. "I'm so glad. I do hope you'll be happy."

"Don't worry about that." Supremely confident, he grinned at her. "I will be."

He turned once more before he passed out of sight and called back to her:

"You plan to take some time off, Jen. The best possible thing you could do."

Stunned, rebuffed, but feeling twenty pounds lighter, she went back alone to the office. Perhaps it had all worked out for the best, she decided a little flatly. Her conscience was light since she had done her duty as she saw it, even though it might have jeopardized her security. If Steve refused to believe her, she couldn't make him change.

So he's finally going to be married, she thought dazedly, feeling a little sorry for the girl, who she knew was a mere child, wondering what her life would be like with him. But he was obviously too happy to let anything bother him and that was the important thing to her. If he had what he wanted—

SWAN'S HARBOR

Maybe I will take a vacation, she thought stiffly, sitting down at her desk, watching the involuntary twitching of her fingers. Steve's right. I've been working too hard. And hereafter, I will mind my own business.

———————

Martha Pierce had given the three boys an early supper and sent them off to the movies. The first show didn't start until seven; but they had left the house eagerly at quarter past six. Half an hour before the lights went out in the movie house, they would be sitting in the coveted front row seats surrounded by what would sound like hundreds but would actually be about twenty other boys and girls of their own approximate age and size. There would ensue the most enjoyable part of the entire evening, a solid half hour of whistling, yelling and general disturbance, paper airplanes and showers of peanut shells, that would subside only when the screen came to life and the thunder from the sound machine drowned them out.

She had finished the few dishes quickly and now she wandered through the downstairs rooms of the big house feeling like a ghost. She was beginning to wish she hadn't been so precipitate about getting rid of the boys. At the time it had seemed the best thing to do; but she felt now, if she could only have heard them shouting around their trapeze under the big maple in the back yard, she would have been assured that she herself was alive.

As it was, she had no such assurance in the underwater silence. Even though she knew Frank was upstairs lying on the bed in their room, she had never felt more alone than she did right now.

He had driven unannounced into the garage that morning at eleven o'clock and Martha could still feel, as she remembered looking out and seeing his little car, that high lift of excitement and relief in the pit of her stomach. For a while, at least, everything would be all right because it always was when he came home.

He had looked so well, so happy and rested, when he'd come into the house. Across his cheekbones an unaccustomed flush of tan had made his long face almost handsome. But it always looked handsome to her.

Pure happiness at the way he looked flooded through her as welcome as rain after a month of dry weather. He held out his hands to her and Martha would have gone willingly into his arms. But she met his eyes first and all the relief and all the happiness curled up into a tight ball that felt like a clenched fist, or like a second heart and one she was physically aware of.

So she took his hands instead as she might have those of an acquaintance of whom she was fond and whom she hadn't seen for a few days. She couldn't stop herself from kissing him lightly on the cheek.

"Hello, Marty." He gave her a poor imitation of a sheepish grin. "Did you miss me?"

"You oaf! You know I always miss you when you're not around. No! I didn't even know you'd gone."

"How're the boys?"

"At the top of their bent. It was so hot this morning, they all took lunches and headed for the lake about an hour ago. I don't expect to set eyes on them again till dark."

Frank sat down at the kitchen table limply and stared at her, obviously searching his mind for something to say. Martha couldn't look at him. The miracle of change she had been praying for had not taken place. Everything was as it had been, only more so. And there he sat, after being away for two weeks, completely incapable of saying anything at all to her, his own wife.

It was quite clear to her that his silence resulted from incapability and not unwillingness. Trying herself to fill in the breach which was contagious, she began bustling aimlessly around the room, giving the appearance of action without accomplishing anything or intending to.

"Are you hungry?" she asked finally. "You sit right there and I'll put on some coffee and get you something to eat."

"Well, I stopped in Centerville and had a lunch," Frank said with difficulty. "But I would like some coffee."

At least that much about him had stayed the same, she thought, feeling like a drowning man who sees somebody slowly getting ready to throw him a rope. If he had refused the coffee, she felt that she might easily have had hysterics right here in the middle of the kitchen floor.

She flung herself at the percolator, filled it and put it on over the gas flame, knowing that she was being clumsier and noisier than usual and that he sat there wincing at, and enduring each clang.

It was a relief when he finished his coffee and got up, stretching and yawning elaborately.

"Lord, I'm weary! I've been on the road since yesterday morning."

"Why—" She fell on the possibility with eagerness. "—don't you go up and have a shower and go to bed?"

"I believe I will."

He gave her another forced painful smile and started instantly up the back stairs. A few minutes later, as she was numbly rinsing out the coffee pot, she heard the hiss of the shower, accompanied by the rumblings and clankings that went on somewhere in the depths of the house whenever large quantities of water were drawn off.

A little later she also heard his steps padding along the hall to the bedroom and then nothing. At three in the afternoon, unable to bear the stillness any longer, she went quietly up the stairs and along to the open bedroom door. Frank was lying on his back on the bed, his hands folded under his head, staring at the ceiling. Obviously he hadn't been asleep at all.

Hastily, before he became aware of her and turned his head and they had to speak, Martha ducked back from the doorway. As she crept silently back down to safety, she felt the lower half of her face begin to quiver. And when she picked up the deserted knitting she had left beside her chair, her fingers were trembling so that she could hardly make them close over the needles. When she did, she was uncertain whether or not she really held them.

What on earth was he thinking, lying up there in the quiet bedroom, staring at nothing? She had seen signs of this particular mood before; but now, seeing it at its worst, knew that they had been only faint signs. He was like a man in some kind of catatonic trance which still permitted him to move and talk; but shut his mind off completely in a little walled-in room of its own where apparently he had as little control over it as she might have had.

At five o'clock, the boys came roaring across the front yard and into the house, their eyes red and blood-shot from a day's constant immersion in water. Hastily she produced large quantities of scrambled eggs and toast and held the bait of the movies out before them, praying they wouldn't notice their father's car in the garage. If they did, no power on earth could prevent their concentrated gallop up the stairs to find him; and if that happened, with Frank feeling as he did, Martha couldn't imagine what he would do or say.

Fortunately she got them out of the house again, thoroughly puzzled as to why they were being permitted to go without being hauled upstairs into the bathroom for the usual scrubbing and forced into clean T-shirts. Taking what the Lord sent them, they went war-whooping off down the street, their voices fading slowly while their mother sat limply on a chair in the empty kitchen waiting for the echoes of tumult to fade from her own whirling head.

My lord, she thought suddenly, staring, what *am* I going to do? I can't keep the kids away from him for the rest of their lives! He will just have to snap out of this ridiculous behavior! It *is* ridiculous, too.

Feeling definite and sure of herself and knowing suddenly what to say to him, she went clattering up the stairs, careless of noise in her eagerness to tell Frank that she understood him and would do everything to help, if only he—

She was halfway across the bedroom, her mouth open to shape the first words, before her mind could take in the information her eyes relayed to it. The room was empty. The only sign she had that Frank had been here was the dent in the pillow where his head had lain. The counterpane was barely ruffled, he had been so still.

She stood frozen by surprise in the center of the room looking carefully at the bed as if she could make him materialize somehow, so that she might say the things she had found to reassure him.

When it didn't work, she turned slowly, and scrutinized the entire room as carefully, feeling that she looked at it for the first time. She found only one thing different and at the sight of it, her heart gave one of those sudden convulsive thuds that re-echo through the extremities of the body.

Propped inconspicuously between two jars of cream on her vanity table where she might easily not have seen it at all until much later, was a small folded square of paper.

Martha put out her hand to pick it up from where she stood. Finding that she was a good ten feet from the table, still holding her hand out stiffly, she crossed the room and retrieved the paper.

Holding it, still folded with its contents safely anonymous, she became aware of a peculiar sound in the quiet house, something like a convulsive whimper. She listened, found that she was making it herself, and could stop it by taking her lower lip firmly between her strong white teeth and biting hard.

The folded paper felt hot in her nerveless hand. Frank had creased it so tightly that she couldn't seem to get it open and when she finally did, it took a conscious effort to make her eyes focus.

There was '*Dear Martha.*' It had been scratched out lightly. A few more words had been heavily marked out. Then a fresh beginning, which, too, was inked over so that she couldn't read it. Finally:

"*I know it's melodramatic to leave a note when you plan to take the step I'm about to take. But I want you to know it has nothing to do with you, Martha. I can't even stand myself any more. Or other people. If you burn this, nobody but you and I will know what I've done because it will look like an accident. Leave that much to me.*"

No signature. Nothing more.

"Oh, my *God!*" Martha said and finding action still available to her, ran for the door and down the stairs. She was still moaning to herself when she gave the number and waited, the phone slippery in her sweating hand. She couldn't stand still. Anchored as she was by the wire, she paced nervously the three steps it would let her go and back again.

"Oh, Lizzie," she said, her heart sinking in disappointment. "This is Martha Pierce. I've got to find Steve quick. Do you—"

"He's down to the wharf." Recognizing emergency when she

heard it, Lizzie didn't give the information as grudgingly as she did to the usual female inquirer. "Want me to call him?"

"No, I'll go down."

Martha left the receiver dangling emptily against the wall with the operator's querulous voice coming tinnily through it. Frank's car was gone from the garage and she realized that he must have rolled it out to the street and started it there since she had not heard him go. But how long ago had he done it?

As she backed her own car out, the bumper caught the door casing and a long splintery piece came away. Looking back she could see it lying on the ground.

Steve would have to help her. Steve would know what to do.

Evening cool and quiet had already settled down over the shore when Steve parked his car and sat looking out across the Harbor. There had been no wind all day. The tide, flooding, surged quietly and greenly under the wharves. Out where the full light struck the calm water, colors like those in watered silk were in constant smooth motion. The hulls of the boats at their moorings looked whiter than ordinary paint could ever have been, and the garish trim on the white gasoline scow had darkened down in contrast.

He sat for a moment remembering the conversation he had had with Ann that afternoon, remembering the notice that had appeared without his previous knowledge, in the Bangor paper. When he had first looked at the stiff, high school senior picture, he'd thought: That looks familiar. Announces Engagement, he read, looked more closely at the picture and recognized it. Hilda had changed considerably for the better since that photograph had been taken. Then, realizing fully what he was reading, finding his own name prominently displayed in that dreadful story, he could think only one thing:

Oh my lord, I should have told Ann!

It had not occurred to him that Hilda would go ahead and put any such item in the paper without asking him. When he had cooled off a little, he saw that probably Hilda had had nothing to do with it. Perl and Dolly were the ones who'd want to make the thing public as soon as possible.

A little later he began to feel a sneaking relief that it had come out that way. He hadn't been looking forward to seeing Ann, not with what he had to say to her. Perhaps it was better after all for her to find it out, reading it coldly printed in the paper.

He felt that way until he went home to dinner and met Lizzie's outraged face.

"All right," he said defiantly, before she could light. "Yes, I've seen the paper. Yes, it's true. And I don't want to hear a word out of you, old lady, because you've been after me to get married and settle down for the last ten years."

"I'm not thinking about me," Lizzie told him. "I'm thinking about somebody else and you know who I mean, too, Steve Swan!"

"You never approved of that, anyhow," he said sharply, out of his own guilty discomfort. "And I'm not going to discuss it now."

"No, I certainly never did approve of the way you carried on. But you never even told her about this. You just let her read it in the paper, didn't you? *Didn't you?*"

"What makes you think so?" Hearing it put baldly into words didn't make it sound very well even to Steve. "How do you know Ann and I didn't just decide to call it quits?"

"I know because she called up here this morning and asked for you. She told me then. And let me tell you, young man, when I think of the mother-in-law *you're* going to have, I think it serves you right!"

"Oh, shut up, Lizzie. I meant it when I said I didn't want to talk about it."

"I shouldn't think you would."

The telephone rang and they stood staring at each other while the jangling bell rang out through the silent house. It rang again before Steve could make himself move.

"You answer it," he said.

"I won't if it never gets answered." Lizzie presented him with a fine view of her indomitable back, going away.

The phone rang the third time and Steve, unable through long habit of running when it did, couldn't let it go unanswered as he would have preferred to do.

"Hello?" he said hopefully into the mouthpiece.

"Steve, I wondered if the story I saw in the paper this morning was true."

He drew a deep breath. At least she wasn't the crying kind. He wouldn't have to cope with hysteria; but her voice was so quiet he found himself almost wishing she might have let it go a little.

"Yes, Ann. I didn't— I wanted to see you—"

"I never realized before what a coward you must be," she said with icy fury. "I think you might at least have told me first. It was a little tough, finding it out like this."

"Ann, please baby— I didn't intend—"

"Obviously."

"Let me come down and see you, please."

"No, I guess not, Steve. I just wanted to ask you about it. I don't want to discuss it at length."

He heard the telephone click in his head and hung up slowly, aware that he had lost completely something that nobody else, not even Hilda, would be able to replace.

Even now, sitting here alone in his car, Steve could feel the hot flush that crept up his face at the memory of Ann's still voice and the scorn she had managed to get into it. Well, it was over and in his imagination, looking forward to that scene with Ann, it had been so much worse than the actuality that he could only be relieved. She would have been justified in saying a lot more than she had.

Life could manage to get so darned complicated, he thought bitterly, climbing slowly out of the low seat. At that moment he was confronted by another complication which was unexpected and the proximity of which drove the first one momentarily out of his mind. One of the six other cars there in the parking space at this hour of the evening, belonged to Frank Pierce.

He examined the little Ford closely to make sure, surprised to find that Frank must have come back from his latest excursion, and dismayed to discover that he might well be down on the wharf right now. Things had been happening to Steve himself so fast he hadn't had time to think how he would meet Frank when he *did* turn up. His mind simply wasn't ready to be disinterested and friendly as it had been before.

"Hell!" he said feelingly. "I don't want to talk to him tonight."

That was the trouble, when you knew things about people they weren't aware you knew. It changed the way you looked and talked. You simply couldn't stay the same with them.

For a moment he was on the point of getting right back into his own car and driving away to put off that meeting until he knew how he could behave. But that was the way he had acted over his own personal affairs and for which he had been called, with justice, a coward.

No, he thought. I might as well meet one of them head on.

He walked reluctantly down the wharf, defiance giving his stride a swagger that wasn't repeated in his mind. He passed the open office door and became aware that there was more activity than he would have expected at this hour.

"No, Minnie, I won't be home for hours," Art was explaining carefully into the phone. "This damned hand-liner turned up half an hour ago with twenty five hundred pounds of fish and the *Sally & Joe*'s on her way in with a load of flat-fish. I'm stuck down here with only Jacky and Pat to help me. All right, then?"

Steve passed on, leaving him to his explanations. At the head of the wharf Jacky and Pat were sullenly unloading. Steve glanced over the edge into the neat boat moored there. Her kid-boards were in place and she was loaded deep.

"Jase, hurry up, for pete sake!" Jacky yelled impatiently. "I've got a date tonight and it's too good to miss."

Jason Wills moved with apparent slowness. He had a stiff knee that swung sideways when he walked; but he could do as much work as anyone else and more than a good many.

"All right, son." His soft, deep, burry voice came calmly up to them. "But my living's a lot more important to me than your date."

"It's a heavy one," Jacky announced lasciviously. "And I'm going to keep it if I have to leave half those fish right aboard there."

"Let me know if you can't carry it," Jason said easily. "I'll lend you a wheel-barrow."

"Ah—" Jacky began. His reply would have been a crude one if he hadn't glanced up, seen Steve, and thought of something else.

"Did you see that feller?" he said slowly.

"What 'feller'?" Steve mimicked.

"That—oh—Frank Pierce." Jacky's red face got redder.

"No, why?"

"He was looking for you a little while ago." Jacky's eyes

flickered thoughtfully across Steve's face and dropped again. "Seemed awful anxious to find you."

"Where'd he go, Jacky, did you notice?"

"Naw. Uptown, I guess."

"That's funny," Pat said suddenly. "Last I saw of him, he was down on the float. I never seen him leave."

Steve shrugged.

"If he wants to see me bad enough, I guess he knows where to find me."

"If you mean Frank Pierce," Jason broke in. "He took your punt, Steve, and rowed off up the Harbor about fifteen minutes ago."

"Oh, thanks, Jase." Steve turned away. He had taken half a dozen aimless steps before he saw Martha. When he did, the look on her face stopped him as firmly as a hard hand set against his chest.

"What is it?" he said, feeling his lips move stiffly around each word.

Her face looked heavy and as stiff as his own felt. She tried to say something. It looked to him as if she tried to take a step toward him and couldn't.

"Martha, for the lord sake!" Regaining his own power of locomotion, Steve walked over to her, trying hard to look unexcited.

"I thought he'd come down here." Her voice was nothing but a whisper rustling dryly in his ears. "He did, too. His car's up there in the parking space."

"I know it." Steve made a patting motion in the air with one hand. "Jase Wills just told me he borrowed my punt and rowed up the Harbor in her. He'll be back before dark."

She shook her head and held out her hand to him. With dismay Steve saw that familiar white flash of paper.

"What's this?" He smiled, but it was nothing but an unamused drawing back of his lips. "Another Jeremiad?"

"Hurry, please."

Steve took the paper from her limp fingers and read it at a glance, feeling the quick jump and pound of blood behind his eyes.

"Jesus!" he said, dropped the note, and ran for the float.

"Let me come with you."

He heard her voice, not the words; but he knew what she would have said and answered that knowledge.

"You stay here," he roared.

Behind him, obedient to his urgency, the quick tap of her high heels on the planking stopped. Steve untied the scrummy green punt the boys used to tend the lobster cars moored out in the Harbor and jumped into her, shipping water over the bow. As he pulled out to the *Eloise*, he was aware that the audience of four at the head of the wharf watched him curiously. Out of the corners of his eyes he could see them frozen into attitudes of attention: Jase in his boat; Art in the door of the cleaning shed; Jacky and Pat at the winch.

For the first time since he could remember, the *Eloise* refused his first jab at the starter. He thrust her into gear, opened the throttle, and jabbed again. This time she responded with a roar and shot forward at full throttle, nearly dumping him on the platform.

There was an outraged yell from the wharf and glancing back, Steve found Art gesticulating furiously. The green punt, which he had forgotten to tie to his mooring, bobbed backward in the boil of water from his thrashing propeller, and began to float lazily toward the Coast Guard wharf.

"Let her go," Steve said savagely and turned his back on the whole watching crew. Already he was well up past the boat yard. He put the *Eloise* closer inshore.

Without having to think about it, he knew where Frank would go, but he would row up close to shore because the shadows there were deep now and there would be less chance of his being seen before it was too late.

At this time of the flood tide, the water would be running fast and deceptively smooth into the entrance of Jim's Gut. Once a punt started in through the Gut, and was at the complete mercy of that tremendous force of water, it would live only until it touched the first rock. In his mind Steve could see what the punt would look like after that, and also what would be left of the human occupant.

For a cold second, as he shivered involuntarily at that mental picture, Steve caught himself wondering if it might not be the best thing to let Frank go ahead. Apparently he'd had it all planned out. It would be one solution.

But he kept his eyes on the green shadows inshore, not pausing for an instant in his search, knowing that he had no intention of letting matters take their course, if there was anything he could possibly do to stop them.

He saw the small white boat when it seemed to him she had already begun to feel the influence of that current that converged on the narrow mouth of the Gut. Frank hadn't seen him. He was sitting calmly at the oars, not hurrying any, but not losing any time either.

Steve had thought the *Eloise* was at full throttle; but when his hand closed on the lever there were still two notches to go. He opened her up savagely and the rise in her engine note attracted Frank's attention. He squinted toward the bigger boat and instantly stepped up his own pace. If he managed to get twenty yards closer inshore, the *Eloise*, because of her draft, would be unable to follow him.

Steve changed his course slightly to cut in ahead of the punt; but he didn't let her slow down. He couldn't spare a second and he knew it. He kept his furious stare fastened onto the small boat as if, by the concentrated force of his gaze alone, he could hold her back.

Frank glanced calculatingly toward the Gut behind him, and back at the *Eloise*, apparently figuring his chances. At the rate Steve was over-taking, it would be clear even to Frank, that he must have room to pass between the punt's bow and the shore in fairly deep water or put the *Eloise* up on the ledges the full length of her hull.

Steve could almost see the shrug. Knowing Frank, he knew there would be one. Frank started backing water hard; but he was too much in the grip of the current to be able to make progress against it. The punt simply stood still.

Hastily Steve swung his boat over and came up with the punt. They rocked together unwillingly in his back-wash. Steve didn't dare cut the throttle altogether. The water boiled and hissed past the *Eloise*'s white side, making her white a pale green.

He reached over angrily and gaffed the punt, giving the *Eloise* a little more gas. She edged slowly out, taking the punt and her occupant with her.

"Pass me that painter," Steve growled.

Frank, with a visible shrug this time, handed up the loose end of the rope coiled in the punt's wide bow. He followed it himself, shipping the oars neatly and climbing over the *Eloise*'s washboard.

"You damned fool!" Steve gritted, not looking at his friend's face. "You know better than that! Two more minutes and you'd have been a goner."

"I forgot what that current was like," Frank lied steadily. "I'm damned sorry, Steve. I guess I nearly made you pile the *Eloise*, didn't I?"

"You needn't think I'd have done it. Anyone who'd do such a cussed fool stunt, I'd let them go first."

He was beginning to cool off a little now and was wondering how he was going to answer the inevitable question when it came. Frank was leaning against the shelter house lighting a cigarette and he looked so normal Steve couldn't believe he had written that note. He couldn't believe it until Frank's first match went out before he got his light. The cupped hands that held the match to the cigarette were shaking uncontrollably. Frank glanced up quickly and met Steve's concentrated stare. His face closed suspiciously.

"I guess I ought to thank you for getting me out of a tight spot, Steve."

"Well, that's all right. I suppose anyone would have tried. I was lucky to catch you before you rowed right into that current. It's hard to realize how far offshore you feel it. Sneaks up on you."

Frank hadn't even heard him. His face was still suspicious and his voice was heavily sullen.

"I was lucky you happened along," he said stiffly. "How *did* you happen to be coming up the Harbor right now?"

Faced with the expected question, Steve groped for only a moment before he found a passable lie.

"I was going over to the factory just on the chance I might be able to get some bait. The *Sammy O.* came in late this afternoon, loaded to the gunwale." He lied with only a slight clumsiness, saying more than was necessary. "Judas Priest," he said rapidly. "I haven't even had time to say hello, Frank!"

Frank gave him a grin that was close enough to normal to be reassuring.

"Well, go ahead and get your bait, you cussed dollar grubber," he said. "I'll go along for the ride. Hello."

Steve gave a snort of nervous laughter and put the boat's nose over. It was only a two minute run to the factory and he spent the two minutes wondering what he would do when they got back to the wharf and found Martha waiting there. Frank had apparently accepted his reason for being out at seven o'clock at night as the true one. But when he found her waiting for him, he would know it for the lie it had been.

Steve pulled in alongside the deep-laden *S. O. Dowdell* and cut the engine. Willie Peck, the night watchman, thrust his wizened curious face overside and looked in silence, thoughtfully. The ever present wad of tobacco in his cheek made it impossible for him to speak until he'd relieved the pressure, which he did expertly, pursing his lips and letting go to leeward.

"Hi," he said experimentally, spit again, and added with more legibility: "What's on *your* mind?"

"They going to unload tonight?" Steve asked. "I wanted to get some lobster bait."

"They're going to start at eight o'clock, if you want to wait around that long."

"Blessed if I do."

Steve let go and the *Eloise* drifted off. He couldn't face an hour of sitting there in the boat staring at Frank and having Frank stare back at him. Frank was doing enough thoughtful staring right at the moment to make Steve uncomfortable. Apparently he had just realized that Steve could have got all the information about the *Sammy O.* unloading if he'd wanted to call the factory. He could have called from the wharf and saved all this running around.

SWAN'S HARBOR

As Steve headed the *Eloise* back across the Harbor, he was actively aware of Frank's presence behind him, still sullen, still suspicious and, worst of all, completely silent.

Evening was closing in. Overhead, as they roared back down the Harbor, the sky was clear; but in the east a low wrack of cloud gathered over the outer islands. Just behind the lighthouse, Steve could see the faint beginning of light that would later be the moon-rise.

He was watching it abstractedly and trying not to think about anything, when Frank came slowly up from the stern and nudged him. Steve glanced at him to find Frank's face puzzled and intent.

"What's that light?" Frank said, nodding toward the glow Steve had been watching.

"Moon rise."

"Moon rise, hell!" Frank said shortly. "Moon won't be up for two hours yet."

"You're crazy!"

Forgetting everything else, Steve turned and looked more closely. Now he could see that it wasn't the right color for moon rise. It wasn't the right color for anything but one thing and as he looked the glow began to grow until it showed faintly reflected on the clouds.

"Something's afire!"

"Whatever it is, it's burning fast."

The *Eloise* was hitting her peak and Steve kept her at it until they swirled past the wharf. Art was waving from the float frantically. Steve circled in. Art jumped and made it. Steve hauled the wheel over and opened her up again.

When they were fully under way, he glanced at Art's face and the stony thrusting look of it gave him a chill of comprehension.

"What is it?" Frank yelled.

"That's the *Sally & Joe* out there," Art told him tightly. "She's out there burning."

As they rounded the bar the picket boat from the Coast Guard base was coming up rapidly astern.

———————

Will Holmes, standing at the wheel of the *Sally & Joe* as she plodded slowly up alongshore toward the lighthouse and the entrance to the Harbor, was wondering how a man could feel as good as he did and feel bad at the same time.

It was very queer and he couldn't analyze it. He should have felt *all* good. The wheel under his hand controlled the forty-five feet of the *Sally & Joe* as ponderously as if she had been forty-five feet of lead instead of anything as buoyant as wood. For the first time since that disastrous week's layover in Rockland when they had been fog-bound, the *Sally & Joe* had a good trip of fish aboard.

About time, too, Will told himself. It seemed to him that layover had been the beginning of his trouble and the trouble had dogged him ever since. Nothing worth talking about really, just things that happened to every dragger now and then. The worst of it was, they had happened to him one right after the other. Gave a boat and the man that ran her, too, a bad name and it took months of the best fishing to wear it out, once earned.

Well, anyone should be satisfied with the trip he had just made. He glanced astern through the lashed open door of the shelter house, stepping away from the wheel until his shoulder was shoved hard against the two hundred gallon gasoline storage tank. The metal surface of the tank felt warm against his back through the thin cotton shirt. It had been hot today, on the water even where you might reasonably expect a cool breath now and then. If it had been that hot outside, it must have been like the white hinges of hell on the mainland. It would have cooled off, though, by seven-thirty when he counted on making the wharf.

Between Will in the shelter house and the stern of the boat, which rode much deeper in the water than it had on the outward trip, lay four thousand solid pounds of sole, dab, and flounders, kept from shifting by the three kid-boards. That was a good haul, especially right now when fish were scarce as hen's teeth. Will was satisfied with it. But still, something wasn't as it should be.

Under his good feeling lay the bad for which he found no reason. He was nearly into the Harbor. Everything was going fine. There wasn't a breath of wind, or any sign of it stirring soon. There was nothing; but he was as nervous as a cat.

Ever since three o'clock Peter, the big yellow coon cat, had been acting funny, too. Watching him, Will was beginning to get the heeby-jeebies. Peter was pacing the washboard, from the stern up the port side, around the bow, and back down the starboard to the stern. Then he'd repeat, in the opposite direction. He wouldn't cross the stern itself because Billy Ratcliffe was lying face down there, apparently asleep. But Peter was wise. Billy didn't care for cats and he'd caught Peter stepping fastidiously over him once. Neither he nor Peter had forgotten the ensuing spitting, howling melee.

Every once in a while, during that constant pacing, Peter would stop, sit down, look at Will, and let out a low doleful howl that Will could hear over the purring growl of the big Chrysler Crown simply because he saw Peter's mouth open and knew that some kind of a sound was coming out of his wide pink throat.

Peter was an excellent sailor, and as far as Will could see there was no reason for his present behavior. He sighed, wishing he were already tied up at the wharf with Art's face glowering down at him. Fifteen more minutes. He glanced toward the shore, found himself abreast the light and cut his estimate to ten. Ten more minutes and he'd be in with the first load of fish he'd had for nearly a month.

His ears, tuned to change, heard the first hesitation that interrupted that reliable roar from the Chrysler. The big eight cylinder engine, seated on its bed above the open bilge, separated from Will only by the forecastle wall, gave another more definite splutter, choked, and stopped dead.

"Oh, thunder!" Will said loudly, almost relieved that finally something had gone wrong. He thrust his head in through the forecastle door and roared: "Arthur!"

Arthur, who had been sprawled out asleep on one of the bunks, came upright with a jump.

"Judas, Will," he said complainingly. "What—what—you yelling for?"

"Shake the lead out, son, and take a look at that engine. Can you see anything wrong? She hot or anything?"

Arthur, scouring sleep from his eyes, staggered over and stood staring down at the mystery of warm metal. He had no idea what he was looking for and Will knew it.

"She's not any hotter than she always is," Arthur said. "The only thing I can see wrong is, she ain't going."

"Ha, ha, ha! You're getting almost too big for your britches, ain't you?" Will glanced astern to see that Billy was getting slowly to his feet. "Hout yourself up outta there," he said to Arthur. "And measure the gas in the tank."

He didn't see how he could be out of gas because he could

have sworn Billy had filled the tank from the storage at two o'clock.

Arthur, still sticky with sleep, crawled up the companionway and used the handle of the small gaff to make the necessary examination. The handle came back up out of the tank bone dry. Arthur stared at it puzzled and even felt the wood doubtfully.

"There ain't a drop of gas in that tank," he announced.

Will, who had reached the same conclusion with his first glance at the gaff handle, thought: Well, that's once trouble sounded just like what it was. And, for once, it was easily remedied. But that fact didn't keep him from turning on Billy with a snarl.

"Didn't I tell you to fill that tank this afternoon?"

"You sure did," Billy bristled right back at him. "And I filled her."

"Well, where's it gone?" Will snapped. "Is she drinking it through a straw now?"

"You got to remember you got a heavy load aboard," Billy pointed out pacifically, too close to the pay-off to want a fight with him.

"Darned if I think it's enough of a load to make her use gas like that! Well, we're too close inshore to take time to argue about it. Fill her up again."

Billy did so in a sullen silence, broken only by the gurgle of gasoline and one more doleful reproach from Peter, seated now on the stern.

"What ails that damned cat?" Billy growled.

"Too close association with you," Will said snappily. "I can't think of nothing else."

He choked the engine hard and ground the starter. She coughed once or twice, hopefully, and subsided. So he choked her again. This time she spun and caught. Then she backfired loudly and settled down to a steady pound.

Arthur, who was still standing at the entrance to the companionway, let out a yell and lurched away from it, scrabbling toward the stern crazily over the slippery fish. Billy watched him, his mouth open; but Will glanced instead in at the engine. He knew instantly what had happened to the tankful of gasoline. The whole bilge, swashing openly beneath the engine, was afire. When he poked his head in the companionway flames shot hungrily up at him, and already the fumes of burning gasoline were acrid in the forecastle and nothing for a man to take into his lungs.

Will staggered back away from that heat as if it were something that could push him.

"Get overboard," he yelled. "Quick!"

Billy let out a string of lurid profanity and dived past him down the companionway into the roaring forecastle. Will reached out and switched off the engine, knowing it was useless to try and turn off the gas because the tank they had just filled was now feeding its load down into the gas-filled bilges, down into the blazing horror that was already making the deck warm under his feet.

He knew what Billy was after. The life belts were all neatly stored in the fore-peak, up beyond the bunks. He reached hurriedly for the fire extinguisher that hung in the companionway, feeling the lick of fire against his hand, smelling the odor of burning hair.

"Billy, come out of there," he said softly. Billy couldn't hear him and he wouldn't come until he'd got the belts. He couldn't swim a stroke and Will didn't know whether Arthur could or not.

Already, in the short time since Arthur had lurched away

from the companionway, the growl of fire had risen to a roar. Already a solid wall of flame stood between Will and Billy Ratcliffe.

"Oh, Billy!" Will could feel himself beginning to sob as he turned the extinguisher and let it go. If only he could keep that flame down until Billy got out. The heat blasting up at him from the mouth of the hell that yawned where the familiar companionway had been made his eyeballs feel like molten glass.

A lifebelt came sailing heavily through the flames and landed at his feet. Will grabbed it just as it started sliding down the ladder, and slung it back at Arthur who was standing on the stern yelling, a steady, high-pitched, hysterical sound he didn't even know he was making.

"Put that on," Will yelled. "Get overboard!"

He had an impression of Arthur slipping into the smoking canvas jacket. There was a splash and Will forgot him. He stood with his own shoulders pressed hard against the storage tank, coldly aware but not even thinking actively that it was only half full and in ten minutes or less, with this heat beneath and around it, it would explode.

He heard then, muffled in the roar from the boat's bowels, what he had subconsciously been listening for ever since Billy had plunged past him and down the ladder. There was a sudden high choked-off scream and then nothing—only the all consuming noise of the fire.

Will's clothes were beginning to smoke when he climbed up on the washboard and ran quickly toward the stern. He stood there a second, wondering if he could do anything. Without being aware that he was going to, he vomited on the scrubbed buff paint. Even here on the stern he could feel the heat. The enclosed shelter house, in the time it had taken him to make the stern, had become an encompassed whirlwind of dark flames, their edges turning instantly to greasy smoke. A lick of it swirled up past the window and the glass disintegrated. Instantly the smoke and flame boiled skyward, geyser-like, into the quiet evening.

Will turned and jumped. When he hit the water he thought for a second that the impact had stripped off every broiled shred of flesh from his face and hands.

When he came up, kicking hard to get rid of his rubber boots, and glanced at the big boat, Peter was on the stern again, yelling. Will tried to purse his lips to whistle; but he couldn't even move them.

He knew he should swim away from her as fast as he could. But there was Peter. He never knew how long he stayed there, treading water, trying to whistle to the cat who would jump only to that sound. While he was still trying, something wound itself in the slack of his shirt at the shoulders and pulled him straight up. He felt his spine scrape over hardness. Then he hit solid deck with a thud and scrambled to his feet. He saw young Arthur huddled in the scuppers. Steve Swan's face, when he tried to focus on it, circled crazily around him.

"Billy?" Steve kept yelling. "Where's Billy?"

Will couldn't speak; but he pointed at the flaming hull and Steve ran for the tiller and swung the *Eloise*'s stern around until it nearly touched the higher one of the *Sally & Joe*.

When the oily smoke poured back over them, Will leaned forward and was sick again over the side.

He was only half aware that somebody had jumped from the stern of the *Eloise* to the burning dragger. He glanced up to see whoever it was grab for the frantic cat and throw him bodily into the smaller boat. Peter landed spitting and made a bee-line for the comparative darkness under the stern.

"Frank!" Steve yelled. "You can't—"

Somewhere in the dragger there was a sound like a muffled cough. Halfway up the washboard to the shelter house, Frank Pierce stood frozen, his arms up against the tremendous heat.

"She's going!" Art screamed. "Get away!"

Steve was leaning over the side yelling wildly at Frank who was beginning to edge in toward the heart of the fire. Art raced past him, grabbed the wheel, gave it a wild swing, and opened the throttle. The *Eloise* put her stern down and shot away from the flaming dragger.

"Jump, Frank!" Steve's voice faded suddenly. From the *Sally & Joe* came a sullen thudding roar in reply. Instantly the growing darkness vanished in a sudden uprush of flame that towered over them in a fountain of heat and showered down again in drops of burning gasoline.

Steve stopped shouting and stood, his mouth open to shout and no sound coming from it. The *Sally & Joe* had been transformed by the explosion into a flaming crater, a shell of a boat, still miraculously afloat, but with a living leaping cargo of fire now and nothing else.

He had closed his eyes at the moment the storage tank exploded and when he opened them again, there was only the black hull against the light of the flames and no sign of life. He had not expected any.

As he watched, the Coast Guard Cutter edged slowly in toward the burning gasoline beginning to spread out on the water around the settling hull.

"Oh, jesus," Will said. "You shouldn't a let him go, Steve. Billy was dead before I jumped."

Steve closed his eyes, feeling the beginning shudder shake him like an aspen leaf in a gale. He shut his teeth hard against the feeling in his throat.

"You might have said so." His voice made the words sound as if they scraped out over a nutmeg grater.

"Oh, jesus!" Will kept saying. "Oh, sweet jesus!"

Steve went forward to stand for a second beside his brother.

"Take her in, will you?" he said, teeth clenched still against the shakes and the sickness. "I can't."

Art glanced at his face and looked away. He nodded, straightened the boat out and headed for the Harbor. Looking back, Steve was just in time to see the *Sally & Joe*'s black hull vanish, leaving only the phenomenon of the burning rose on the surface of the dark water and the silhouette of the cutter as she circled waiting for it to burn out.

On his hands and knees he crawled up onto the bow where nobody could see him and lay there face down, retching dryly and trying, through sheer physical force, to make himself stop that deep shaking. He would think it had finished; then, in a place just below his stomach, he would feel the knot begin to grow and shake and spread until his fingers and toes were twitching. It would stop for a blessed second and instantly begin all over again.

He lay wondering how he would tell Martha that Frank had died to save a cat and a man already dead.

He felt the *Eloise* slow under him and lifted his head to see the wharf looming ahead. The crowd of silent people who had gathered there looked only like a row of white faces under the flood light, a row of featureless white balloons.

He got to his feet stiffly and waited until the *Eloise* was nearly in to the lobster car. Art was uncertain about her and was coming in too fast; but that was all right because nothing mattered deeply. Steve bent and grabbed the bow line and jumped for the car.

Too late he saw that the end of the car, under the weight of the crowd, had been under water. Already in the air, he saw the shine of water on the slick wood and braced his body against the inevitable skidding fall.

He nearly saved himself at that. But he had braced backward in mid-air against the direction of the fall and he couldn't stop himself from going to his knees. His left leg went into the water to the thigh and the *Eloise*, coming in too fast under Art's nervously uncertain hand, scraped the full length of her white hull along the front of the car and bounced off.

Steve was conscious long enough to hear a woman scream, high and thin like a hurt rabbit, and know that he himself had never before known what physical pain was like.

——————

Lizzie never knew who had called her up from the wharf to tell her about Steve's accident. The young masculine voice was unfamiliar to her and the boy was too excited to do anything but stammer the details into her ear.

Fortunately there was a chair in the hall next to the little stand where the telephone sat. In the middle of the babbled story of the *Sally & Joe*, Lizzie sat down carefully, saying nothing, clinging to the phone. So she was already sitting when the voice said:

"Oh, my lord, I don't know but what it cut his leg off."

It was so hard to concentrate on the fact of consciousness with that swirling black edging in behind her eyes.

"Miss Hawkes!" the voice said frantically. "Miss Hawkes, you still there?"

"I—yes, I'm here. Where is he now?"

"He's still down here. They've called the ambulance. They're going to take him over to the hospital. Doc says he won't lay a finger on him till they do."

"Is he conscious? Does he know?"

"He's out like a light. Has been ever since it happened."

"Please God he stays that way till it's over," Lizzie said and put out a nerveless hand to hang up the receiver. The hand wasn't hers. She watched it with a curiosity that lay completely outside her mind.

Moving slowly like an automaton, she got her old coat sweater from the hook behind the stove in the kitchen and went out. Stumbling down the hill to the street, she stood looking carefully both ways in the soft lapping blue dusk that would get no darker because the moon had risen in the east. It was bright enough already to cast Lizzie's shadow across the empty macadam. Feeling as if she were no more solid than that shadow, she crossed to the far sidewalk and started downtown.

There was only one person who could help her now, only one she wanted to turn to now. She pushed open the white gate, staggered up the path, and rang the door-bell. Unable to wait without doing something, she started banging with her clenched fist against the unresponsive door.

The light came on quickly, pinning her in the center of the yellow glow like a fly in a pan of cream. Ann's face, when she opened the door, was stony and cold. She took one look at at Lizzie and the coldness was gone, but the stoniness was still there. Lizzie thought she could see the warm color run out from under the fine skin.

"What is it?" Ann moved to one side and let the older woman come in past her. Lizzie stepped into the hall, shut the door carefully, and told her, her voice sounding like a rusty gate hinge in a slow wind.

"Steve is hurt bad. They've lost the *Sally & Joe*. Frank Pierce and Billy Ratcliffe are both dead."

Ann thought for a wild minute, if she could only make the silence last, after that awful voice had stopped, she could make the words be unsaid.

"How bad?" she asked hoarsely.

"I'm not sure. His leg. Quite bad. They're going to take him over to the hospital. I've got to go, Ann. You're—you'll take me."

"Naturally."

They went quietly out to the garage and got into Ann's small car. A mile outside of town, they met the ambulance, going the other way, its red light over the driver's cab flashing. When the driver saw their lights approaching, he touched the siren and the long car flashed past them, efficient, swift, its motor a purr of sound. The low warning growl died and almost before Ann could pick up the lights in the rear view mirror, the ambulance was out of sight on the road to the Harbor.

Lizzie started to talk, fast and tonelessly, repeating exactly what had been told her over the phone. When she finished, she began all over again, apparently unable to stop.

They had two miles of the eighteen still to go and Ann had long ago closed her ears to that toneless voice babbling endlessly beside her and was driving with dogged attention to the road when the ambulance overtook them on its return trip.

The siren wailed behind them. Ann started and pulled over to the shoulder to let the big, tan Reo scream by. The lights were on in the back this time and she caught a distorted glimpse of Will Holmes's face, only it really didn't look like Will's face and she was never sure afterward how she recognized it so certainly in that sharp flash of light. She saw nothing else, and that much was snatched out of sight before she could assimilate it. There were two more cars following the ambulance closely and she waited for them. One was Steve's Cadillac. She couldn't tell who was driving it; but it gave her a cold feeling of emptiness to know that it roared over this circling mountain road while he lay unconscious in the ambulance ahead of it.

In silence she pulled back onto the hard surface. The siren had turned off Lizzie's voice. She just sat now, staring after the fading tail-lights.

When they drove into the circular turn in front of the hospital, the ambulance had vanished; but the Cadillac stood before the wide steps alongside the No Parking sign.

Looking at those steep stone steps, Ann was sure she'd never be able to climb them. Her knees felt as if the tendons holding them in place had turned to water. Then she decided if Lizzie could do it, she could.

The heavy door opened silently and closed with a little swish of air. Minnie and young Arthur were sitting in two of the straight chairs on one side of the waiting room. Their faces looked as white as Ann's felt. Across the room, closer to the desk, Perl and Dolly Washburn were waiting, too. Perl looked sheepish and shocked and as if he wanted to be anywhere else. Dolly, when the door opened, glanced up mournfully. Her bony face froze into a mask of disapproval, and she began whispering angrily to Perl who looked even more sheepish. There was no sign of either Hilda or Art.

Ann crossed rapidly to Minnie and stood waiting, not even finding it necessary to ask the question.

"He's in the operating room," Minnie said hoarsely.

Wordlessly Ann drew up a chair for Lizzie who sank into it and sat huddled and humped over, looking like a sackful of old bones somebody had tossed down carelessly and hadn't bothered to arrange into a semblance of humanity. Ann sat down herself and stared at her hands, knowing how Lizzie felt, knowing that when something terrible happened to somebody you loved it made you feel as if all the virtue had run out of you, as if there were none of the emotions left to make you sure you were human.

Hesitating steps came down the invisible corridor and when Will Holmes appeared in the double door, Ann was halfway to her feet.

He moved slowly toward them, his singed face shining with some white salve. The skin, where it showed, was red and tight-looking. His eyes were bloodshot and sunken and his walk uncertain.

"Oh, Will!" Ann said softly.

"Pretty sight, ain't I?" He held his hands out toward her. "Look at that! They look like hot-dogs." Somebody might have picked him up by the heels and doused him into boiling water.

"You ought to go right home, Will!"

"No way to go till you folks do," he said shortly. "Besides, I want to wait and see how he comes out."

The seven people sat for another hour in the quiet waiting room, not talking; with no sound except the occasional sibilant hiss from Dolly when she leaned over to communicate some further bit of her resentment to her silently protesting husband. Perl seemed to get smaller in his chair, until Ann began to feel that he might just shrink up into himself and vanish altogether. Looking at the two people who had produced the girl Steve had left her for, she felt as if she ought to hate them and everything they represented. But she couldn't rake up any feeling whatsoever about anything but Steve.

What was happening to him as he lay unconscious and helpless somewhere in the efficient bowels of this quiet building with the bright lights bearing down on him and the impersonal heads poring over him?

An hour and twenty minutes by her watch from the moment she had opened the heavy door, the surgeon appeared and came striding briskly over to Minnie. A short, broad, red man with competent stubby hands and a wide impassive face, he stood before them for a moment waiting to see if anyone would ask him the question. When nobody did, he said quickly:

"He will be all right in a couple of weeks. Just shock now."

"What about his leg?" Young Arthur's voice was hoarse and it startled Ann who couldn't remember ever having heard it before. Clutching at anything to keep her from hearing what the surgeon would say, she turned her head frantically to look at the boy. He was pale under his tan. His face looked taut, not flabby; but his light eyes were glassy and staring. Her concentration on his face couldn't make her deaf.

"There was nothing that could be done to save it. We had to amputate just above the knee."

Dolly Washburn screamed and the sound echoing through the quiet corridors, brought protesting nurses on the run from every direction, like furious disturbed white hens. The surgeon turned on her savagely.

"That's enough!" he said. "There are very sick people here."

"Oh, my poor boy!" Dolly's voice subsided; but it still throbbed with feeling. "Let me go to him! I must go to him!"

"*Nobody* will go to him, at least until tomorrow afternoon and maybe not then. It depends."

Ann got quickly to her feet, feeling Lizzie come up beside her like a shadow.

"Will," she said levelly out of a great weariness that had filled the hollow from which her humanity had drained. "You better come home now."

"All right." Will stumbled obediently after them out to the car. Ann didn't wait to see how the others were going. She couldn't bother.

Steve lay uselessly in his chair in the big front window surrounded by the hated appurtenances of invalidism, staring with a consuming inert rage at the small brown booklet Art had just dropped into his lap.

During the two weeks he had spent fretting in the hospital, Art hadn't been over once; but now, the first day he was home, here was Art with his ridiculous pad and pencil, and with this absolutely infuriating little book.

Steve found, since his accident, that rage was the hardest emotion for him to cope with and the one that descended most often upon him. He couldn't go out, now, and work like a fury until he'd worn off its edge. He had to bottle up his rage somehow, and he felt often as if the inward pressure would shatter his body into pieces. The first week in the hospital, after he realized fully what had happened to him, had been the worst seven days he had ever lived through. There were times when he had felt he wouldn't make it, when he had desired actively not to make it, to die. The second week, unable to overcome the tremendous barrier of his normal good health, he had spent in a red fury at everyone and everything concerned with what had happened; the surgeon who had cut his leg off; the nurses who attended to his helplessness; the dead and vanished *Sally & Joe;* Frank Pierce who was well out of it all. But the rage was greatest of all against his brother who had actually done this terrible thing to him.

He lay for two weeks trying to think of something that he could do to Art in retaliation. Nothing enormous enough occurred to him now that he was incapable of carrying out physical revenge. But he was still thinking.

Sitting here now, in his own living room, staring at that stubborn face, he hated Art actively with a hatred he felt must be as apparent as a halo around his head would be.

He snatched the booklet and opened it. His eyes, traveling down the list of entries, bulged slightly. It was a savings bank pass book made out to Stephen Swan and the entries in it went back to a date shortly before their father's death. The total, by this time, was impressive.

"So she was right." Steve turned narrow angry eyes on his brother. "You've been holding out on me all this time!"

Art had his note ready and handed it over. Steve took the paper angrily from his hand and read:

"*This wasn't my idea. Pa said years ago when you were in college he was afraid you'd never save anything. So he started doing it this way for you. Told me to keep on till you needed it. He held out ten per cent. Half of it's here. Half my name. He knew sooner or later you'd need it. He was right, wasn't he?*"

"You bastard!" Steve said. "I don't need you for a guardian."

Art flushed and started to write busily.

"*Not my idea. Pa's. I wouldn't care if you starved to death.*"

"Oh, shove those notes, will you! I'm sick and tired of the things! I know damn well the only reason you've come up here today is to sit there and gloat over your handiwork. Made a good job of it, didn't you?"

"*Not on purpose,*" Art printed rapidly. "*I swear.*"

"Don't give me that! You've been laying for me for some reason ever since we were kids. Well, you've ruined me this time. You ought to be satisfied. I'm done for and you did it."

Art lost his temper so obviously that Steve jumped. Art got up slowly and came over to stand looking down at his helpless brother, his eyes narrow and red in his flushed face, his jaw muscles working. Steve thought for a whirling second that Art was going to haul off and hit him. What he did was almost as shocking. He smiled and thrust his face closer to Steve's and began to talk in a low taut voice that didn't sound like his own.

"I didn't do it on purpose," he said levelly. "But now it's done, I'm glad of it. You hear that, Steve Swan. I'm glad it happened. If I'd tried for years I couldn't have thought of anything that would have served you out better. Now if you want to sit there and persuade yourself I did it apurpose, go ahead. It'll be the pay I'll take for giving *your* brat *my* name, for letting people think all these years that boy was mine when I knew damn well he was yours. Yeah! Go ahead! Believe I did it on purpose!"

Steve was too astonished to take in the fact that Art had finally spoken to him directly and with intent.

"Are you crazy?"

"Not any more," Art said calmly. "I feel a lot better now. I'll even go on with it. It's worth it."

For a shattering minute Steve saw clearly how he could take his revenge. All he had to do was keep his mouth shut now and let Art go on, all the rest of his life, thinking the boy who carried his name belonged to his brother. But he thought of something else. His imagination had never been particularly vivid, especially when it came to seeing how other people felt, or how his actions would affect somebody else. Now, suddenly, he did. He saw if he let Art go on with this ridiculous supposition, three innocent people would be made miserable for the rest of their lives, too. He wouldn't want to be either Minnie, young Arthur, or Millie, living in the same house with Art.

"So *that's* what was wrong with you the night you got married," he said.

"You must have thought I was blind, both of you. Well, Minnie's known for a long time I wasn't. Now you know."

"For what you've done to me," Steve said musingly, "I ought to let you go on thinking that. And I could do it."

Art's face, not hard now, but defenseless and stricken, told him he could. Steve sat tasting his bitter triumph before he gave it up.

"No son of mine could ever look like Arthur." The absolution was as cruel as he could make it. "Set your mind at rest, Art. He's all yours. I never in my life laid a finger on Minnie."

Art got up, moving slowly. He was forced by the bitterness of his brother's voice to believe him. If what he had believed all these years had been true, Steve would have told him so now. He was carrying on his shoulders the weight of fourteen wasted years as he went across the room to the door. Listening to his feet go out along the hall, Steve thought they might have been the steps of an old, old man.

He glanced thoughtfully down at the bank book he still held. Well, he thought wryly, it will come in handy now I'm laid up. Hilda and I can still go ahead and—

His thoughts stopped abruptly there. He didn't know what Hilda and he could still do. He hadn't seen her since the week after the accident. She had been to see him once only. And she had seemed different; but perhaps he was the one who'd been different. He wouldn't know until he saw her again and he didn't know when that would be. If she didn't come today, he would forget his pride and ask Lizzie to call her. Then she would either have to come or have to refuse. He would know where he stood then.

Thinking that he could no longer use that phrase without

233

knowing that he didn't stand at all, Steve bared his teeth angrily at the impersonal sky on the other side of his glass cage. He would never stand anywhere again.

———

Hilda came slowly down the stairs from her bedroom to the wide gloomy hall feeling as if she might be going to be sick to her stomach. At the big front door, separated only by the thin mesh of the screen from the outside and what she was supposed to go and do, she hesitated, half-turned, and glanced hopefully up the stairs. Up there was safety, uncomplicated and waiting for her. Once she stepped out of the house into the blinding sunshine, that was behind her. She would have given anything she had for the ability to turn and go back up those stairs. She glanced down at her hand on the door latch and the big square green stone flashed its message of assured possession hatefully back at her.

There was a rustle in the doorway at the back of the hall, giving into the kitchen. Hilda didn't have to look in the direction of the sound. She knew that her mother stood there watching, her eyes like some hard black stones, her face stiff with the driving force that was sending Hilda out of the house.

Feeling like a rabbit whose place of safety has turned to a trap, Hilda went hastily out the door and down the path to the gate. Once that had closed behind her there was no possibility of retreat.

She walked slowly, feeling sun strike against her eyes like a blow when she passed from the shade of the elms into the light.

She had been over to the hospital once, a week after Steve's accident, and she still felt, when she couldn't help thinking about it, that involuntary chill that had fingered its way down her spine when she stood in the door looking at the great hump of protecting wickerwork under the covers that kept the weight of the bedclothes off his stump.

She had looked at that first with sick fascination. Then she had seen his big brown hand, lying idly on the white spread, like something that a casual caller might have put down there and forgotten. As she watched it, it turned over slowly and started to pick up and pleat tightly tiny folds of the cloth.

Looking at his face had been hardest of all and, once she had taken her eyes off that dreadful mound under the bedclothes, she couldn't force herself to look at it again although she was as aware of it as if it had been another person in the room with them. She had never before seen Steve's face when it didn't look as if he intended to smile in a second, or had just stopped smiling. It didn't look like that now. It was thinner yet, in some way difficult to define, it was heavier. His eyes, sunken and dark, rested on her face with an expression of brooding suspicion that didn't change during the entire half hour she sat in the cell-like little room trying to think of something to say to him.

She couldn't make herself talk about the accident and it was the only thing Steve could think about. They avoided all mention of it out of an identical childish reaction that made them understand each other's reluctance perfectly.

At the end of half an hour, Hilda got up gratefully to go, thinking that she had got through this first meeting all right, the next would be easier. Steve let her go as far as the door. Then he said hoarsely:

"Hilda, you know what they've done to me, don't you?"

Hilda had turned on him the tortured sullen face of an adolescent confronted with embarrassment.

"Yes."

"Will it make any difference to you?" he asked heavily.

She shook her head No.

"Yes," he said, suspicion thickening his clear voice. "You look as if it wouldn't!"

How she got out of that room and out of the building, Hilda could not remember. But she knew, at this moment, walking up the quiet street alone and cold in the hot sunshine, that she had been mistaken. The second meeting was not going to be easier. She had thought that the plunge, once taken, would harden her as the first dive into icy water makes the second seem warmer.

She had put it off too long. She hadn't gone again to the hospital in spite of Dolly's recriminations. She had written Steve short notes each day, saying that she wanted to come; but there was always something to prevent it. Besides the smell of the building made her feel faint.

Even when she knew he was home, she put it off, letting the first day go by like twenty four hours in a nightmare. But this morning Lizzie had called her and asked her to come. Lizzie's voice, in spite of her message, had told Hilda clearly that Lizzie didn't want her any more than she herself wanted to go; but Steve had left neither of them a choice.

Across the street she hesitated again, looking up the hill to the big white house. In one of those rooms he was sitting now waiting for her like a spider in a web. Perhaps he was even somewhere where he could look out the window and see her hesitating here. During the last two weeks Hilda had forgotten about the last evening they had spent together and could remember only the times before when she had been half afraid of him. She was more than half afraid now. If she had once admitted the unreasoning horrified terror that lay under the surface ready to consume her once its existence was recognized, she would never have been able to cross the street and climb the hill to that door.

The mere idea of him sitting in that house, perhaps with the awful maimed leg propped up somehow so she'd have to look at it or, even worse, concealed in some way so that lack of visibility would make it even more apparent, made her feel as if the blood in her veins had turned to solid ice.

Lizzie let her in without comment, except for a barely civil greeting.

"He's in the front room." She nodded down the hall. "Go on in. He's expecting you."

Rather than point out that she had never set foot in this house before, Hilda went uncertainly down the hall toward the big light opening at its end. It was a lovely house, she thought with reluctant regret. It smelled so clean, like furniture polish and fresh air. There were so many glowing wooden surfaces that she, who was more accustomed to the hard yellow shine of varnish, thought she had never seen such beautiful wood and wondered what kind it was that could look as if it would feel like satin to her fingers. It was all terribly bare, though. None of the little things around that would make you feel at home here, no lacy cloths on the dark surfaces of tables, no little glass dishes, no porcelain figurines, nothing to break the straight clean lines of the handsome furniture. It was more like a barn than a house. It didn't look lived in.

As she came into the light she saw with relief that Steve was sitting up in a big chair facing the window. She could see the back of his head silhouetted there. That was better than having him in bed. She thought she had made no noise; but he had heard her.

"Come in, Hilda."

Feeling like a child she stepped down into the room and

crossed to his chair. Steve didn't turn his head, waiting for her to come to him. As she rounded the side of the chair, Hilda sighed softly. It wasn't as bad as she had expected. He looked almost normal unless you knew what to look for. His trouser leg wasn't cut off or sewed over in a flap. It was where it should have been and looked almost all right and only a little limp until you looked for the foot, until you looked for the foot—until—

Everything inside her head felt as if it had started to go around in concentric circles and only Steve's sharp hard voice kept her from dropping right there beside him.

"Sit down, Hilda," he said loudly.

His tone, not gentle as she could remember it, worked like a slap across the face. She groped carefully for the arm of the chair that had been drawn up beside his and sank into it gratefully, looking everywhere but at the place where his left foot should have been and wasn't.

"I wondered when you'd come to see me."

"Steve—"

"I kind of gave up, so I asked Lizzie to call you."

"I was coming, anyhow," Hilda lied hastily.

He let that go. Instead, he reached out and took a fold of the loose cloth of his trouser leg between his fingers and began to pleat it the way he had the bed-spread.

"How do you think it'll be?" he said softly. "Doesn't look quite natural, does it?"

"Steve, please," Hilda said hopelessly. The circling was starting inside her head again and she was utterly thankful for the hard physical presence of the chair beneath her. "I can't— You've just got to let me get used to it before—"

"Let *you* get used to it!" His voice was that of a man examining a totally new idea.

"If we could only talk about—for just a little while first—talk

238

about something else." Pleadingly she looked at his face and saw with dismay that she hadn't said the right thing.

He grinned at her, showing his teeth; but the grin made no difference to the look in his eyes.

"That's not the way," he said. "You have to grow up sometime, Hilda. The only thing to do is face things. Head-on, see? We will talk about it. The doctor said I had remarkable regenerative powers. He said it was a beautiful stump. See?"

Before Hilda realized what he was going to do, Steve had grasped her limp right hand firmly by the wrist and laid its whole length on the emptiness where his left knee had been.

Hilda screamed, jerked her hand away, and was halfway across the room before her own scream had died into the relief of hysterical tears.

"I can't. I can't." She stood there shouting at him. "It's horrible! I can't!"

When the sound of her voice died Steve was silent for so long that she had time to realize what she'd said and to see what she'd done.

"It's all your fault," she babbled at the back of his head. "I would have been all right if you'd only given me time, Steve. I didn't want to hurt you. I can't help the way I feel, can I? I can't help the way I feel about crippled people, can I?"

"Keep right on, Hilda. You're making it so much better with every word."

"I can't help the way I feel," she repeated sullenly and stood waiting.

"All right," Steve said, each word sounding like a drop of ice. "Only get the hell out of here, Hilda. I don't want to see you again. Just get out of my sight!"

She stood there hearing him say the words she had wanted to say and lacked the courage for. She looked around the big room, seeing what she had irrevocably lost because he had hurried her and was filled with relief almost matched by the volume of her resentment against him for forcing her before she was ready to be forced.

She could see his hand lying palm up on the maimed leg, the fingers curled slightly. She glanced thoughtfully down at the big green stone on her own finger. She might at least save that out of the wreckage; but she hated the sight of it. She wrenched at it furiously and went over and dropped it in that hand, seeing the fingers close on it reflectively before she turned and ran back through the hall the way she had come.

Lizzie, in the kitchen, had heard her scream and had started in to see what was wrong. She'd thought better of it when their voices started, and had returned to her kitchen. Now, hearing Hilda's flying steps, she looked up to see her flash past and out the back door. It slammed forcibly behind her.

Well, Lizzie thought, at least he's taken care of that himself, once and for all. There had been a finality about the way Hilda had slammed that door that told beyond a doubt she would never willingly open it again.

Hilda flew blindly down the hill, not even seeing the man and woman who had started slowly up it, until she ran head-on into the man who, because of his awkward limp, had been unable to avoid her.

They stood clinging to each other in a clumsy staggering dance of mutual support and Hilda, looking over his shoulder met the level, scornful gaze of the woman squarely. Angrily she pushed herself away from her unwilling supporter and stood, shaking with fury and despair, waiting for the words she knew were coming.

"Oh my god," she said. "I can't!"

"You've run out on him, haven't you?" Ann asked icily.

"It's what *you've* wanted all along. You've just kept hanging around hoping it would happen. Now it has and you don't like that either."

"Yes, I'll take what's left," Ann said. "Gladly. If I can get it."

Jason Wills glanced quickly from the girl who had run into him to Ann's tight face and, like a prudent man, continued up the hill, leaving them to it.

"Well, then," Hilda said furiously. "Well, then, what—"

"Obviously," Ann's voice was cold, "you never really loved him, did you? Or it wouldn't make the slightest difference to you whether he had one leg or three. You really make me wonder how you would have behaved if it had suddenly turned out that he was a poor man. Just the same way, I have no doubt."

She brushed past the breathless Hilda and went on without a backward glance. Jason had stopped in the kitchen, she saw, and sat there talking quietly to Lizzie. Ann went on down the hall to the front room.

Steve was sitting in his chair and he didn't glance around when he heard her, but he stiffened all over, and she could tell from the back of his head that he, too, was angry. That would be an advance over the impenetrable inertia she had been battling for two solid weeks. It made her feel good to know that he was sitting there boiling.

"I said I didn't want to set eyes on you again," he grated.

"You've made a mistake I hope, Steve." She went quickly over to him, seeing his start of surprise and immediate relaxation at the sound of her voice.

"Yeah, I guess I did. Consider that unsaid, will you?"

"With pleasure. But as long as you don't mean me—"

"Well, I don't." His left hand was clenched shut; but he reached out with his right and his fingers closed strongly on hers. "Judas, Ann, I don't know how I'd have gotten through these last two weeks without you! You put up with an awful lot from me."

"Yes," she agreed. "And I'm getting a little weary of it."

She sensed his withdrawal. His hand loosened and slid away from hers. Instead of using the excuse she had given him to flare into vocal anger and get rid of it, uncharacteristically he slid into pathos.

"Yeah, I can see how you would. But, lord, Ann, you don't know what it's like to depend on somebody else for everything. The only thing I can do for myself is breathe. Believe me, if I had any way to do it, I'd knock myself off and put an end to it."

"You damned fool!" she said hotly. "If I ever hear you say such a ridiculous self-pitying thing again, I'll—I'll—"

"Well?" He stared up at her sullenly. "What the hell else is there to do? I'm a cripple, Ann. I'm a *cripple!* I'm disgusting. I can't do anything. I can't ever go in my boat again."

Her chance had come before she was ready for it and she nearly let it get by her.

"Oh!" she said. "Jason."

Steve stared.

"What?"

Jason's voice came quietly from the hall.

"Be right with you."

"Keep him out of here," Steve said fiercely. "I don't want to see anyone. Get him out of here, Ann!"

He was beginning to move frenetically in his chair in a futile attempt at escape. Ann watched his ineffectual efforts for a moment, wanting nothing more than to humor him, to tell Jason not to come in, to let Steve sink back into his comfortable, self-deluding inertia. Instead she said, making her voice as even as she could:

"Listen to me, Steve. If you sit here feeling sorry for yourself much longer, you'll never move again."

"I *can't* move," he yelled at her. "I *can't!*"

"You will. That's why I want you to talk to Jase."

"What the hell has he got to do with it?" Breathless, he stopped trying, sank back into his chair braced hard against its back, sweat beading out on his forehead.

"Listen. He's been going in his boat for the last twenty years, hasn't he?"

"That's a little different." His eyes flared yellow at her. "All he's got is that limp. I haven't any leg, Ann."

"He hasn't, either."

"Oh, damn you. What a dirty trick to tell me a thing like that! I know you're lying. I—"

Jason thudded down the steps across the room. His eyes on the young man's face were pitying; but not very much.

"No," he announced loudly. "She ain't lying, Steve. I got a wooden leg. Have had for years. See?" He proceeded to prove the truth of his statement. Steve was silent. "I always say it's ar-thuritis," Jason said softly, now, into his silence. "So as not to embarrass people, you know."

After Jason's tread, firm and hesitating so slightly you wouldn't have noticed the drag unless you were listening for it, had died away along the hall, Ann stood waiting through the longest, most important silence of her life.

What Steve said when he finally broke that silence would make no difference to her own next action; but it would make all the difference in the world to the rest of her life. If he said one thing, she would spend the remainder of her life catering to a complete invalid; if he said another, they would have a rich and completely normal future to look forward to. In either case, they would do it together. She found herself holding her breath; but the silence lasted so long she finally had to let it out in a little windy sigh.

Steve hadn't looked at her since Jason had gone. Now he did, and relief made her limp. She felt for the chair, without daring to take her eyes off him, and sat down because her legs would no longer support her.

"Well, the pair of you have taught me a lesson," Steve said.

"No," she contradicted. "We haven't. We've just proved to you that you've made a mistake. There's no teaching on our side, Steve. Any *lesson*, you'll just have to learn without a teacher."

"You'll help me, won't you, Ann?"

"I'll do my best and you know it; but it'll be hard for me, too, Steve. I'll say and do a lot of things that'll hurt you because I can't imagine what it will be like for you with only one leg."

She said it with calculated brutality and waited for his reaction.

"I should think the first thing you might try to do," —her eyes were as even as her voice—"is to get over wincing visibly whenever anyone uses that word. For the lord sake, Steve, you're alive! What's a leg?"

Steve swallowed.

"Less than I thought, apparently," he said. "It'll take time, though. I can't change all at once." He paused and added, experimentally, watching her narrowly: "Or alone, either."

"There's no need for you to do it alone."

"Do you mean you'd really let me come back to you now?"

"Well," she looked away. "I don't know how clearly I'd have to say it before you got the idea."

"I mean really serious, Ann. I mean will you marry me?"

She sat wordless and into her silence, Steve said hoarsely: "Ann, *please*."

"Darling, don't! It's all right. I was just trying to think how to say yes in four or five different ways at once."

He thought of something else suddenly and opened his clenched left hand. He had been holding so tightly to the ring that Ann could see the deep impression the square corners of the big stone had made in his palm. He looked at it thoughtfully and then at her.

"Do you—" he began. "You don't, do you?"

"No, damn you, I don't!" She struck at the hand and the stone made a parabola of living green light. "I've got a little pride left."

Steve didn't even turn to see where it had gone. He held his empty hand out to her and she took that gladly, coming to kneel beside his chair.

Ten minutes later when Lizzie came noisily down the hall, neither of them had moved.

"Well!" Lizzie said, on a surprised breath.

"Lizzie!" Steve roared. "Lizzie, we're going to be *married!*"

"I am glad to hear it." Lizzie accepted the news grandly. She and Ann exchanged a mutually admiring look; one which gave no ground on either side, but established firmly their future relationship.

Unable any longer to pretend disinterest, Lizzie gave them both a wide forgiving smile.

"I'm sure," she said gently, "I'm as pleased as you two look. Only I've made you both a good hot cup of coffee. It's time we calmed down. Too much been going on here this afternoon."

"*I* wouldn't care," Steve told her grandly, "if it was twice as much."

Lizzie shrugged.

"Maybe it is," she said. "You won't know for sure for a while yet."

www.ingramcontent.com/pod-product-compliance
Lightning Source LLC
Chambersburg PA
CBHW070928260626
47162CB00007B/2828